THE
GATHERING

Lisa Stone lives in England, has 3 children, and has several books published under the pseudonym Cathy Glass, many of which have become best-sellers. This is her sixth Lisa Stone thriller.

Website: lisastonebooks.co.uk
Email: lisa@lisastonebooks.co.uk
 /lisastonebooks.co.uk
@lisastonebooks

D1336073

Books by Lisa Stone

The Darkness Within
Stalker
The Doctor
Taken
The Cottage

Books by Cathy Glass

True stories

Cut
The Silent Cry
Daddy's Little Princess
Nobody's Son
Cruel to Be Kind
The Night the Angels Came
A Long Way from Home
A Baby's Cry
The Saddest Girl in the World
Please Don't Take My Baby
Will You Love Me?
I Miss Mummy
Saving Danny
Girl Alone
Where Has Mummy Gone?

Damaged
Hidden
Mummy Told Me Not to Tell
Another Forgotten Child
The Child Bride
Can I Let You Go?
Finding Stevie
Innocent
Too Scared to Tell
A Terrible Secret
A Life Lost
An Innocent Baby
Neglected
A Family Torn Apart
Unwanted

Novels based on true stories
The Girl in the Mirror
My Dad's a Policeman
Run Mummy Run

Self-help guides
About Writing
Happy Kids
Happy Adults
Happy Mealtimes for Kids
Happy Kids & Happy Mealtimes

THE GATHERING

LISA STONE

HarperCollins*Publishers*

HarperCollins*Publishers*
1 London Bridge Street,
London SE1 9GF

www.harpercollins.co.uk

HarperCollins*Publishers*
Macken House, 39/40 Mayor Street Upper,
Dublin 1, D01 C9W8, Ireland

First published by HarperCollins*Publishers* 2023
1

Copyright © Lisa Stone 2023

Lisa Stone asserts the moral right
to be identified as the author of this work

A catalogue record for this book is available from the British Library

ISBN: 978-0-00-861185-9

This novel is entirely a work of fiction.
The names, characters and incidents portrayed in it are
the work of the author's imagination. Any resemblance to
actual persons, living or dead, events or localities is
entirely coincidental.

Typeset in Sabon by Palimpsest Book Production Ltd, Falkirk, Stirlingshire

Printed and Bound in the UK using
100% Renewable Electricity at CPI Group (UK) Ltd

All rights reserved. No part of this publication may be
reproduced, stored in a retrieval system, or transmitted,
in any form or by any means, electronic, mechanical,
photocopying, recording or otherwise, without the prior
permission of the publishers.

MIX
Paper | Supporting
responsible forestry
FSC™ C007454
FSC
www.fsc.org

This book is produced from independently certified FSC™ paper to ensure
responsible forest management.

For more information visit: www.harpercollins.co.uk/green

Phasmophobia is a fear of ghosts.

ONE

'It's right next to a graveyard!' Sarah exclaimed. 'I don't believe it! What the heck was Austin thinking of?'

She thrust her phone into Roshan's line of vision. He glanced at the image and quickly returned his gaze to the road ahead.

'I mean, how spooky is that!' Sarah said, frantically scrolling through the images of the graveyard she'd just discovered online.

'I thought you'd looked at the link Austin sent us showing the property?' Roshan, her husband, said. 'He posted it on our WhatsApp group.'

'I did but there weren't any pictures of graves. For good reason! Who wants to spend their holiday next door to dead people?'

'The rooms are nice though,' Roshan replied easily. He was always so chilled and laid-back, the opposite of Sarah, who could be intense and easily provoked. They got on so well because they complemented each other.

The traffic ahead slowed and the satnav flashed a warning of congestion a mile further up.

'The rooms are nice,' Sarah agreed. 'Or were. But

knowing the graves are there has rather taken the shine off it for me.'

'We'll keep the windows closed,' Roshan said with a smile.

'I'm serious,' Sarah said, continuing to study the photos. 'I wouldn't have agreed to renting the place for a week if I'd known.'

'Don't be daft,' Roshan said affectionately, glancing at her. 'It will be fine.' The traffic ground to a halt. 'Here, let me have a look.'

Sarah passed her phone to Roshan and he spent a few moments looking at the images before handing it back.

'The graveyard is very old,' he said. 'I doubt anyone has been buried there for years.'

'And that makes it OK?' Sarah asked.

Roshan shrugged. 'You don't think you might be over-reacting, love?'

'Probably, but that's me.'

'And I love you for it.' He smiled at her. 'I suppose we might have guessed that a converted eighteenth-century church could have a graveyard close by.' The traffic began moving again, although slowly. 'I'm sure it will be fine once we get there.'

'Hopefully, but if I really don't like it can we book in a B & B and just go to the place to meet the others?' Sarah knew it sounded pathetic, but she couldn't help herself. As a child she'd been convinced she'd seen a ghost in a church-yard, and the memory had stayed with her.

'I think that might be taking it a bit far,' Roshan replied in his calm, deferring manner. 'What would be the point of us all getting together after all these years if we're not there for a large part of it?'

He never raised his voice or lost patience, some of the many reasons Sarah loved him as much now as when they'd first met ten years ago. They'd been seventeen then, studying for A-level examinations in the sixth form. They'd begun dating, and married after college when they both had jobs. They were two of a group of five who'd become good friends and had promised to meet up ten years after their graduation. They'd all moved away, but that date had finally arrived.

There was Austin, who'd organized the reunion, his wife, Leslie, who they didn't know, and Megan and Brandon, who Sarah had stayed in touch with on social media since school.

'How much further?' she asked, glancing at the satnav. The traffic was still moving very slowly. She hoped they'd arrive before it was dark.

'There seems to be a hold-up on the slip road,' Roshan said, also looking at the satnav. 'Once we're off the motorway it's about an hour. Can you text Austin and tell him we're running late? He wanted us all there by four o'clock so he could serve dinner. Nice idea to have us all sit down to dinner when we arrive.'

'What time shall I say? Around four thirty?'

Roshan nodded.

Sarah sent the text to Austin: *Sorry, running late. Aim to be with you at 4.30.* She looked at the skyline ahead. It was already a grey, overcast day, and the sun had begun its descent, turning the clouds even darker. The last week in October it was dark by five thirty – even earlier if there was a lot of cloud cover. She shuddered at the thought of arriving at the converted church with its graveyard in the dark, but said, 'Pity Austin didn't arrange our get-together in the summer.'

'That's partly our fault as teachers, if you remember,' Roshan reminded her. 'We're the ones limited to school holidays, and there was nothing available for this summer that had four bedrooms, so half-term was the next best slot.'

Sarah's phone bleeped, and she read out the message. 'Austin says fine, drive safely, and he's looking forward to seeing us.'

3

'As we are him.'

Sarah placed her phone in her lap and gazed out of her side window at the slowly passing grassy bank as the car inched forward.

'To be honest, I was surprised he invited me,' Sarah said after a few moments. 'You were much closer to him than I was.'

'But we were all part of that group, and that's what we agreed before we left and went our separate ways – that in ten years' time we'd meet and see what we'd made of our lives. I was surprised he'd remembered. Last year I wondered what Austin was doing and tried to find him on social media, but there was nothing – not on Facebook, Twitter or LinkedIn. It even crossed my mind he might be dead. Then suddenly he appears on social media and finds us all.'

'I wonder what he's been doing?' Sarah asked absently.

'You mean apart from qualifying as a psychiatrist? That takes years.'

'I was thinking more in his private life. I mean, you and I have kept in touch with Megan and Brandon, but no one has heard from Austin since we left.'

'He didn't say much about his private life, but he's bringing Leslie.'

'Yes, the only one of the group we don't know. Why didn't he add her to the WhatsApp group he set up?'

'I suppose he thought it wasn't necessary; that he could tell her the arrangements for meeting.'

Roshan touched the brake as the traffic in front ground to a halt and the sun continued its descent.

TWO

It was dusk as they pulled into the village, the sky a murky grey. 'Take the next turning on the left and you have reached your destination,' the satnav announced.

Roshan followed the directions as Sarah peered through her side window. The trees were losing their leaves but between the semi-bare branches she could make out the outline of the church. It looked exactly as it had online, except instead of sunlight shimmering on the stained-glass windows they were now illuminated from within. Austin had raved about the lattice windows in his text messages, as they were among the many original features that had been sensitively restored.

Roshan took the left turn and the car bumped over the single-track gravel lane and then onto the hardstanding in front of the gate. He parked next to the other two cars and cut the engine. 'I need to use the bathroom,' he said, opening his car door. 'Out you get.'

Sarah didn't move. Although the small eighteenth-century converted church was like its picture, she now saw it wasn't next door to a cemetery – it was in the middle of it. The graveyard loomed to the right and left of the building, at the front, and as far as she could see in the dusk, to the back. Roshan had been right when he'd said it probably hadn't been used for years. The headstones that she could see from the car were covered in moss and lichen and at odd angles from where the ground had subsided. It would have been so much better if they'd arrived in daylight with the sun shining, she thought.

Roshan was taking their suitcases from the boot and now appeared at her side window. She gingerly opened the door.

'Come on, love, hurry up, I'm dying for a pee,' he said.

She stepped out and drew her jacket around her. The air was still and quiet. A damp mist was forming over the unkempt graveyard. Trees and countryside lay behind them and the road they'd just been on was somewhere to their right.

'We're not that far from the road,' Sarah said, trying to reassure herself, closing her car door. Every sound seemed to echo out here.

She followed Roshan to the wooden gate with its carved arch. A low stone wall ran off either side.

'Beautiful. It looks original,' Roshan said, admiring the gate as he pushed it open.

Sarah followed him in and along the slate path, keeping her gaze away from the graves either side. She'd been a child when she'd had that dreadful fright, aged seven. She was an adult now and needed to get a grip, she told herself.

'The door could be original too,' Roshan said as they stepped into the porch and faced the solid oak door of the church. He set down one of their cases and, raising the wrought-iron door knocker, gave a loud rap, which made Sarah jump.

The door suddenly opened and there stood Austin.

'I heard your car. Good to see you both. Do come in.'

He shook Roshan's hand and kissed Sarah's cheek. 'Let me take your jackets and cases.'

Setting down the cases, Roshan slipped off his jacket and passed it to Austin. Sarah did the same.

'I'll need to use the bathroom first,' Roshan said. 'Sorry we're late.'

'No problem, you're here now. The cloakroom is just there,' he said convivially, and pointed to a door further along the hall. 'I'll put your cases in your room for you shortly.'

'Thank you,' Roshan said, and disappeared into the cloakroom.

Austin turned to Sarah. 'So we meet again after all these years.'

'We do,' she said, feeling slightly uncomfortable, although she wasn't sure why.

She'd seen Austin's photograph on Facebook and the WhatsApp group he'd set up to arrange this gathering, but even without them she would have recognized him anywhere. Tall, lean, clean-shaven, with high cheekbones and piercing blue eyes. Just as charismatic now as he had been all those years ago. A charmer and smooth-talker, but he'd had a habit at school of standing too close and invading your personal space. It was no different now. Sarah found herself taking a step back.

'Go through and meet the others,' he said, 'while I hang up your jackets.'

Placing a hand on the small of her back, Austin guided Sarah along the short hall to a door on their right. She stepped into what had once been the nave of the church but was now the main living area.

'Sarah!' Megan cried, rushing to her.

'So good to see you again,' Sarah said as they hugged.

'And Brandon,' Sarah said after a moment. Letting go of Megan, she moved toward Brandon for a hug.

'Great to see you,' he said, smiling warmly. 'You haven't changed one little bit. I think I've put on a few pounds since you last saw me.'

He was fuller in the face, but Sarah didn't say so. Brandon had been a lovely guy, and she was looking forward to getting to know him again. They'd had some contact through social media, just acknowledging birthdays, 'liking' holiday photos, and so forth. They hadn't seen each other in person in seven years. Sarah had seen Megan five years earlier, just after she'd had her daughter Ella. Around the same time, Roshan had met up with Brandon. They all had a lot of catching up to do.

'Where's Roshan?' Brandon asked, looking around.

'In the loo,' Sarah replied.

'Good. I thought for a moment we were going to be two down.'

'Two?' Sarah asked, puzzled.

'Leslie couldn't make it,' Austin said, suddenly appearing in the room behind her.

'Oh dear, and after all the trouble you've gone to, organizing this,' Sarah said. 'What a pity. I was looking forward to meeting her.'

'It can't be helped,' Austin said stoically. 'Just one of those things. She woke not feeling so well.'

'Is she all right to be left on her own?' Sarah asked, concerned.

'Yes. She'll join us later if she feels up to it. Now what can I get you to drink? I've brought most things. Is yours still vodka and lemonade?' he asked Sarah.

'You remembered that!' Sarah exclaimed.

Austin nodded.

'Probably because of the number of vodkas you drank on your eighteenth birthday,' Brandon quipped.

'Oh my! Yes,' Sarah said. 'I remember. How embarrassing. I could really knock them back in those days.'

'I think we all could then,' Megan said. 'I stopped drinking alcohol completely when I got pregnant. I only drink occasionally now.'

'Roshan and I limit it to weekends,' Sarah said, settling easily into conversation with Megan. 'You can't go into school and teach with a hangover.'

'I guess we've all grown up,' Austin said. 'But there's no need for us to be sensible this week. This is our big reunion. So what's it to be, Sarah?'

'OK. Vodka and lemonade would be great,' she said, with a small laugh. 'A real trip down memory lane.'

'And a refill for you?' Austin asked Megan, taking her glass before she could protest. 'Brandon, do you want a refill?'

'No, thanks. I'm OK for now.'

Austin disappeared through a door on the far side of the room into what Sarah assumed must be the kitchen. Warm air floated in with the smell of something delicious cooking. Austin was going to so much trouble to make them feel welcome. The perfect host, Sarah thought.

As she was talking to Megan and Brandon, Roshan came in from the cloakroom.

'Good to see you,' he said, hugging Brandon, then Megan. 'Sorry we were late. There was a hold-up on the motorway.'

'Austin told us,' Brandon said.

'Have you been here long?' Roshan asked.

'About an hour and a half,' Brandon replied. 'But Megan was here earlier.'

'I came by train,' she said. 'I don't own a car. Austin collected me from the station, which was nice of him.'

'How is little Ella?' Sarah asked.

'Great. She's spending the week with my mother where she'll be spoilt something rotten.'

'But nice for you to have a break,' Brandon said. 'It can't be easy bringing up a child alone.'

'No, but now I have her I wouldn't change anything. She means the world to me.'

Austin reappeared with Megan and Sarah's drinks. 'What would you like, Roshan? I've got a selection of wines, bottled beers and spirits. Do you want to come and choose?'

'Great, thanks, mate,' Roshan said, going with him.

'Amazing place, this,' Brandon said, gazing up into the apex of the roof. The three of them were standing in the centre of what was now the living room.

'It is,' Sarah agreed, also looking up. The white emulsion plaster set off the dark wood of the exposed beams all the way into the high roof.

'Austin showed me around when I first got here,' Megan said. 'He knows a lot about the place. He researched it all online.'

'He gave me a guided tour, too,' Brandon told Sarah. 'Typical Austin, researching everything. Do you remember he was always involved in one project or another while we were at school? I guess that's why he's done so well.'

'I think we've all done well in our own ways,' Sarah said. 'I mean, we can't all be brain surgeons.'

'He's not a brain surgeon, he's a psychiatrist,' Brandon pointed out.

'I know, it was just an expression.'

The door to the kitchen opened and Austin and Roshan returned, both carrying wine glasses.

'We were just admiring this room,' Sarah said, taking a sip from her drink.

'It is impressive,' Austin said. 'They've done the conversion well. I had a look at the plans online. It was only completed last year. They kept the height in this room, and put in a false floor and walls on the second floor to create four bedrooms. The kitchen-diner is where the old vestry used to be. Do you want a quick tour before we eat?' he asked Sarah and Roshan.

'Yes, good idea,' Sarah agreed. She had to admit that now she was inside the warm building, well-lit by numerous fashionable lamps, and among friends, she was starting to feel more relaxed about staying the week.

'Kitchen-diner this way,' Austin said, and proudly led the way. Megan caught Sarah's eye and threw her a knowing look.

'Anything we can do in the kitchen?' Brandon called after them.

'No, just relax and enjoy your drinks,' Austin replied. 'I'll see to it.'

Sarah and Roshan followed Austin into the kitchen-diner. The original walls, ceiling and wooden beams were in keeping with the building, but the rest of it was sparklingly new and expensive. It had a designer kitchen, the likes of which Sarah usually only saw in glossy magazines. Yards of gleaming glinting granite work surfaces, matching floor tiles, oak cabinets, a central island, subtle concealed lighting, and a long cream marble table with cream-coloured upholstered wooden chairs. Little wonder the rental on the place had been so high, Sarah thought.

'Beautiful,' she said admiringly, taking it all in.

'Dinner smells good,' Roshan said, nodding at the range cooker.

'Typical guy, can only think of his next meal,' Austin said, smiling at Sarah.

Sarah laughed, then wished she hadn't. It felt wrong, having a joke with Austin at Roshan's expense. 'I wouldn't have him any other way,' she said, and kissed his cheek.

'I'll show you your room now, then I'll serve dinner,' Austin said, a little stiffly. 'Best leave your drinks down here. The spiral staircase is narrow and you'll need a hand free for the rail.'

Sarah and Roshan did as they were told and left their

glasses on the central island, then followed Austin into a stone alcove at the far end of the room where a wrought-iron spiral staircase lay out of sight. Austin went first, Sarah followed, then Roshan, their shoes clipping on the metal stairs.

'I see what you mean about holding on,' Sarah said, halfway up. The staircase, while full of character, was just wide enough for one person, and the steps narrow. She was holding the metal handrails on both sides.

'This is my only issue with the renovation of this place,' Austin said as they continued up. 'I would have applied for planning permission to run another staircase off the living room.'

The top of the staircase gave way to a spacious landing, carpeted in dark blue, with four oak doors leading off.

'All reclaimed wood,' Austin said, referring to the wooden beams and doors. 'Two double bedrooms and two singles, each with their own en suite. I've put you in here,' he said, opening a door directly ahead of them. He stood aside to let them go in first.

'Very smart,' Brandon said, looking around, impressed.

But Sarah's gaze had gone to the window. She was uncomfortable. She knew from the online photographs that the bedrooms, like most of the rooms, had at least one stained-glass window. It added to the character and charm of the place, the description read. But whereas in the photograph the sun had been streaming through the glass, casting colourful patterns onto the walls and floor, now it was pitch dark outside. The glass had become opaque. Impossible to see out, but with the light on inside presumably anyone outside could see in.

'Aren't there any curtains or blinds?' she asked.

'No. But you're on the second floor,' Austin said, clearly amused.

'Oh yes,' Sarah said, embarrassed.

Feeling foolish, she drew her gaze from the window and looked at the beautiful, expensively decorated room, with its designer soft furnishing, brass bedhead, and velvet chair. The type of room she would normally have loved to have stayed in, but without curtains to hide the dark outside she knew she wouldn't sleep a wink.

'I'll leave you to freshen up,' Austin said. 'The en suite is through there. Dinner will be ready in ten minutes.'

'Cheers, mate,' Roshan said, and Sarah managed a very small nod.

THREE

'The bedrooms are gorgeous, aren't they?' Megan enthused as Sarah and Roshan returned downstairs.

'Very impressive,' Roshan said. He'd come down the narrow spiral staircase first in case Sarah tripped and fell.

Megan and Brandon were seated at the dining table and Austin was busy at the range cooker. Their drinks, which they'd left on the island, were now at their places on the table. They'd been topped up. Open bottles of red wine and white wine were also on the table, which was set immaculately and traditionally: cutlery settings for three courses laid precisely either side of the bone-china dinner plates, with a linen napkin placed centrally, and a side plate each with its own butter knife for rolls. The finishing touch was a beautiful centrepiece of roses. Austin certainly knew how to play host, but as they took their places Sarah wondered what it had all cost. They'd paid Austin their share of the rent for the place, but they'd need to settle up with him for all the food, drink and trimmings he'd bought.

Austin served the starters in ramekin dishes. 'Cheese soufflé,' he announced. 'Megan, yours is dairy free – I know you're vegan. And Sarah, you don't eat meat, but you're happy with fish and dairy, yes?'

'That's right, thanks,' Sarah replied, wondering how Austin had known this. Roshan must have told him, for she was sure she hadn't.

'You shouldn't have gone to all this trouble,' Megan said, looking both slightly embarrassed and quietly pleased that he had.

'I wanted to,' Austin said, sitting at the table, holding her gaze for a moment too long. Megan blushed. 'I thought I'd make our reunion meal special, and after this, if everyone is happy, we can set up a rota for cooking.'

'Absolutely,' Megan agreed.

'Sure,' Brandon said. 'But don't expect too much from me.'

'Yes, of course we'll all cook,' Sarah said. 'And you must tell us what we owe you for all of this.'

'Nothing,' Austin said. 'Our reunion meal is my treat.'

'That's generous of you. This is delicious,' Brandon said, tucking in.

Austin shook out his napkin in a little flurry and laid it over his lap. Brandon and Roshan had put their napkins to one side and Sarah had dumped hers onto her lap, still folded.

'I think a toast is in order?' Austin said, and picked up his wine glass.

The others stopped eating and picked up their glasses.

'To our reunion and our future health, happiness and lasting friendship,' Austin said. 'And one of my favourite quotes by Freud – "Out of our vulnerabilities will come our strength."'

They toasted their future, and if anyone thought the quote was slightly odd, they didn't say.

Austin refused their help to clear away the empty ramekin dishes after the first course. The starter had been delicious.

Megan took the opportunity to check her phone, having explained that she was checking for messages from her mother about Ella. 'She's fine. I'm just a bit over-protective,' Megan said. Then looked at her phone again. 'You'll never guess what. The newsfeed on my phone says that Chanel Woman struck again yesterday. This time she's robbed a village post office as they were cashing up.'

'That must be thirty robberies by now?' Brandon said.

'Thirty-two, it says here,' Megan replied.

'Good business for the perfume company,' Roshan added with a smile.

'You've got to admire her tenacity,' Brandon said. 'She must know the entire police force is looking for her, and she's running rings around them.'

'And it says here the only thing the witnesses can agree on is that she wears Chanel No5 perfume while she commits the robberies,' Megan said.

'What's that?' Austin asked as he worked in the kitchen. 'I haven't been following it.'

'You must have heard of Chanel Woman?' Roshan said. 'She's been robbing small businesses, shops, garages, and banks for over two years and has completely evaded the police.'

'And they don't have a description of her?' Austin asked.

'Not really,' Roshan said. 'Average build and about five feet six inches tall. They think she's in her early thirties, but that's all. Apart from the fact she always wears Chanel No5 when she commits the robberies, and a lot of it. It lingers long after she's gone, and the smell is often still there when the police arrive. It's the only evidence they have so far.'

They all laughed.

'Perhaps she works for Chanel,' Brandon joked.

'It says here,' Megan continued, 'that they now think she is wearing wigs, a different one each time. And possibly prosthetic masks or prosthetic make-up. The police have put out an appeal asking the public to think about anyone they know who has bought these unusual items, or has them in their possession, or if they know of someone who has access to them through their work.'

'Maybe someone in the movie business?' Sarah suggested.

'I'm guessing they could easily be bought online,' Brandon said.

'The police say although she hasn't used the gun she carries, she could if cornered,' Megan added, reading from her phone. 'So the public shouldn't approach her.'

'She's clever, but she'll get caught before long,' Roshan said.

'What makes you say that?' Austin asked as he began bringing dishes of steaming hot food to the table.

'She'll get overly confident and make a mistake.'

'Perhaps they could put out an appeal for anyone who's bought Chanel N°5 in the last two years to come forward,' Brandon joked.

'That should narrow it down to a few million,' Roshan laughed.

Megan put away her phone as Austin finished arranging the dishes on heatproof mats down the centre of the table, then took his seat at the head of the table. Sarah and Roshan were on one side, with Megan and Brandon on the other.

'This looks amazing,' Megan said.

'That's the vegetarian goulash with rice,' Austin said. 'Rack of lamb for the meat eaters, mint sauce. And fresh vegetables for all. That's your dairy-free spread for the rolls,' he said to Megan. 'And that's the butter.'

'You've thought of everything,' Megan said appreciatively. 'Thank you so much.'

'Yes, thanks, Austin,' Sarah said. 'You've gone to a lot of trouble for us.'

'I think another toast,' Roshan said, picking up his glass. 'To Austin and this wonderful meal.'

'To Austin,' was repeated around the table.

'To our little gathering,' Austin said. 'Now let's eat. Help yourselves.'

As they ate and drank, with Austin refilling their glasses, they swapped details of their lives over the past ten years. Sarah wondered more than once how Austin knew so much about them when he hadn't kept in touch and had only recently appeared on social media. Eventually, having drunk slightly too much wine, she asked.

'Austin, how come you know all this about us? I mean, the rest of us have kept in touch online, but you haven't.'

He smiled convivially. 'Just because I don't have social media doesn't mean I don't keep abreast of things. People share so much online.'

'So you've been stalking us?' Sarah asked, which she wouldn't have done had she not had so much to drink. She felt Roshan tap her thigh to stop.

'I wouldn't call it that,' Austin replied good-humouredly. 'I hadn't seen you all for so long, and when I realized you'd all kept in touch, I did my homework. Otherwise I could have been Billy-no-mates and have had little conversation to offer about the things that matter to you.'

'That's so thoughtful,' Megan said.

'Don't you use social media for your business?' Roshan asked, steering the conversation onto safer ground.

'Yes, of course. It's necessary. I have a website and email address. But in my line of work it's not advisable to be too accessible. Some of my patients are very troubled, some quite disturbed.'

'But not dangerous?' Megan asked.

'It depends on what you mean by dangerous. I think we

18

all have the potential to do bad things. It's the severity and motive that has more of a bearing for me. That's what I look into when I'm assessing and treating a patient.'

'I see,' Brandon said thoughtfully. 'I like to think I always strive to do the right thing.'

'Me too,' Megan agreed.

'Most of us do think that, most of the time,' Austin replied. Then, leaning back in his chair, he began to outline some theories on moral psychology and ethical behaviour, which led to a heated discussion on what we perceive as right and wrong.

'What you said earlier about vulnerabilities leading to strength?' Brandon queried, slightly sceptically. 'How does that fit in with these theories? As a civil engineer I pride myself on practical problem-solving, not theorizing.'

'Agreed, I'm glad you asked me that,' Austin said, sitting upright, ready to meet the challenge. It was already obvious he loved nothing more than a hearty discussion about psychology. 'If we are able to confront our fears and vulner-abilities they are no longer frightening,' he said. 'When I first see a patient, I start by looking at where their problem originated. What triggered it. I then carefully help them to dismantle the root cause until it lies in pieces, shredded, and is no longer threatening. Much of my work is taken up with helping clients identify and come to terms with their innermost fears and phobias. We all have them, but some of us have them to a degree that they impact on our lives.'

'That's me and spiders!' Megan declared with a shiver. 'When I first arrived here there was a large spider on the wall in the porch. Austin had to remove it before I could walk past.' She gave a small embarrassed laugh. 'Austin has offered to help me overcome my phobia. What about yours, Sarah? I am sure he would help you, if you want him to.'

Austin looked at Sarah. 'Would you like my help? I can teach you some relaxation techniques so you wouldn't panic when something frightens you.'

'No, thank you!' Sarah said indignantly. 'I don't panic and I don't have any fears or phobias.'

Austin held her gaze, then leaning ever so slightly into her personal space, said, 'We could perhaps address your fear of the dead, which is more likely a fear of dying – a common phobia.'

'I don't have a fear of the dead or dying,' Sarah cried, her eyes flashing in anger. 'And I'd appreciate it if you didn't discuss me here.'

'I am so sorry,' Austin said immediately, seeming genuinely apologetic. 'Please forgive me. That was completely out of order. Let's change the subject. I promise I will try not to talk about my work in future. The problem is that I am so passionate about it, I take it everywhere I go.'

'It's fine,' Roshan said. 'It's interesting and I know you meant well.'

'Thanks,' Austin said. 'Now I will try to make amends by serving dessert. My pièce de résistance: Strawberry and Elderflower Fraisiers. Megan, yours is dairy-free.'

They fell silent as he stood and went into the kitchen where he removed a chilled tray from the fridge and brought it to the table. Six perfectly round Fraisiers, each topped with a fresh strawberry and piped cream.

'Six?' Roshan queried.

'Just in case Leslie felt up to joining us. But I've received a text from her saying she won't be coming today, and hopes to join us later in the week. So there's one spare if anyone can manage a second.'

It was nearly midnight by the time they said goodnight. The dishwasher was running and all that remained were the coffee cups and brandy glasses which they'd left in the sink to wash in the morning.

'Thanks again for everything, Austin,' Megan said.

'Yes, thanks,' Brandon and Roshan echoed.

'You're very welcome. I'll lock up and switch off the lights,' Austin said. 'I suggest you take water up with you. You don't want to be stumbling down the spiral staircase in the dark.'

'Good idea,' Brandon agreed. 'Does everyone want a glass of water?'

'Yes please,' Roshan, Megan and Sarah said.

'I'm OK,' Austin said.

Brandon poured four glasses of water and handed them out.

'See you all in the morning,' he said, and disappeared into the alcove then up the spiral staircase.

Megan said goodnight and followed him. Sarah went next, then Roshan.

'Sleep tight,' Austin called after them.

'And you!' Roshan replied, while Sarah said nothing.

'Sleep tight!' she exclaimed once they were in their bedroom and the door was closed. 'Who does he think he is? My mother?'

'He's just being friendly,' Roshan said. 'You know, you were quite rude to him at times tonight. What's the matter?'

'There's something about him. Yes, he can be charming, and he went to all that trouble, but sometimes he really gets under my skin. I remember we used to clash in sixth form. I'll try not to let him get to me.'

'Good. But let's not talk about Austin any more. We're on holiday and if you're not too tired, neither am I.'

'I'm never too tired,' Sarah said with a seductive smile. 'Just a bit tipsy.'

She went to Roshan and, standing with her back to the

window, slipped her arms around his waist. She felt the warmth of his body pressed against hers, then his moist lips covering hers. And as he gently eased her onto the bed and began to remove her clothes, all thoughts of Austin and the graves outside vanished.

FOUR

Sarah knew where she was even though she dared not open her eyes. Terror gripped her. She could feel the coolness of the night air on her bare skin, the damp soil beneath her feet. She could hear the silence of the dead. She knew she was in the graveyard. The recurring nightmare from her childhood where she was at the mercy of her worst fear – death.

'Confront it,' she could almost hear Austin saying.

'I can't,' she cried, close to tears.

She could not confront the paralysing horror of seeing a spirit in the churchyard as a child. It was better left alone. Austin didn't understand that not everything could be explained by psychological theory and rational debate. Sometimes you had to accept what couldn't be explained. And Sarah had accepted that there was another world out there in a different place and time, a spiritual world, that we went to when we died. And sometimes people returned and showed themselves.

'But I was a child then,' she said out loud. 'Now I'm an adult and I have Roshan.' He was here beside her, in the safety of their room. She needed the nightmare to end now. 'Roshan?'

She reached out for him but felt nothing. He wasn't there. 'Roshan?'

Her body stiffened as her fear grew. He was always there for her when she had the nightmare.

Heart pounding, tense and trembling, she covered her face with her hands as she had done as a child, then slowly parted her fingers, revealing the scene in front of her a little at a time. The mist that had been forming in the churchyard when they'd arrived had thickened now. It hung between the trees and shrubs, and around the headstones of the graves, reducing visibility to a few yards. Something small ran through the undergrowth that made her jump. A mouse? She looked down, but the nightmare didn't break. She was wearing the lacy nightdress she'd packed, but her bare feet were caked in mud. This was far too real. She needed to wake.

'Roshan?' she said, reaching out again.

There was still no one beside her. Where was he? She needed him now.

An owl hooted far off in the trees, and Sarah became aware of another movement, closer now. There was someone there, but it wasn't Roshan. Through the haze a figure passed at the edge of her vision. Female, transparent, with no substance, and not made of flesh and bones. She screamed. It drifted fully into view, gliding effortlessly through the graveyard, passing through the headstones, then stopped. The spectre from her childhood, back to haunt her, as realistic now as it had been then.

Reality hit her. This was no dream. She really was in the churchyard, and the spirit was real.

'Confront it,' she heard Austin say. 'You can do it if you want to.'

Shaking from cold and fear, Sarah took one step forward

and stopped. The spirit raised a hand and beckoned for her to follow.

'No!' she screamed. 'I don't want to die yet.' And burying her face in her hands, she fell to her knees sobbing.

FIVE

Inside the converted church Roshan woke with a start. The bedroom was pitch black and it was a few moments before he remembered where he was. Lying on his side, he was facing the stained-glass window, now opaque at night. The room was very quiet. Too quiet, he thought.

He reached out to touch Sarah, but the bed was empty. He couldn't hear her moving in the bathroom either.

'Sarah?'

No reply.

Switching on his bedside lamp, he hauled himself up the pillows. The room tilted. He'd had far too much to drink the night before.

'Sarah?' he called again, then drank some of the water from the glass on his bedside cabinet. Where was Sarah?

He reached for his phone and checked the time – 2.05 a.m. 'Sarah?'

Easing back the duvet, he got out of bed, his head aching. He gingerly crossed the room and switched on the main light. Sarah was nowhere to be seen, but her clothes were where they'd fallen as he'd undressed her. He pushed open the door to the bathroom. It was empty. There was nowhere else she could be. Their bedroom door was still closed. Where the hell was she? Perhaps she'd gone downstairs for more water? But as he looked, he saw her glass was still full.

'Sarah?' he asked again.

This wasn't like her, not up at night in a strange place. Feeling ridiculous, he checked under the bed. Of course she wasn't there. What would she be doing under the bed? He pulled on his pants and trousers, opened the door to the room, and nearly jumped out of his skin. In the dim glow of the night light on the landing he could see Brandon and Megan had just come out of their rooms.

'Did you hear that scream?' Megan asked anxiously, pulling on her dressing gown.

'I did,' Brandon said. He was tying his bathrobe.

'Something woke me, and Sarah's not in our room,' Roshan said, more worried than ever now. 'I'm going to take a look downstairs.'

'I'll come with you,' Brandon offered. 'Although I thought the scream came from outside.'

'Where's the main light switch here?' Roshan asked, searching the walls.

'Here,' Megan said, and switched it on. 'Shall I come too?'

'If you want,' he replied.

The light from the landing gave enough of a glow for them to safely navigate the spiral staircase.

'Sarah?' Roshan called as they descended.

At the foot of the stairs he switched on the light. The kitchen-diner was empty. He went into the living room.

'She's not in there either,' he said, returning. 'This is completely out of character.'

'Do you think she could be in Austin's room?' Megan suggested.

'Why would she be in there?' Roshan asked, a little too aggressively.

27

'I don't know, perhaps she wandered in there by mistake. There's nowhere else she could be. Did you check the cloakroom in the entrance lobby?' she asked. 'Perhaps Sarah thought she'd use the toilet in there rather than wake you.'

But Brandon was already at the back door that led outside. 'It's unlocked,' he said, and turned the handle to open it. The cold night air rushed in.

'Why would she be out there?' Roshan asked, worried. He went out first. Brandon and Megan followed. 'Sarah!' he called into the night. 'Sarah, are you out here?'

An old stone path led from the back door into the churchyard. Roshan began walking along it, calling Sarah's name. The others followed. There was no lamp outside, just the glow from the kitchen light, now partly absorbed into the mist.

'Sarah!' Roshan cried again, and stopped to listen. They were in the middle of the churchyard now.

Silence.

'There's no way she'd come out here by herself at night,' Roshan said. 'She's petrified of graveyards. She was ready to go home when we first arrived and realized where we were staying. She must be inside somewhere.'

'There's only the cloakroom and Austin's room left,' Brandon said as they continued along the path.

'Unless there are outbuildings we don't know of,' Megan suggested uneasily. 'But why would Sarah come out here at all?'

'I don't think she has,' Roshan said, and stopped.

They'd come to the end of the path, countryside, dark and forbidding, lay beyond. The graveyard stretched out either side of them.

'Let's check indoors again,' Brandon said. 'If Sarah's not there then we need to call the police and report her missing. If she's wandered off she could be anywhere.'

28

'Does Sarah sleepwalk?' Megan asked, her voice slight.

'No, never,' Roshan replied. 'She has a bad dream from time to time, and wants a hug, but that's all.'

'Come on, let's go in then,' Brandon said.

'Yes,' Megan agreed. 'It's horrible out here.'

'Sarah!' Roshan tried one last time and waited. There was no reply. They began to retrace their steps along the path.

A few steps and they all heard it. A noise, coming from the graveyard to their right. A sound that could have been a choked sob as if a child might be quietly crying, but could have been an animal in distress. They stopped where they were and listened.

'Sarah?' Roshan called, desperation in his voice.

'Just a moment, I've got my phone in my pocket. I can use the torch,' Brandon said, taking his phone from his bathrobe.

He shone the beam in the direction the noise had come from. It fell on gravestones scarred from years of weathering, weeds, overgrown grass, a broken china angel, a rusting grave vase, and one with flowers suggesting someone still visited the grave. He raised the beam slightly and shone it deeper into the churchyard until the mist sent the beam back again.

'Sarah!' Roshan called.

'Sarah!' Brandon shouted louder.

Nothing.

'There's no one here,' Megan whispered, standing close to them. 'Let's go back indoors.'

'I agree,' Brandon said. 'We'll search thoroughly and then call the police.'

'Sarah!' Roshan cried one last time.

Suddenly a movement. They froze and listened. The noise of breaking twigs coming towards them through the dark and mist, from somewhere in front. Brandon quickly raised his phone and shone it straight ahead. Nothing for a few seconds, then another noise, a whimpering, and the faintest outline of something or someone coming towards them. Very slowly, a step at a time, out of the mist. White, like an apparition. Megan gasped and grabbed Brandon's arm. The figure continued towards them.

'Sarah!' Roshan cried, running to her.

'What the hell!' Brandon said.

'It's her,' Megan shrieked.

Sarah, her flimsy white nightdress wet and stained and clinging to her. No shoes, her feet were covered in mud. Her hair wet and bedraggled, her face pale, her eyes staring, disorientated, almost deranged, as though she didn't know where she was.

'Does Sarah take drugs?' Brandon quietly asked Megan.

'No, not as far as I know,' Megan replied, staring in horror.

Roshan had his arm around Sarah, holding her close, trying to comfort and support her as he led her back to them. She seemed to be more conscious of them now.

'Whatever are you doing out here?' Brandon asked.

'Where's Austin?' Sarah mumbled, her head on Roshan's shoulder.

'In his room asleep, I would think,' Roshan replied. 'Why?'

'I thought he was here.'

'No, love. Come on, let's get you indoors.'

Brandon went first, shining his phone torch just ahead of them and highlighting the way. Roshan followed, supporting Sarah, helping her over the uneven stones of the path and towards the back door. Megan kept close. As they neared the building a light came on in a room on the second floor: Austin's room. Roshan helped Sarah over the doorstep and into the kitchen-diner.

'Get Sarah washed and into something warm,' Brandon said, locking the door behind them. 'I'll switch off the lights down here.'

'I'll make her a hot drink first and bring it up,' Megan offered.

'Thanks,' Roshan said.

He helped Sarah across the kitchen-diner and then up the spiral staircase. Since it was only wide enough for one, he kept his hands on the small of her back to support her in case she stumbled. She still seemed disorientated. They arrived on the landing as the door to Austin's room opened and he came out.

'Austin?' Sarah asked, puzzled.

'Jesus! What's happened to you?'

She looked at him, dumbfounded and confused.

'Sarah seems to have been sleepwalking,' Roshan said, helping her across the landing to their bedroom.

'She's been outside?' Austin asked incredulously.

Roshan nodded and opened their bedroom door.

'Anything I can do?'

'No. Sorry to have woken you,' Roshan said, embarrassed that Austin had witnessed Sarah like this.

'No problem. Probably best to lock your bedroom door to keep her safe. That's what I advise my clients who sleepwalk.'

SIX

Safely inside their room, Roshan turned on the shower, adjusted the temperature, and then helped Sarah take off her dirty nightdress and step into the shower.

'Do you remember what happened?' he asked, worried.

'Some of it,' she said. The warm water ran over her body, washing off the mud and grass, but not the full horror of the night.

'I woke at two o'clock to find you gone. I was worried sick,' Roshan said. Usually when he was in the shower with Sarah he was caressing her body and making love to her. But now nothing was further from his mind. He was far too tense and anxious.

'To begin with I thought it was that dream I have sometimes,' Sarah said, slowly recovering. 'But it wasn't a dream. It was real. I could see the ghost from my childhood very clearly, feel her presence, and I could hear Austin telling me to confront it. I know he was out there somewhere.'

'Sarah, we both know that's impossible.'

'But I was outside, wasn't I? So that bit was real.'

'Yes, but that's where it ends, love. Sarah, I think you should get help. You've had that same dream – nightmare

32

– on and off since your childhood, and tonight was horrendous.'

'I know. I suppose I could ask Austin for his help.'

'No, I was thinking more that when we got home we could find someone local who could help you.'

'Yes, you're probably right, I should,' Sarah agreed.

She was clean now, and she switched off the shower. Roshan held out the bath sheet and Sarah stepped into it. He gently wrapped it around her and then passed her a hand towel to dry her hair.

'I'm being very well looked after,' she said, finally able to raise a small smile.

He kissed her lightly on the nose. 'I was so worried, Sarah. Please don't do that again.'

'I didn't do it on purpose.'

'I know.'

'I felt I had to go,' she said. 'Like I had no control of it. As if someone was telling me what to do.'

Sarah sat on the edge of the bed and began absently towel-drying her hair. A knock sounded on the door, which made her start.

'It'll be Megan with your hot drink,' Roshan said.

He opened the door.

'How is she?' Megan asked. She was carrying two mugs on a small tray.

'Not too bad. Come in.'

'We're all going to be so shattered tomorrow,' she said. 'I've made you both a hot chocolate. I thought something sweet for shock. How are you?' she asked Sarah, putting the mugs on her bedside cabinet.

'OK. Thanks for the drink,' Sarah said. 'Sorry for having you all up. What a first-night reunion!'

'Don't worry about us. It's you we're concerned about. Brandon and I have just been talking, and we think it's not surprising you had a nightmare. It's our first night in a strange place, and Roshan said you're not happy around graves. We all had far too much to drink, and Austin was talking about confronting our fears. It's a wonder I didn't wake in the night seeing spiders!'

'You could be right,' Sarah said, grateful there might be a rational explanation. 'But it was so real. I was that petrified child again in the graveyard. I felt sure Austin was there, but it's more likely it's what he said at dinner and during the evening that preyed on my mind.'

'I think that makes perfect sense,' Roshan said, relieved. 'Thanks, Megan. Have you and Brandon ever thought about becoming psychologists?'

Megan smiled. 'I'll leave you to it then and see you both tomorrow. Austin wants to show us around, but that can wait until the afternoon.'

'Absolutely,' Roshan said. 'We'll have a lie-in. Thanks again.'

Roshan went with Megan to the door and said goodnight, then locked it behind her, leaving the key in the lock. Sarah finished her hot chocolate and got into bed. Roshan drank some of his, then switched off the main light and climbed into bed beside her.

'Can you leave your lamp on until I'm asleep?' she asked.

'Yes, of course.'

He put his arm around her and she snuggled close, resting her head on his shoulder.

'You're safe now,' he murmured.

He held her to him. Gradually her breathing grew more and more shallow and she slowly relaxed into sleep. Only when he was sure she was fast asleep did he reach out to switch off his lamp. Before doing so he checked his phone. There was a text message from Austin – just to him, not their WhatsApp group.

I'm very worried about Sarah. Happy to offer my professional help.

He was about to text back when he noticed what time the message had been sent: 12.13. Strange. That was just after they'd said goodnight and had gone to bed – before Sarah went missing.

Austin didn't know Sarah, Roshan thought as he lay awake in the dark. So why had he thought she needed help before her nightmare? They hadn't seen each other in ten years and had only been together a few hours yesterday. Had Austin spotted something that he, being so close to Sarah, had missed? Something Austin's professional eye had seen. But what? Roshan prided himself on knowing Sarah better than anyone. He was too tired to think about it now. Perhaps when the chance arose and he and Austin were alone he could ask him what he meant and then take it from there.

SEVEN

Sarah woke gradually the following morning. Sunlight was streaming through the stained-glass window, sending colourful patterns onto the floor and duvet. It was beautiful, just like in the photographs online, and reminded her of the kaleidoscope she'd had as a child. The various shapes and colours created a magical moving world of wonder and delight. What a difference the daylight made to their room, she thought.

She sat up in bed and drank some water. She could hear Roshan in the shower. What time was it? She checked her phone: 10.40. Little wonder they'd slept so late after last night. How embarrassing. She'd have to apologize to everyone. Whatever had she been doing? A recurring nightmare was one thing, but to go wandering around in the middle of the night convinced it was true was definitely something else!

And yet . . .

It had seemed so real. The feel of the wet grass and soil beneath her feet, stumbling through the graveyard in the mist. Running from the woman in white. She couldn't recall leaving their room or the building, just being outside. What would have happened if Roshan, Megan and Brandon hadn't come looking for her? It didn't bear thinking about. Best not dwell on it, she decided. Put it behind her and enjoy the rest of the week.

Sarah swung her legs out of bed and savoured the room afresh. It was certainly grand, well beyond what their usual holiday budget allowed. Splitting the bill for the place between them all had made it affordable. Although Austin clearly didn't have to worry about cost as he'd done so well for himself. She heard Roshan finish in the shower and he came out with a towel wrapped around his waist, the hair on his chest still damp. For a second he looked at her with concern. 'You're awake, love.'

'Yes, and I'm fine. Don't worry. I'll apologize to everyone and we'll enjoy the rest of our week together.'

His relief was obvious and he kissed her lightly on the lips. 'I think the others are up. I heard some movement when I first woke. Once you're ready, we'll go down. I'm dying for a coffee.'

'Me too.'

Twenty minutes later, dressed in jeans, trainers, and similar long-sleeve polo shirts, Sarah and Roshan walked down the spiral staircase. The smell of coffee and cooking greeted them. Brandon was alone in the kitchen-diner, at the range cooker frying eggs.

'Good morning,' he said. 'Coffee's there.' He nodded to the coffee without looking at Sarah.

'Sorry about last night,' she said, getting it out of the way.

He met her gaze. 'Are you OK?'

'Yes, I'm fine. Just embarrassed. Least said, soonest mended.'

'Of course.' He looked relieved. 'Do you two want these eggs? I can put some more in for me.'

37

'No, you have yours. We'll sort ours out,' Roshan said. He poured coffee for himself and Sarah and topped up Brandon's mug. The coffee tasted delicious.

'Trust Austin to get the best ground coffee,' Roshan said.

'Absolutely, but there's no brown sauce or tomato ketchup. I doubt he uses them,' Brandon said with a smile. 'I've started a shopping list – there. Add what you want. There's plenty of food for today, so we can go shopping tomorrow.'

'Are Megan and Austin up?' Sarah asked, dropping bread into the toaster.

'They're in the living room,' Brandon replied. 'They've had something to eat and Austin is giving Megan a session to help her with her arachnophobia – fear of spiders. I've been keeping out of their way. They shouldn't be long now.'

Brandon took his cooked eggs from the frying pan and sandwiched them between two slices of buttered bread, then carried them with the coffee to the table.

'Do you want eggs?' Roshan asked Sarah, cracking one into the frying pan.

'No thanks, I'm just having toast.'

'There's honey, but no marmalade,' Brandon said. 'In that cupboard beside the fridge-freezer.'

'That'll do me.'

Sarah buttered her toast, spread on honey, and joined Brandon at the table. Roshan brought over his cooked breakfast. The sun was shining through the window in the kitchen too, catching little dust motes in its beam.

'It's a lovely day,' Sarah remarked.

'It is,' Brandon agreed. 'Austin is eager to give us a guided tour. I've said I'll go.'

'That'll be nice. Learn about the area,' Sarah agreed.

'So how are things with you?' Roshan asked Brandon as they ate. 'We didn't get much chance to talk last night. What's your latest news?'

'Not a lot really. I haven't managed to meet the love of my life yet. I'm not one for clubs or singles holidays, and there aren't that many women in my line of work. But I have managed to buy a small house with a mortgage.'

'Well done,' Roshan said. 'We're still renting and saving for a deposit.'

'I had a bit of help from the bank of Mum and Dad,' Brandon admitted. 'I'm an only child and they wanted me to have it now. I was grateful.'

As they talked, ate, and drank coffee, renewing their friendship, normality returned for Sarah. She was reminded why the three of them had got on so well at school and in the sixth form. Brandon was a lovely guy with a good sense of humour, just like Roshan. The boys had a lot in common: open, sincere, kind and empathetic, and it crossed Sarah's mind that if she hadn't dated and then married Roshan she probably would have ended up with Brandon.

It was 11.30 when the door to the living room opened and Austin and Megan came in at the end of Megan's therapy session. Both were smiling and relaxed, and appeared at ease in each other's company.

'Hi guys, did you both manage to get some sleep?' Megan asked.

'Yes, thanks,' Sarah replied. 'I'm sorry I had you all up.'

'No problem. At least you're OK.'

'Sorry, Austin, I woke you too,' Sarah added, meeting his gaze.

'I was concerned for you,' he said, more earnestly than Sarah would have liked. 'Do tell me if you want my help. My sessions would be free, of course. They always are for my friends.'

'That's kind of you. I'll think about it.'

Roshan hadn't told Sarah about Austin's text message, and he wouldn't. Sarah had recovered from her ordeal last night

39

and was back to her old self. If she did want to talk about her recurrent nightmare to a therapist, they would find someone when they returned home. For reasons Roshan couldn't say, he felt that was preferable, even if they'd have to pay.

'Are we all ready to go on Austin's guided tour?' Megan asked enthusiastically.

'Nearly,' Sarah said. 'Just give us a few minutes to freshen up.'

'And me,' Brandon said.

'So let's meet back here in fifteen minutes,' Austin suggested. 'And remember, sensible footwear for our walk.'

'It's like going on a school outing,' Megan laughed, and Sarah agreed.

Fifteen minutes later, suitably dressed for walking in the countryside in autumn, they assembled in the kitchen-diner.

'We'll start at the front of the church where you came in,' Austin said.

He led the way through the living room, then the lobby where they'd come in, out the main door and down the front path. They stood in a line just the other side of the gate so, as Austin said, they could see it in 'all its glory'.

There was no mist now; the sky was blue with the occasional fluffy white cloud passing behind the church tower. 'This church is typical of many in the area,' Austin said. 'And is thought to be built on the site of an earlier Anglo-Saxon church that was recorded in the Domesday survey of 1086.'

'That's incredible,' Megan enthused.

'It is,' Austin agreed. 'So much history. This place has seen a lot. The ruins of a wall belonging to the original church can still be seen in the graveyard at the rear. We'll go there in a minute.' He continued with a history of the church and the site it was built on over the centuries, then paused. 'Any questions so far?'

'No, I think you're being very thorough,' Brandon said, with only the merest hint of irony, and exchanging a small smile with Roshan.

'Good. So we'll go into the churchyard and do a circuit of the building from outside,' Austin said, and headed off, closely followed by Megan.

'I'm guessing that flashy BMW is Austin's,' Roshan said quietly to Brandon, nodding to one of the cars parked on the hardstanding.

'It's certainly not mine,' Brandon said. 'How much did that set him back? Must be £50K plus.'

'It could be financed,' Roshan pointed out.

'Maybe, but from what I've seen he's doing very well. There's money in sorting out people's heads.'

They followed Austin and Megan through the graveyard to the left of the church, where he paused, not far from where Sarah had been found last night.

'This is the oldest part of the existing church,' Austin said. 'It was the north aisle and became part of the living room in the reconstruction. The south doorway which is now our back door is later, suggesting the church could have been extended by the addition of the central nave.'

They nodded.

'The tower,' he said, looking up, 'was probably built around 1500, and that arch is Tudor brickwork. The church was then allowed to decline until the great Victorian restoration in the nineteenth century.'

They continued round the back of the church, where he paused again. 'There are the remains of the original wall that I mentioned. The roof is new, the original was lead. I picked up an interesting fact while researching. In 1839 lead was stolen from the roof, and the church warden caught and

41

prosecuted the thief. He was found guilty and sentenced to be deported for twelve years.'

'That wasn't very Christian,' Sarah remarked. 'Times were hard then. I've been covering this period with the children in my class. He was probably trying to feed his family and keep them from all starving.'

'Very likely,' Austin agreed. 'There wasn't much leniency shown then, they were still hanging teenagers for some crimes.'

'That's shocking,' Megan gasped.

'Do you know what happened to the man's family?' Sarah asked.

'No, it didn't say,' Austin replied. 'If the family had no income, then they would have likely ended up in the work-house at the best, or living on the streets.' He turned, ready to move on. 'This way. We'll complete our tour of the outside, then I suggest we walk up that hill over there.' He pointed. 'I understand it gives an excellent view of the church, village, and surrounding countryside. Then we could go to the village pub for lunch.'

'Best idea you've had all morning,' Brandon said.

'Yes, a nice pub lunch. Sounds good to me,' said Roshan, and the others agreed.

They followed Austin to the only side of the church they hadn't seen yet, where he pointed out period features. He'd certainly done his homework, Sarah thought. But she was starting to get a little jaded, as she sensed Brandon was. The church had a lot of history, but most rural villages in England had a church like this. There were hundreds, if not thousands, dotted around. She allowed her gaze to wander to the graves nearby, absently reading the inscriptions that were still legible on the headstones. Her gaze fell to a patch in the grass where a grey marble memorial stone from a cremation lay. Beneath it would be a cask containing the deceased's ashes. Although the grass was growing over the edges, there was no weather damage, suggesting the stone was more recent. The sun bounced off the polished marble and Sarah squinted to read the inscription.

In loving memory of Michelle Warner

Her heart stopped and her mouth went dry. It couldn't be. That was impossible. It was her mother's name. She must have misread. She looked again but there was no mistake. A coincidence? They must both have the same name. Then she read the date of her birth and death.

Sarah's head began to swim and her stomach churned. She grabbed Roshan's arm to steady herself. How could that be? Her mother's ashes lay in a different cemetery in another part of the country miles from here, close to where she'd lived. But there it was.

She squeezed Roshan's arm and he looked at her questioningly as Austin continued his lecture.

'Look at that memorial stone,' she whispered.

Roshan followed her gaze to the memorial stone and then back to her. He frowned, puzzled. 'What's the matter?'

'It's my mother's.'

His eyes widened in disbelief and he reread the inscription. Then he looked at Sarah again.

'It's not your mother,' he whispered. 'It's a Michael Wilson and he was seventy-nine years old when he died. Your mother was thirty-four. Whatever is the matter, Sarah?'

She looked again at the inscription, and as she did, the previous one showing her mother's details slowly disappeared, morphing into the one Roshan had seen.

She swallowed hard and took a deep breath. Get control, she told herself, but she knew what she'd seen.

'Sorry, it must have been the sun shining on it,' she said.

'Yes, and Michelle is similar to Michael,' Roshan added.

But Sarah was so sure of what she'd seen, just as she had

been last night, that it made her afraid. Her eyes could be deceiving her on other matters. She continued to hold Roshan's arm and looked around, hoping that what she was seeing was real.

EIGHT

On Monday morning, Detective Constable Beth Mayes sat at her desk in the open-plan office above Coleshaw police station. She was concentrating on her computer screen. Opposite her was Detective Constable Matt Davis; his gaze was fixed on his screen too. Their morning briefing meeting had finished an hour ago and had largely focused on the spate of robberies committed by the woman the media had labelled Chanel Woman. Leading the briefing, Detective Sergeant Bert Scrivener had said it was their priority to catch this woman, as questions were now being asked about police competency: she had evaded them for two years, and was still continuing her robberies right under their noses.

Beth had been tasked with going through the witness statements again to see if there was anything they might have missed that could give them a clue to Chanel Woman's identity. Matt was checking orders for prosthetic masks. These were laborious tasks, but the bedrock of good detective work is often tedious. If their diligence paid off and led to the culprit being brought to justice, then it would all be worthwhile and might even lead to promotions. Beth and Matt had joined the police force around the same time and had worked together for most of their career. But as they and others in the room continued to sift through two years of reports, nothing new came to light.

Beth's desk phone rang, 'DC Beth Mayes,' she said, answering.

'Hi Beth, I've got Danny Able from the *Coleshaw Times* on the phone,' the call handler said.

'Put him through, please,' Beth replied without hesitation. They needed the media's help in identifying Chanel Woman, and Beth had a good working relationship with Danny. 'Hi Danny, how are you?'

'Good, thanks. And you, Beth?'

'Fine, considering it's Monday.'

'You'll have had your morning briefing by now,' he said, 'and a chance to gather the evidence from Friday's robbery. What's the latest on Chanel Woman?'

'There is something,' Beth said. 'We believe she's local.'

'How local?'

'Within about a thirty-mile radius of Coleshaw.'

'I see. Can you tell me how you know this?'

'Sorry, I can't, but you can use it. You're the first to know. We'll be putting it out later.'

'OK, Cheers.'

Beth pictured the front-page headline in their local paper: *Chanel Woman Lives Locally!* Or similar. Danny didn't need to know why the police thought she was local. In fact, it was better he didn't, for the truth was it was nothing more than a hunch of DS Scrivener's based on how well she appeared to know the area.

'Anything else?' Danny asked.

'We think she visits the shops and businesses she targets for some time before making her move,' Beth said. 'We're re-examining all the CCTV footage. You can print that too.' But again, she knew it wasn't a lot. An opportunist thief might chance to go into a property where there was an open front door or smash the window of a car where valuables had been left on display, but no experienced thief would. They would spend time getting to know the layout of the premises they were going to burgle, familiarizing themselves with the routine of those working there so they knew when they were at their most vulnerable. However, Danny seemed pleased he was getting this information first.

'Thanks, Beth. I'll upload this to our digital newspaper straight away, then it will be front page in the printed edition on Wednesday. Let me know if anything else comes through.'

'Will do.'

The call ended and Beth returned her attention to her computer screen.

Matt sighed. 'It's like looking for a needle in a haystack,' he grumbled. 'There's thousands of outlets selling these prosthetic masks online. Apart from masks going to film sets, sales spike at this time of year for Halloween. We're looking at hundreds of thousands sold globally, but I'm expected to match one with those Chanel Woman wears?'

Beth nodded sympathetically.

'Everything OK?' DS Bert Scrivener asked, arriving at Beth's side and looking at Matt.

'Yes, sir,' he replied, and returned his attention to his screen.

'This could be something or nothing,' DS Scrivener said to Beth, handing her a printed sheet with a name and address on it. 'Following our last appeal we've had a call from a man who owns a bargain buy type of shop that sells everything. He says a woman matching the description of Chanel Woman was in on Saturday. She bought a mask. Not a cheap gory Halloween mask, but a high-quality latex mask of an attractive woman in her twenties. They don't sell many of those. The last one was sold two years ago to a local amateur dramatic company. He was intrigued and asked her what she wanted it for. She said she liked to change her appearance. He'd seen our appeal and it set alarm bells ringing. She paid in cash, but he followed her out of the shop and noted the registration of the car she was driving. This is her name and address. She lives in Drayten, which is within my thirty-mile radius. It's a long shot, but you never know. Obviously, don't take any chances. If it looks dodgy, phone for backup.'

'Yes, sir,' Beth said.

DS Scrivener went off to talk to someone else. Beth closed the computer file she'd been working on and stood, picking up the sheet of paper.

'Lucky you,' Matt said. 'A change of scenery and some real policing.'

'I'll ask for you if I need backup,' Beth replied with a smile, and left.

Ten minutes later Beth had picked up the pool car from the yard at the back of the police station and was heading towards Drayten. The satellite navigation system showed it was twenty-five miles and the route was clear. The DS had clearly thought that this 'lead', like all the others over the last two years, would go nowhere. If he'd really believed this could be the Chanel Woman who carried a gun when she committed her crimes, he would never have asked her to go alone.

You had to hand it to the woman, Beth thought as she drove. She used simple but very effective techniques. Know your target well, use a prosthetic mask which looks like a real face but not your own, wear gloves so there are no fingerprints, and carry a gun so people are scared into doing what you tell them. She was in and out of the premises in minutes, leaving behind no clues whatsoever, apart from the perfume she always wore. That had become her trademark and a fingers-up at the police: *Hi, it's me, Chanel Woman. I've struck again, and you can't get me.*

She must be very rich by now, Beth thought as she followed the satnav's direction and turned left. The cash she'd stolen from businesses, post offices, and banks amounted to over £5,000,000, which she must have been laundering, although no one had reported any money laundering concerns. She'd also robbed jewellers of an estimated £2,000,000, some of which she surely must have sold. But where? None of it had come onto the market yet, as far as they knew. Yes, she was a cool, calculating, successful thief with style and panache, a rare breed. But her luck would run out soon. She would be getting overconfident by now and hopefully slip up before long. Could it be that buying that mask from the Bargain Buys shop where the owner had had the good sense to note her registration was her downfall? In which case, it would be Beth who caught her.

The road remained clear, and twenty minutes later Beth pulled onto the estate at the edge of Drayten. It was a relatively new development built about ten years before, she guessed, with a selection of detached and semi-detached houses, each with their own neat front garden and integral garage. A pleasant leafy suburb where its middle-class residents might aspire to more than they could afford, she thought, and where husbands bought their wives decent perfume for their birthdays, Christmas or Valentine's Day to go with some sexy underwear.

Beth parked the unmarked police car outside 22 Cherry Tree Close, the home of Rita and Jim Tod. The car registered to Rita Tod stood on the driveway, and an upstairs window was open, suggesting someone was in. All Beth knew of the couple was that Rita was forty and her husband was forty-one, that they were the first and only owners of this house, and according to the Police National Computer neither of them had criminal records. Number 22, like its neighbours, had a neatly trimmed front lawn. But unlike its neighbours it had net curtains at all the windows so no one could see in.

Beth got out and walked up the path to the front door. The street was quiet. Those working would be at their jobs by now. She pressed the doorbell and heard it chime. She waited, but no one answered. She pressed the bell again, and a few moments later the door opened.

'Mrs Rita Tod?' Beth asked.

'Yes, that's me.'

'I'm Detective Constable Beth Mayes,' Beth said, showing her ID.

'What's the matter?' Mrs Tod asked, immediately concerned. 'Is it my husband, Jim?'

'No. Can I come in? I need to discuss a purchase you made.'

'A purchase?' she said, puzzled, but invited Beth in.

She was the same height and build as Chanel Woman, Beth thought. And her short blond hair would easily tuck under a wig. The decor in the hall took Beth by surprise. The walls were wallpapered with a lavish floral print, possibly designer, a bit at odds with a modest house on a modern estate. The smell of air freshener hung in the air.

Mrs Tod showed Beth into the main living room, which stretched from the front of the house to the back. This room was also lavishly decorated with a different floral print, and it had an expensive-looking cream sofa, matching chairs, and, unusually, a well-stocked cocktail bar. Did they do a lot of entertaining, Beth wondered. There was no clutter or sign of others living here.

'You can sit down,' Mrs Tod said, a little apprehensively.

'Thank you.'

Beth sat in the chair closest to the door as Rita took the sofa. She showed no sign of nervousness.

'The last time I saw one of those cocktail bars was in the house of a well-known celebrity,' Beth remarked.

'We often have guests at the weekend,' Mrs Tod replied.

'Nice.'

'You mentioned a purchase?'

'Yes, I understand you bought a high-quality prosthetic mask from a shop called Bargain Buys in Drayten?'

The colour drained from Mrs Tod's face. 'How do you know that?'

'The owner of the shop noted the registration number of your car.'

'Why?' she asked.

'It was an unusual purchase, and he'd seen our appeal on television for those selling prosthetic masks and make-up.'

Mrs Tod stared back, apparently uncomprehending. Did she really not understand, or was it a ruse, allowing her time to think?

'In connection with Chanel Woman,' Beth added.

Mrs Tod maintained eye contact. 'I'm sorry. I don't know what you're talking about.'

'You must have heard of the Chanel Woman robberies?'

'I think I saw something on the news, but I didn't take much notice.'

'She's evaded police capture for two years, largely because she wears a very good prosthetic mask. Just like the one you bought.'

Mrs Tod's gaze darted around the room then returned to Beth. She seemed to be weighing up her options. Beth watched her carefully for any sudden movement. If she tried to make a run for it, Beth would call for backup.

'We know you bought it,' Beth said. 'Can you tell me for what purpose, so we can eliminate you from our enquiries?' Mrs Tod (or was it Chanel Woman?) licked her bottom lip, the first sign of nervousness. An admission of guilt that she'd finally been caught?

'My other mask tore,' she said, her voice slight. 'It was a replacement.'

'Why do you need a mask at all?' Beth asked.

'I would prefer not to tell you,' Mrs Tod said, fidgeting with her fingers.

'I need to know,' Beth said, and touched her phone, ready to press the distress button that would summon all available officers in the area, if necessary. 'Perhaps you would prefer to answer my questions at the police station?'

'No, of course not. I haven't done anything wrong. The reason I need the mask is embarrassing. I'd rather not tell you, that's all.'

'It takes a lot to embarrass me,' Beth said, and waited, senses alert. If the woman lunged at her or produced a gun, would she have time to press the distress button? Perhaps she should have brought Matt with her after all.

'If I tell you, you won't tell anyone else?' Mrs Tod asked. 'I mean the press, or put it on social media?'

'There shouldn't be any need to,' Beth replied carefully.

'Very well. If you must know, my husband and I are members of a swingers' club. We meet on Saturday nights, when we dress up and have a good time. We wear masks so we can't easily recognize each other, and the sex is more fun that way. Your inhibitions go. My previous mask split after some rather rough sex, so I had to get another one in time for this Saturday.'

Did the woman take her for a fool?

'I can show you it upstairs if you like.'

'Yes, please.'

Finger hovering on the distress button of her phone, Beth followed Mrs Tod up the carpeted stairs and into a bedroom at the rear of the house. There was a king-size bed with shiny black satin sheets, and a leather chair with bondage straps beside it. Mrs Tod opened the wardrobe where the prosthetic mask lay on a shelf, on its side as if beheaded. Its hollow eyes stared back at them. Beside it were trays of dildos and other sex toys.

'Do you want to see the torn mask? It's in the bin,' Mrs Tod said.

'No, that won't be necessary,' Beth said tightly. 'Thank you for your cooperation. I'm sorry to have troubled you.'

And as Beth made her way downstairs she steeled herself to break the news to DS Scrivener and the rest of the team their suspect ran a swingers' club. They were going to have such a laugh at her expense.

NINE

Ten miles from Coleshaw police station, where Beth's colleagues were still joking about her false lead, Chanel Woman was pouring herself a large gin and tonic before she phoned her husband. He was going to be so disappointed when she told him what she'd done, for, as he'd pointed out before on many occasions, she had everything she needed, so why did she need to steal? They lived in a luxurious five-bedroom house standing in its own grounds. She didn't have to work; he provided everything, so her time was her own to do with as she wished. It was a lifestyle most could only dream of.

The truth was, she didn't know why she stole, and she'd promised him and herself many times she'd stop, but she couldn't. Something came over her: a compulsion, an irresistible urge to plan and commit a robbery. They'd researched possible causes online and found she wasn't the only one who stole for the fun of it, without needing the money. It was an illness, and it had a name. Kleptomania. She knew she needed help before it was too late and she got caught. He'd even suggested that she hand herself in to the police, but she knew she would never survive prison, even if it was a reduced sentence due to illness being the cause of the crime.

She'd promised him she wouldn't leave the house while he was away, but she'd broken that promise the minute he'd gone. Now she had to phone him and confess before he saw it on the news.

She took another large sip of her drink and absently touched the scar on her face. It was bothering her more than usual today. Most likely the latex from the last mask she'd worn. She reacted more to some than others. Her cheek was probably red and inflamed but there were no mirrors downstairs where she could check. The only mirror in the whole of the house was upstairs in their dressing room. She didn't need constant reminders of what she looked like. The ugly scarring covered most of the right side of her face, a result of being trapped in a burning car at the age of seventeen. Her boyfriend at the time had just passed his driving test and borrowed his father's car to take her for a ride. He'd approached a bend too fast, braked too hard on a slippery road surface and lost control of the car. It had rolled – she could still remember it rolling, over and over again – and then burst into flames. He'd been thrown clear and had gone for help, leaving her trapped upside down by her seat belt to burn alive.

She'd only survived thanks to a passing motorist who'd risked his life to pull her out, seconds before the car exploded, but not before the flames had melted half her face. Despite skin grafts and some reconstructive surgery, she was scarred for life. She wondered if that was the reason she wore attractive masks when committing the robberies. But that didn't explain why she stole when she didn't need the money. It was a wonder her husband put up with her.

The holdall containing the cash from the last robbery was hidden at the back of her walk-in wardrobe. He'd help her take care of it when he returned, just as he had all the other times. She knew she had a lot to be grateful for and hoped his patience wouldn't run out.

Finishing the last of the gin and tonic she took a deep breath and called his mobile. He answered immediately. 'Hi, love.'

'Can you talk?'

'Yes. But I think I know what you're going to tell me. I've seen it on the news.'

'I'm so sorry,' she said, and burst into tears.

He waited, as patient as ever, until she'd composed herself.

'I'm disappointed in you, yes,' he said. 'But it's not your fault. I'll make sure you get the help you need. Don't touch anything, we'll deal with it when I get home.'

'Thank you. I'm so sorry.'

'I know.'

TEN

That same Monday at 4.40 p.m., the autumn sun was beginning to drop as Sarah let herself out the back door of the converted church. She set off along the path that ran through and around the graveyard. It would have been unthinkable two days ago when she'd first arrived, but now she was forcing herself to walk alone in the graveyard every few hours. Austin was helping her to confront and overcome her fears, and she had to admit it was getting easier. *Face your fear, confront it, breathe deeply*. Bit by bit, a step at a time, she was making progress.

This was the latest she'd been out, though, and she doubted she'd ever manage to walk here alone at night – the target Austin had set for her. But, on the other hand, Megan had made huge progress controlling her arachnophobia after just three sessions with Austin, so anything was possible.

Although sceptical at first, Sarah had agreed to try Austin's sessions, for as he'd pointed out she had nothing to lose. Brandon had too – to help curb his appetite. Sarah had noticed when they'd first arrived that he'd put on weight, but she hadn't said anything. After just one of Austin's sessions he'd stopped constantly snacking, and here Sarah was doing the unthinkable and going for a walk alone in a churchyard. It had been so simple. All you had to do was sit comfortably in a chair in the living room and listen to Austin's soothing voice as he taught you how to relax and conquer your fear. Simple but effective techniques.

Brandon and Megan were out shopping, Roshan was in the bedroom, chilling, and Austin was in his room answering some emails. There had been an unspoken agreement that Brandon and Megan would go shopping alone, since it was becoming increasingly clear they fancied each other. And why not? Sarah thought as she walked. They were both single and looking for love, and they had been friends since school. Brandon accepted Megan was a single parent so came with a child. Sarah thought Brandon would make an excellent father, and Megan had said she'd like more children.

Sarah paused to read some of the headstones as she had on her previous walks. Many of them were familiar now. Albert and Florence Wright, Henry and Bertha Shaw. Some of the graves had many family members listed, some included babies, which was sad. She remembered teaching her class about the high infant mortality rate in the 1800s, with so little known about disease control and before antibiotics. *Together forever* read the headstone on a grave where a family of four had been laid to rest.

As Sarah entered the place in the graveyard where she'd been found wandering distressed on the first night, the temperature noticeably dropped. She shivered. It always did just here; she told herself it was because the overhead branches of the evergreen trees stopped any sunlight getting in. The soil was wet; it smelled dank, like rotting leaves. She pulled her jacket closer, quickened her pace, and was soon out of the dark patch and round the back of the church. It was warmer and brighter here, and the air smelled sweeter. She continued to the far side of the church, the final part of her walk.

She made herself stop at the memorial stone that had caused her so much anguish. The one she'd thought was her mother's. *Confront your fears, Sarah*, she heard Austin telling her, and she did. Looking at the marble stone she could see how she'd made the error of misreading Michael Wilson for her mother – Michelle Warner. The outline of the names was similar, and the sun had been shining on the marble, not like now. Had she not panicked and bothered to read the rest of the inscription, she would have seen that Michael's beloved wife was also buried here: Constance Mary Wilson.

Yes, it must have been the sun glinting off the stone, and her heightened state of alert caused by her fear of graveyards, Austin had said. Coming just after her first night here and that horrendous sleepwalking episode, when she'd been at her most vulnerable.

But if that was so, why was the inscription changing now?

Sarah stared in horror as the lettering formed her mother's name – Michelle Warner, not Michael Wilson. She blinked hard, looking away and back again, but the letters refused to revert. *Relax, breathe deeply*, focus, she told herself, *remember what Austin taught you*. She took a few slow deep breaths then looked again. It was still her mother's name. Impossible. What was happening to her? She screwed her eyes tightly shut and prayed the words would change back. But when she looked again it was still her mother's name, and Michael and his wife were nowhere to be seen. *It can't be*, she told herself. But this was real, there was no mistake. Her heart pounded, her head swam, and the air temperature dropped further.

'Sarah,' she heard her mother say, as clear as if she was standing next to her. 'Sarah, where are you?'

'I'm here, Mummy,' she said in a small voice that came from her childhood. 'Where are you?'

'I'm here, right behind you,' she replied.

Hardly daring to breathe and petrified of what she might see, Sarah slowly turned and looked straight into the eyes of Austin.

'Are you all right?' he asked with concern, touching her arm. 'What's the matter, Sarah?'

The fuzziness in her head began to clear and she looked at the memorial stone. It had returned to normal. 'It's nothing,' she stammered. 'I'm all right. I've probably just overdone it.'

'Maybe. Why? Did you see something you shouldn't have done? Heard something you knew wasn't real? You know you can tell me. Indeed, you *should* tell me. I can help.'

'I'm fine,' she said, feeling foolish and wanting to get away. 'I've finished my walk for today, so I'm going inside now.'

'OK, if you're sure I can't help.'

'No.'

'I'll see you later then.'

'Yes, see you later,' she said, and hurried down the path and in through the back door.

She wouldn't tell Austin what she'd seen, admit that she'd failed to control her fears. She didn't want to disappoint him. She wouldn't tell Roshan either; he'd said he'd had enough of Austin's psychoanalysing everything, that they were here to chill for a week, not rummage in the murky corners of their minds. He'd told her if she wanted to talk through her phobia about graveyards then they'd pay for her to see a therapist when they got home, that this wasn't the time or place. So, for now at least, she'd keep what happened to herself and pray it didn't happen again.

ELEVEN

At 6.45 p.m. that evening Megan and Brandon were in the kitchen sharing a bottle of wine as they made the evening meal from the food they'd bought together that afternoon. Sarah, Roshan and Austin were in the living room sipping their drinks. The television was on, although Austin was spending more time checking his phone and texting than looking at the screen. Sarah was trying to put the events of her last walk out of her mind.

'You're popular,' Roshan remarked drily to Austin after a while.

'Work, I'm afraid,' he replied. 'Some of my clients need support in addition to our face-to-face sessions. It helps them if they know I'm at the end of the phone, especially if they're in crisis.'

'Do you charge them extra?' Roshan asked. Sarah glared at him. It was none of his business, but Austin didn't seem to mind.

'Not for text messages,' he replied easily. 'Just for the actual sessions.'

'Is all your work private or is some National Health Service?' Roshan asked. Sarah knew where this was leading.

Roshan didn't believe in a two-tier healthcare system where those who could afford it received prompter, some would say, better, care.

'It's all private,' Austin confirmed, unruffled.

'Why?' Roshan persisted.

'I like being my own boss and choosing which patients I accept. Also, I'd need extra certificates to work in the NHS.'

Roshan looked ready to respond, so Sarah raised the volume slightly on the television, effectively silencing him. Once Roshan got going on one of his pet subjects there was no stopping him. Private health and private education were top of his list. He let go of what he was about to say and returned his attention to the television. The news was on, but Austin was concentrating on his phone.

The international news had finished and the regional news had begun, some segments with outside reporters standing against a backdrop of where an incident had taken place. A house fire in Sutton that was being treated as arson; the police were appealing for witnesses. A charity runner who'd just completed a marathon, running from one end of the country to the other. An annual carnival – late this year because of flooding in the village. There was a photograph of the main high street decorated with bunting. Then back into the studio for another police appeal.

'Coleshaw police have issued a statement. They believe the suspect they want to interview in connection with the Chanel Woman robberies lives locally,' the presenter said. 'They also believe she visits the premises she targets, possibly a number of times, before making her move. They have asked for those living in the area to be especially vigilant and report anyone acting suspiciously or suddenly frequenting a premises they hadn't before. If you have any information the number to call is . . .'

Austin glanced up from his phone. 'What wouldn't I give

to have Chanel Woman as a patient,' he said. 'The criminal mind is fascinating.'

'If you did some NHS work, you might,' Roshan said, unable to resist a dig.

Thankfully, at that moment the door to the kitchen-diner opened and Brandon, apron tied around his middle, announced, 'Dinner is served.'

It was two hours and far too much wine later that Sarah finally had to admit that Megan was flirting with Roshan. She'd thought it was her imagination to begin with, but now that Austin had caught her eye after another flirtatious comment from Megan to Roshan, she knew she wasn't the only one noticing it. Megan was sitting next to Brandon and opposite Roshan. They'd been keeping the same places since the first night, just out of habit. But the seating arrangements allowed Megan direct eye contact with Roshan, and she was making the most of it.

What the hell does she think she's doing? Sarah thought, her annoyance and irritation building. Megan had been all over Brandon like a rash, and now here she was, outrageously flirting with Roshan – her husband – and more or less ignoring poor Brandon. Was Megan trying to make Brandon jealous? *Treat them mean and keep them keen* approach? Or was she trying to make Sarah jealous? If so, why? Megan and she were friends. In fact, they were all supposed to be friends – good friends. So why was she going out of her way to upset the dynamics of their group? Roshan seemed oblivious to Megan's flirtatious behaviour, but that didn't surprise Sarah. Such nuances were lost on him and would need spelling out. But that wasn't the point. Brandon had also noticed and was looking hurt.

It wasn't just what Megan was saying either, Sarah thought, her anger increasing as Megan's performance continued. Not just suggestive remarks and innuendos, but her behaviour too. Those slightly parted pouty lips, her seductive lingering looks from beneath those dark, heavily mascaraed lashes. The way she was now toying with her dessert spoon as she licked the last of the cream from it. At some point during the evening she must have undone more buttons at the top of her silky blouse, for she certainly hadn't been showing that much cleavage when they'd first sat down to eat.

Austin caught Sarah's eye again and she knew she had to speak out now. Megan was making a fool of them all, especially her.

'Megan, back off!' Sarah said, with more aggression than she'd anticipated. 'He's married and he's mine.'

'Sorry?' Megan said, surprised, and in a way that was a question, not apologetic. 'Have I said something wrong?'

'Don't play the innocent,' Sarah retaliated, aware her voice was too loud. 'You've been flirting with Roshan all evening. It's embarrassing. Just cool it, will you.'

'Sshh, Sarah,' Roshan hissed, placing a hand on her arm to silence her.

'No, I won't sshh,' she said, shaking it off. 'Poor Brandon, sitting there being made to feel a fool.'

Sarah glanced at Austin, who was looking at her approvingly, which gave her the incentive to continue.

'I've sat here and kept quiet all this time, but I'm going to have my say now. Keep away from my husband, and if you no longer fancy Brandon then tell him. Don't lead him on. He's a nice guy. He'll find someone else.'

'Sarah, stop it!' Roshan said.

'Fuck off!' she snapped. He looked shocked. She'd never spoken to him like that before.

'You need to calm down and let it go,' he said.

Sarah glared at Megan. 'Now, see what you've done! Little

wonder you ended up alone with a child when you behave like this.'

'Sarah!' Roshan said, standing. 'That's enough! You need to apologize, now!'

'I won't. I've nothing to apologize for. It's her who should be apologizing to me and Brandon.'

'I'm OK,' Brandon said quietly, and looked very uncomfortable. 'Let's forget it, shall we.'

Sarah looked again at Austin, who was concentrating on the others, apparently gauging their reactions.

'We'll go and make some coffee,' Roshan said, trying to draw Sarah from the table.

'I don't want coffee,' she said, and released her arm again.

'I'm sorry if I've behaved inappropriately,' Megan said in a small voice, close to tears. 'I don't get to go out much, what with working, going to college, and being a single parent. It seems I've forgotten how to behave. I thought I was just having fun, a good time.' A tear slipped from her eye. 'I didn't mean to upset you, Sarah. I like Roshan, but only as a friend. And I wouldn't do anything to hurt *you*,' she added, turning to Brandon.

'I know,' he said. 'It didn't cross my mind.'

'That's fine then,' Austin said. 'It seems Sarah misread what was going on – the many and complex signals of interpersonal communication. It happens a lot.'

Sarah looked at Austin, dumbfounded, and then at Brandon. Until that moment she was sure Austin and Brandon agreed with her. Had she got it so very wrong? It seemed so, judging from their reactions. In which case Roshan was right and she needed to apologize, and then she'd disappear up to her room and hope the world would swallow her up. She'd made a complete fool of herself. She stood, ready to leave.

'I'm sorry,' she began. 'I don't know what—' She stopped. The doorbell had rung.

65

'Who can that be at this time of night?' Roshan said, checking his watch. 'It's nearly nine o'clock. We don't know anyone here.'

'Perhaps it's Leslie?' Brandon suggested to Austin. 'You said she'd join us when she felt better.'

'She'd have phoned first,' Austin said.

The doorbell rang again, more insistent this time.

'I'll go,' Austin said, and left his seat.

'I'll come with you,' Roshan said, and followed Austin out of the kitchen-diner.

'There's nothing from my mother,' Megan said, checking her phone. 'So it can't be anything to do with my daughter.'

'Good,' Brandon said.

They heard the front door open, voices, then footsteps coming through the living room. The door to the kitchen-diner opened and Austin appeared first, followed by Roshan, and a police officer.

'We've got a problem,' Austin said.

TWELVE

'Good evening, I'm Police Constable Jackie Owen,' the female officer said, her expression sombre. 'I'm sorry to disturb you, but I have reason to believe two members of your group were in Grenville's this afternoon? Judging from the description I've been given, I think it was you, sir, and you, miss,' she said, looking at Brandon and Megan.

'Grenville's?' Brandon asked, puzzled and concerned.

'The village shop,' PC Owen clarified.

'Yes, we were there. Why?' Brandon asked, wondering if he'd mis-parked his car. But wouldn't there have been a ticket on his windscreen? Unless it had blown off.

'We received a call from the store's owner, Mr Grenville. It seems you left the store without paying for some of your shopping.'

'We certainly did not,' Brandon said indignantly. 'We paid for everything, on my card. I have the receipt here somewhere.'

'I remember you paying,' Megan said as Brandon took out his wallet. 'What is it we're supposed to have taken without paying for? It must be a mistake.'

'Two bottles of wine,' the PC said. 'It seems you paid for

two, but after you left Mr Grenville saw that four were missing from the shelf.'

Brandon found the credit card receipt and passed it to the officer.

'Did you keep the till receipt?' she asked, glancing at it, and handing it back.

'No, I didn't ask for one,' Brandon said.

'Here's a copy,' the officer said, giving him a lengthy paper till receipt which listed all the items they'd bought. 'If you check it, you'll see that only two bottles of wine have been paid for, but Mr Grenville says you left the store with four bottles.'

The PC's gaze had gone to the empty wine bottles that littered the dining table; there were more on the work surfaces in the kitchen too.

Brandon concentrated on the till receipt, feeding the paper through his fingers as he went down the list of items until he got to the bottom. 'Shit. How on earth did that happen?' he asked, looking up horrified. 'There are only two bottles of wine here and we bought four.'

'His till couldn't have been working properly,' Megan suggested. 'Or he just missed them when he checked everything through. We bought a lot of stuff.'

'I'm afraid not, miss,' PC Owen said sombrely. 'When Mr Grenville checked the CCTV in the shop it showed you taking two bottles of red wine from the shelf and placing them in your shopping bag. You didn't present them at the till and then left the shop without paying for them.'

'I didn't!' Megan cried, her hand shooting to her mouth in alarm.

'She wouldn't do that,' Roshan said.

'Have you seen the CCTV yourself?' Austin asked, the only one of their group who was managing to remain calm and clear-headed.

68

'Yes, I have,' PC Owen confirmed. 'The CCTV clearly shows the young lady taking the wine.'

Megan burst into tears. 'Oh my God, I can't remember doing that. It must be all the alcohol I've been drinking. I'm not used to it.'

The PC threw her a sceptical look suggesting she'd heard most excuses in her time with the police and this one wouldn't work either. Sarah went to comfort Megan, slipping an arm around her shoulders.

'What's going to happen?' Megan sobbed. 'I've never done anything like this before, and I've got a young daughter. I can't go to prison, I just can't.'

'You're very lucky, miss. The store owner, Mr Grenville, has said he's willing to accept it was an oversight on your part, and he won't press charges if the wine is paid for in cash.'

'That's decent of him,' Brandon said. 'Of course we'll pay for it, but I don't carry cash.'

'I have cash,' Roshan said. 'How much do we owe?'

'The two bottles come to twenty-three pounds ninety-eight pence,' PC Owen said. 'The same price as the two you paid for.'

Roshan took thirty pounds from his wallet and gave it to the officer.

'I'll tell Mr Grenville to put the change in the charity box, shall I?' she said.

'Yes, of course,' Sarah replied tersely, irritated by the woman's manner.

'Thank you for your cooperation,' the PC said, getting ready to leave. 'Enjoy the rest of your stay, but I suggest if you need any more shopping you use another store.'

'Yes of course,' Austin said. 'Out of interest, how did you know where to find us? I mean, we're new here; no one knows us.'

'That's exactly how we found you,' the officer replied. 'It's a very small village where everyone knows everyone else. We knew you weren't local and that the church was being rented, so we put two and two together. Thank you again for your cooperation, But, miss,' she said, to Megan, 'if I were you I wouldn't drink so much. Not being able to remember is a sign of alcoholism.'

Megan hung her head in shame as Austin saw the officer out. Brandon and Roshan joined Sarah at the table to sit close to Megan and offer what support they could.

'I don't know what I'm doing any more,' Megan cried, head in her hands. 'This isn't me. First I upset Sarah and then I steal. I honestly can't remember putting those bottles of wine in my bag, I just can't.'

'I can guess how it happened,' Brandon offered.

'You can?' Megan asked, looking up.

'We bought a lot of things. We had three baskets between us, overflowing. We chose the wine last. There was no more room in the baskets, so you put those two bottles straight into your shopping bag with the intention of paying for it at the till, only you forgot.'

'Do you really think that's what happened?' she asked.

'I'm sure of it,' Brandon replied kindly.

'It makes sense,' Roshan added.

'It does,' Sarah agreed, and passed Megan a tissue to dry her eyes.

'The bottles must have been quite heavy though,' Megan said as she wiped her eyes. 'It's a wonder I didn't realize they were there. And why didn't I see them when I put the other shopping into my bag at the till?'

'Because you were preoccupied,' Sarah said. 'Your thoughts were on buying what you needed to cook us that lovely meal. And maybe you were still hung-over. We have been putting it away.'

Austin returned and quietly took a seat at the table a little away from where the others were grouped.

'I just wish I could remember,' Megan said. 'That officer's comment about being an alcoholic . . . I never normally drink. Do you think she's right?'

'No,' Sarah said.

'Stop me if I'm having too much. I'm not a nice person when I've been drinking. I could have been prosecuted and gone to prison.'

'It's highly unlikely you'd have received a custodial sentence for a first offence,' Austin said, looking at Megan. 'Assuming it was a first offence.'

'Of course it was,' Sarah said defensively. 'Megan doesn't steal.'

'Not that I know of,' Megan said. 'Apart from once when I was five and an older kid told me to take a chocolate bar. But I can remember that clearly, even now. Whereas I can't remember putting those bottles of wine into my bag. I really can't. Perhaps I'm not coping. Shall I go home tomorrow?'

'No of course not,' Austin said firmly. 'And break up our gathering? I wouldn't hear of it.'

THIRTEEN

Brandon groaned in pain, pushing himself onto his side and reaching for his phone. By the light of the moon coming through the stained-glass window he saw it was 3.03 a.m. He groaned again. God, he was ill. He'd never felt so bad. He drew up his knees to try to ease the pain in his stomach, but it cramped again, squeezing the air out of him. It felt as though he was being stabbed with a red-hot knife.

It must have been something he'd eaten the night before, he thought, but what? They'd had a very healthy dinner – vegetarian – that he and Megan had cooked. Unless it was because he wasn't used to vegetarian food. Could it have upset his stomach this much, resulting in this intense pain? He was in agony. Perhaps it wasn't the food but the wine. Could it have been off? But surely they would have noticed? Austin certainly would. He was a connoisseur. He knew all about wines and always poured a little first to smell and taste it before filling their glasses. No, it couldn't be the wine.

So what was making him feel so ill? He hoped the others weren't affected.

Perhaps it was the emotional upset from the evening before, Brandon wondered as he clutched his stomach and groaned.

But they'd dealt with it, put it behind them with a nightcap and had gone to bed friends, ready to move on. Could he have picked up a stomach bug – norovirus? Did that make you this ill? He shivered, feeling hot and cold at the same time. Another burst of pain shot through him, nearly tearing him apart.

He tried taking deep breaths, but he couldn't. The hard mass in his stomach was stopping him. Then bile began to rise in his throat. He was going to be sick! Throwing back the duvet, he rushed into the bathroom where he knelt before the toilet and vomited repeatedly into the bowl. Again and again, relentless and intense, as if his very insides were trying to eject themselves. Then it passed, at least for the time being. He flushed the toilet and sat back exhausted, struggling to get his breath.

Could he have been poisoned, he thought, his mind hot and confused from being sick. But why, how, when and by whom? What motive could anyone possibly have for wanting to harm him? His thoughts went to Megan and the meal they'd prepared. She'd done most of the cooking as she knew the recipes. He'd helped. But it was ridiculous to think she'd poison him. Or was it? She'd been behaving oddly all day, a bit Jekyll and Hyde, coming on to him and then flirting with Roshan – although he'd claimed not to have noticed. Then there was the matter of her stealing the two bottles of wine, which may or may not have been an accident. While they'd been shopping she'd talked about what vegetarians could safely eat that was growing wild and that some plants were highly poisonous. Were there poisonous plants growing here?

Sweat trickled down his back between his shoulder blades. The nausea was starting to rise again, building up in his stomach. Oh no, not more! His stomach was cramping uncontrollably, getting ready to expel its contents again.

Brandon grabbed the toilet bowl and pulled himself onto his knees. He got over it just in time. Vomit gushed out, thick strands of green slime that seemed to go on forever. What the hell was it? Nothing he'd eaten, surely? He grabbed more toilet paper to wipe his mouth and caught sight of what was in the toilet. Dear God! He stared in disbelief. Something was moving. Something that had come out of his mouth was alive and wriggling around in the bowl. Not one but many. He screamed and backed away in horror and disgust.

But he was going to be sick again.

'Someone help me!' he cried, and clutched the toilet.

More were coming, making their way up from his stomach into his throat. He could feel the writhing mass and tried to swallow. They squealed and continued squirming out of his mouth, long green worms hanging from his lips. He frantically tried to pull them out, but they lodged in his throat and slipped through his fingers. He could taste and smell them, unimaginably foul. They were coming out of his nose now. He couldn't breathe or swallow. He was going to die. Choking, he fell onto his side as the worms continued to pour from his mouth and nose. He was going to be eaten alive, die in a pool of writhing carnivorous worms that were of his own making.

'Brandon?'

Austin tapped lightly on his bedroom door so as not to wake the others. 'Brandon, are you OK?'

There was no reply.

'Brandon?' he tried again.

Nothing.

Austin slowly turned the door handle. It wasn't locked, and he eased open the door. 'Brandon?'

The only light came from the moon, but it was enough to see Brandon's bed was empty. He must be in the bathroom,

Austin thought, continuing into the bedroom. So he'd been right when he'd thought he'd heard noises coming from Brandon's bathroom. The rooms shared an adjoining wall, and in the silence of the night, noise was amplified. Austin had woken a short while ago to hear what sounded like Brandon gagging, and then he thought he'd heard him call out for help.

'Brandon?' Austin tried again as he made his way across the room. The bathroom door was closed. 'Brandon?' he asked, and knocked on the door. He didn't want to burst in if the guy was taking a crap.

There was no reply and no noise. Concerned, Austin turned the door handle, but it would only open a little. Something was blocking it on the other side. He quickly put his shoulder against the door and pushed with all his might. It gradually opened until it was wide enough for him to enter.

'Brandon, mate!' he exclaimed, and pulled him away from behind the door.

He knelt beside him and checked he was breathing and then took his pulse. He was either deeply asleep or unconscious. Wearing only his boxer shorts, he must have come in to use the toilet and then passed out. Austin checked his head for any sign of injury, but there was nothing to be seen. Brandon belched and Austin could smell alcohol on his breath. Drunk people did all sorts of silly things, and Brandon had been very drunk. He'd probably needed a pee in the night and then his befuddled mind hadn't remembered where his bed was, so he'd laid down and fallen asleep here.

'Brandon,' Austin said, and began gently shaking him. 'Come on, mate, let's get you back to bed.'

Brandon groaned but didn't open his eyes.

'Come on, wake up. You'll get cold lying on the tiles and I can't carry you.'

Last night Austin had wondered about the wisdom of them having crème de menthe as a nightcap, on top of all the wine they'd drunk. It wasn't a liqueur he would have chosen, green and mint flavoured. But they were adults. He'd declined one and, wishing them goodnight, had gone to bed, leaving them to it. He wasn't their keeper. Later he'd heard them stagger up the stairs, then nothing further until he'd been woken a short time ago by Brandon in his bathroom. Austin wanted to get back to bed and was tempted to leave Brandon on the floor. But that wasn't the way to treat a friend.

He shook Brandon's shoulder again, this time more robustly. He moaned, then suddenly his eyes shot open with a look of sheer terror, and he backed away, scuttling crab-like until he'd lodged himself in the corner between the washbasin and the shower.

'It's OK, mate,' Austin said calmly, in a tone he might have used on a patient. 'I heard you through the wall and came in to see if you were all right.'

Brandon stared back, uncomprehending. Then his frightened gaze travelled over the floor, and up the walls, apparently trying to make sense of what he was seeing. He touched his mouth and nose and swallowed hard.

'Do you want a drink of water?' Austin asked.

Brandon nodded.

Austin took the glass that was on the shelf above the washbasin, filled it with cold water and gave it to him. He watched as he took a tentative sip and then another. Eventually he'd recovered enough to talk.

'Was there anything here when you found me?' Brandon stammered, still sitting on the floor and in shock.

'Like what? One of Sarah's ghosts?' Austin asked with a smile.

'No, not a ghost,' Brandon said and was about to explain but stopped. He drank some more of the water and, putting the glass on the floor, hauled himself to his feet. He swayed and Austin reached out to steady him.

'I think I was having a nightmare,' Brandon said. He looked into the toilet at the clear water. 'Did you flush it?'

'No, and I'm not wiping your arse either,' Austin said. 'You're old enough to do it yourself.'

'God. It was awful, so real,' Brandon said, his face creasing at the memory. 'I thought I was vomiting green worms. It was disgusting. Putrid. I could see, feel and taste them.' He shuddered.

'Do you want to talk about it?' Austin offered. 'I'm good at analysing dreams.'

'Now?'

'If you want to. I'm wide awake and you look like you need to get it off your chest.'

'Thank you. I'd appreciate that.'

'Let's go and sit in the bedroom then where it's more comfortable.'

FOURTEEN

Austin and Brandon sat in the chairs either side of the low coffee table that was just in front of the stained-glass window. The moon had disappeared behind clouds and Austin had dimmed the lights in Brandon's bedroom to low. Brandon, who was now wearing his bathrobe, was pouring out his heart to Austin. It had been easy to begin. Austin knew what to say and do. He'd told him to sit comfortably in the chair with his hands loosely resting on his lap, close his eyes and concentrate on Austin's voice. Low, even, soporific and very close, telling him to imagine himself walking along the most beautiful beach in the world. The air was warm, the fine sand almost white, the sea calm and blue, matching the cloudless sky. It was heaven, and with each step Brandon took he could feel himself becoming more relaxed until he'd been ready to talk.

'Now you can tell me about your dream,' Austin said quietly from close by.

In his super-relaxed detached state, Brandon found himself able to describe his nightmare calmly and objectively, without reliving the horror of the green worms pouring from his mouth and nose. He was able to answer Austin's questions honestly and came to understand the cause of the nightmare.

'So often our unresolved issues are processed by the subconscious through our dreams,' Austin said. 'It's the mind's way of cleansing itself. The symbolism in your dream is clear. You couldn't "stomach" Megan's outrageous flirting with Roshan but you weren't able to say anything to her at the time, so you literally "swallowed" your feelings and emotions. They lay in the pit of your stomach, festering, writhing around in your subconscious. Only once you were asleep did your mind feel safe enough to deal with it. Your feelings of revulsion at what Megan had done began to rise to the surface in the form of those disgusting worms. Then you were able to expel them by being sick and rid yourself of the way she treated you.'

'Yes, it's true,' Brandon said lightly, eyes still closed and his voice far off and unreal.

'Your subconscious chose the metaphor of vomiting because you've been worried about over-eating, and we've been working on that, haven't we?'

Brandon nodded.

'And the fact that the worms were green I'm guessing is because of the crème de menthe you insisted on drinking.'

'Megan said mint was good for digestion,' Brandon said in his dream-like state.

'That's when the mint is infused to make tea. Not a couple of drops added to a bottle of alcohol.'

Brandon finally managed a small smile.

Austin sat back slightly in his chair. 'I think that's enough for now,' he said. 'Unless there's anything else you want to share?'

'I don't think so,' Brandon said dreamily.

'OK. Perhaps another time. We need to get you to bed now. I'm going to count to three and when you wake you will be happy and at peace with the world, having forgiven Megan. One. Two. Three.'

Brandon opened his eyes. He felt good. He knew exactly where he was and what had happened, and everything was fine now. All those bad thoughts had gone and he liked Megan again.

'Thank you so much,' he said.

'You're welcome. Now let's get some sleep.'

Thanking Austin again, Brandon saw him to the door, and then climbed into bed. As he lay down and felt the soft cool cotton pillow mould around him, the light duvet and ridiculously comfortable bed, he thought how at peace he was. He couldn't remember ever feeling this relaxed before. Light and carefree, as though he hadn't a worry in the world. He knew he would sleep well now. Thank goodness Austin was there and had come to his rescue. What was it he'd said about Roshan? Brandon couldn't remember. He was too tired. Doubtless it would come to him in time if it was important. Goodnight, world.

FIFTEEN

'Do you think Leslie is all right?' Sarah asked the following morning as she poured herself coffee. 'I mean, Austin doesn't seem bothered that she's by herself. I'm sure Roshan wouldn't have gone away and left me home alone if I was ill.'

'Austin phones her regularly,' Megan said, slightly defensively. 'I've heard him talking to her on the phone.'

It was nearly midday on Tuesday and the four of them were in the kitchen-diner. After the late night they'd only just got up. Austin had risen at his usual time and gone for a walk.

Sarah took her mug of coffee and joined Megan at the table. Brandon was drinking his coffee standing by the back door. It was open a little on another fine day and the fresh autumnal air drifted in.

'Perhaps Leslie doesn't exist,' Roshan suggested, dropping two crumpets into the toaster. He was the only one who wanted something to eat at present. 'Maybe there is no Leslie and she's a figment of Austin's imagination.'

'That's a bit harsh,' Brandon said, feeling some loyalty to Austin for the help he'd given him during the night.

Roshan shrugged.

'Why would Austin want to make Leslie up?' Megan asked. 'I don't see it.'

'To save face, who knows?' Roshan replied. 'But think about it, none of us was invited to the wedding. We've never spoken to her or seen a photo, and there's no sign of her on social media. I checked.'

'We weren't in touch when Austin got married,' Megan pointed out. 'And perhaps Leslie didn't change her surname when she married.'

'I also searched on just her first name,' Roshan said. 'Leslie, twenty-seven, works in retail and lives with Austin.'

'Was that enough?' Megan asked.

Sarah nodded. 'I've found old friends online with less information than that.'

'What have you got against Austin?' Brandon asked Roshan from where he was standing by the back door.

'Nothing, I haven't got anything against him,' Roshan said. 'But I don't understand why you lot are in awe of him. It's like the sun shines out of his arse. If anyone has a problem, it's "ask Austin".' He knew he was sounding confrontational and perverse, but the revere in which Austin was being held was really starting to irritate him.

The others had fallen quiet and Roshan guessed he'd overstepped the mark again. He was finding he was doing it more and more, making harsh comments. He knew he needed to rein himself in. He was doubting this gathering was such a good idea, but he didn't want to be the one to ruin it. The toaster popped and he concentrated on buttering the crumpets, then he took his plate and coffee to the table where he joined Sarah and Megan. Megan avoided his gaze and Sarah looked at him pointedly.

'It's nothing personal,' he said to no one in particular, and concentrated on eating.

'You could ask Austin about Leslie,' Brandon said a

minute or so later. 'I can see him. He's coming back from his walk.'

'I think we just let it go,' Sarah said.

Megan agreed. 'We're all hungover and saying things we don't mean.'

'Good walk?' Brandon asked Austin as he stepped aside to let him in the back door.

'Very good, thanks,' he said, slipping off his jacket. 'I'm ready for a fry-up. I'll cook it. Does anyone else want anything?'

Sarah groaned at the mention of fried food.

'No, thank you, Austin,' Megan replied politely.

Roshan continued drinking his coffee.

'I'll join you,' Brandon said, and left the back door. 'But first I think Roshan has something he'd like to ask you.'

'For fuck's sake!' Roshan exclaimed, and slammed down his mug, making it slop.

'Troublemaker,' Sarah hissed at Brandon.

'Don't talk to him like that,' Megan said, coming to his rescue.

Austin looked at them bemused, a smile toying on his lips. 'Whatever is the matter? It's like kindergarten, I can't leave you alone for five minutes.' His gaze travelled from one to the other. 'So who's going to tell me what happened?'

'I don't have a problem telling you,' Roshan said. 'I suggested Leslie could be a figment of your imagination.'

Austin began to laugh. 'Is that what's made you argue? Incredible. How cute and interesting.'

Put like that, their behaviour sounded pathetic.

'I was concerned that Leslie was by herself when she was ill,' Sarah said in justification, feeling Roshan needed her support.

'But you also said Austin didn't care about Leslie,' Megan replied accusingly.

'You little snitch!' Sarah said, rounding on her.

'OK, children, enough,' Austin said, clapping his hands to bring them to order. 'We can clear this up here and now. You can all speak to Leslie.'

He took his phone from his trouser pocket and made the call.

'Hello, love,' he said. 'I know I've just finished talking to you, but my friends have some doubts you exist.' He listened, and then smiled. 'That's what I said, but if I put my phone on speaker do you feel you can talk to them? Just for a few moments. Thanks, love.'

Austin took the phone from his ear and engaged the speaker. 'They can hear you now.'

'Hi, Leslie here,' a female voice said.

'Hi, it's Megan. Nice to meet you.'

'And you.'

'Hi, I'm Sarah.'

'Hi Sarah.'

'Hello, Megan,' Brandon said. 'How are you feeling?'

Roshan stood and left the room.

'Much better, thank you,' Leslie replied. 'I'm so sorry I haven't been able to join you. I hope you're all having a great time. I'm sure you are.'

'So are you feeling better?' Sarah asked.

'Getting there, thank you. Not perfect. I must have picked up a stomach bug or got food poisoning, I can't ever remember being this sick before. I've only just started eating again. Austin didn't want to leave me here, but I persuaded him to go. I knew how much he'd been looking forward to meeting you guys again after all this time. All the planning that has gone into it. If I feel up to it, I'll join you for a couple of days at the end of the week.'

'That would be great,' Megan enthused. 'We'd like that.'

'Thank you. You're kind to worry about me. Austin's been

telling me what good friends you all are and how good it is to be together again. Enjoy the rest of your week and hopefully I'll see you soon.'

'Yes, take care,' Megan said.

'Look after yourself,' Sarah called.

'Bye, Megan,' Brandon added.

'Bye, everyone.'

'Thanks, love,' Austin said, ending the call, and returned the phone to his pocket.

The silence was deafening. Sarah could feel Megan gloating, hear her unspoken, 'Told you so.' Austin went to the kitchen and, taking a large frying pan from a cupboard, placed it on the hob to cook himself breakfast. Brandon joined him. Megan poured herself another coffee. Sarah quickly finished hers, then stood and without speaking quietly left the room. She went swiftly through the living room and into the lobby where they kept their outdoor wear. Biting back her anger, she pushed her feet into her boots, put on her waterproof coat, and let herself out. She needed fresh air and time alone. Constantly being with the others was claustrophobic and, while no one would admit it, they were all getting on each other's nerves. She was annoyed with Roshan for making a fool of himself by suggesting Leslie didn't exist, and then leaving her to deal with it. She was angry with Megan for snitching on her, and angry with Brandon for betraying Roshan to Austin. It was like a war zone. Whatever was the matter with them? Their behaviour was childish and pathetic. If they didn't pull together to make it work, then they may as well go home before the end of the week.

SIXTEEN

Hands thrust deep into her coat pockets, Sarah continued walking up the hill, following the route Austin had taken them on their first full day together. How long ago that day now seemed, when she hadn't minded Austin behaving as if he were in charge of a school outing. Indeed, they'd all appreciated the trouble he'd gone to to find somewhere nice for them to stay and learn about the church's history and the surrounding area. After their walk they'd gone to the village pub for Sunday lunch. It had been so much fun. They'd laughed and joked, pleased to be together again after ten years, and vowing to stay in touch and meet up more often in the future.

How and why had it gone so badly wrong so quickly, Sarah thought as she walked. Ironically, Austin would probably be able to answer that since he was qualified to do so and loved all that interpersonal behaviour stuff.

Sarah continued up the hill, looking back every so often to get her bearings until the church came into view. This was more or less the same place they'd stood on Sunday to admire the view. Drawing her coat beneath her, she sat on the grass. It was autumnal damp, not wet. She gazed at the church and surrounding scenery. A tranquil English scene that had probably remained unchanged for centuries. Timeless, evocative and nostalgic of a bygone era, she thought, like the Constable paintings she'd been teaching her class about. She could see their cars parked on the hardstanding at the front of the church, like an anachronism, out of place in time. Horses and carts would have been more appropriate.

As she gazed at the peaceful setting, she found herself starting to relax. A kite soared high above her, its huge wingspan carrying it effortlessly across the sky as it circled looking for prey. She watched it glide on a current of air until it disappeared from view. She drew her gaze back to the church and its surrounding graveyard. Some of the very large headstones were just about visible from here. Was her phobia getting any better with Austin's help? She honestly wasn't sure. She didn't feel the same panic and could walk through the graveyard, but her imagination was still getting the better of her. She avoided the memorial stone for Michael and Constance Wilson. Once they returned home, she'd do as Roshan suggested and find a therapist.

As Sarah looked, the front door of the church opened and Austin came out, closing the door behind him. Although he was some distance away, she could see he wasn't wearing a jacket or coat, so presumably wasn't going for another walk. He moved away from the entrance and put his phone to his ear. He must have stepped outside to make a call; they all did that if they wanted some privacy. It was probably one of his patients. He moved around as he concentrated on the conversation, taking a few steps one way and then the other. Then he looked up and possibly straight at her. She kept very still. Could he see her? She assumed he could as she could see him. No use trying to hide now.

As she watched, the call ended and he looked at his phone as if making another. Suddenly her phone rang. She picked it up. The caller display showed Austin. Shit. She really didn't want his company right now. She was enjoying the peace and solitude. But she could hardly not answer if he'd seen her.

'Hello, Austin.'

'Sarah, is that you sitting up there all alone?'

'Yes.'

'Are you all right?'

'Yes.'

'We were worried about you. You left in a hurry without saying anything and seemed to be upset.'

'No, I'm fine, thank you,' she said, irritated by the thought they'd discussed her. 'Just having some time out.'

'Do you want to talk?'

'No, thank you.'

'All right, if you're sure, I'll leave you to it. We all need our own company sometimes.' He said something else which Sarah didn't catch, then ended the call. He gave a little wave, which Sarah felt obliged to return, and he disappeared indoors.

Sarah supposed she should be grateful that Austin, Megan and Brandon were concerned for her, but she couldn't quite manage it. Perversely, she pictured the three of them discussing her hasty exit, and maybe Roshan's too. She should be getting back to him to see how he was. He'd been annoyed by Brandon's betrayal and had left the room before he could say something he regretted. She knew how his mind worked. They all needed to regroup now and patch things up. Perhaps go out for a meal tonight? A change of scenery on neutral territory. The village pub they'd gone to for Sunday lunch was nice.

Sarah stood and brushed off the grass from her coat and jeans. A noise came from behind. She turned, but there was no one there. Maybe it was a bird or small animal, or another walker some way off? Then why was she feeling so uncomfortable, almost scared. And why was the air temperature dropping as it did just before – she could barely say the word – in the short time before the ghost appeared.

Fear kicked in and she began running down the hill, going as fast as the damp grass would allow without losing her footing and slipping. That feeling she wasn't alone. Something was following her. Every few seconds she turned, but there was nothing there. *It's your over-active imagination at work again*, she told herself over and over, like a mantra. *Don't panic, breathe like Austin taught you to. You are in control.*

But it wasn't helping. Someone or something was behind her, even though she couldn't see them. 'Confront your fears,' she heard Austin say. But fear of the unknown, and what she might see, stopped her.

Sarah continued to slip and slide down the hill, but the church was still some way off. Why was she making such slow progress? Her legs felt heavy. It was as if she was running through mud or quicksand. *Calm down or you'll make yourself worse*, she told herself, trying to take deep breaths. Not too far now.

Suddenly she screamed as ice-cold fingers touched the back of her neck. Without looking behind she ran as fast as she could, running for her life. But it was keeping up, she knew. The ghost from her childhood was here again, just as it had been on that first night. It wasn't a dream any more than it had been then. Austin was wrong. It was real. She felt its cold touch again, its malevolent presence, and ran for all she was worth, her chest heaving as though it was about to burst. Down the last of the hill, not far now. Then finally through the gate and into the churchyard. She instinctively went to the left of the building, not the right where the memorial stone lay, then round the corner – and straight into Roshan.

'What the hell!' he said, shocked, and took her in his arms.

He knew her distress, she didn't have to tell him, and without saying anything further he helped her in the back door and across the kitchen-diner, which was thankfully empty. Brandon's and Megan's voices could be heard coming from the living room. Austin was nowhere to be seen. Sarah clung to the rail for support as Roshan helped her up the spiral staircase and into the privacy and safety of their bedroom.

'What is it?' Roshan said, easing her onto the bed. 'I've been worried sick. Where have you been? I tried phoning you but you didn't answer.'

Sarah leaned against the bedhead as she slowly got her breath back. 'Can you get me a glass of water please?'

She took a few sips before speaking. 'I went for a walk but it was up there, waiting for me.'

'So you saw something again?'

'I didn't see it, but I felt it. I was petrified.'

'Why didn't you answer my calls? I would have come to you.'

'I didn't get any calls from you, only one from Austin,' Sarah said, and took out her phone. She stared at it in disbelief. There were three missed calls from Roshan. 'It must have been when I was running back. I wasn't thinking straight.' Yet she'd run with her phone in her hand, and even if she hadn't heard it ring she would have felt it vibrate. 'Roshan,' she said, 'what's the matter with me? I feel I'm going mad here.'

SEVENTEEN

Half an hour later, Sarah felt much calmer and her tears had subsided. She and Roshan were lying side by side on the bed, propped up on pillows as they talked. He still had his arm around her, holding her close, and her head rested on his chest. She felt safe like this.

'Promise me you'll get some professional help when we return home,' Roshan said gently.

'I will. Definitely. I thought Austin's relaxation techniques were helping, but now I'm not so sure.'

'He's not a qualified doctor,' Roshan said.

'What do you mean?' Sarah asked, looking up at him. 'He's a psychiatrist.'

'No. You have to qualify as a medical doctor and then specialize to become a psychiatrist. Austin has never qualified as a doctor. I checked. He's not listed on the General Medical Council's list of practitioners. It shows all doctors in the United Kingdom. He's not there. That's why he can't work in the NHS. He's not qualified.'

Sarah paused thoughtfully before replying. 'I think he refers to himself as a psychologist?' she said. 'Is that different?'

'Yes. You don't need to be a doctor to be a psychologist,

but you have to have a relevant degree and then post-graduate qualifications in clinical psychology.'

'Well, that's it then,' she said, feeling she was stating the obvious.

'No, it's not,' Roshan said flatly. 'In order to practise as a psychologist you need to be registered with the British Psychological Society, and Austin isn't. I've looked. I've also been reading his website. It's worded very carefully. While he mentions the word psychology a number of times, and says he has a long-standing interest in psychology and helping others, he never actually claims to be a psychologist. I'll show you if you like.'

Sarah moved her head slightly so she could see Roshan's phone screen. He had Austin's website marked as a favourite so he could easily return to it. Clearly, he'd done so quite a lot, for he knew the layout of the web pages well. Sarah listened as he read aloud, sometimes paraphrasing lines where relevant. '"When assessing a new patient, I carry out a full psychological assessment through observation and psychometric testing . . . From this I am able to analyse the patient's psychological problems . . . then suggest appropriate treatments. I have successfully treated victims of abuse, acute stress, trauma, phobias, anxiety, grief, low self-esteem and depression. Psychotherapy" – that word again,' Roshan said – '"helps people understand how they can improve their life choices and confront their fears leading to a more healthy lifestyle and behaviour." Then there is a lot of stuff about relaxation techniques that we already know about.'

'What are you saying?' Sarah asked, feeling that perhaps Roshan had become a little obsessed with this. It was comforting that he was being so supportive and understanding, but did they need all this talk of Austin? Now that she was feeling better, Sarah thought she would like to take off her clothes and make love to Roshan. They were on holiday, after all. She snuggled closer.

'What I'm saying is that Austin is claiming to be something he's not,' Roshan said bluntly.

'But he's always done that,' Sarah replied. 'And been full of himself. Remember how he used to exaggerate at school? You and Brandon were always catching him out.'

'I remember, and he always had a smart answer for everything – which let him off the hook.'

'And we forgave him because he's charming, charismatic and we like his company. We would never have had this get-together if it hadn't been for Austin. He took the initiative and arranged it. I really don't see the problem.' She nuzzled Roshan's ear. 'Megan swears he's helped her,' Sarah murmured. 'And look at all those positive reviews on his website.' She kissed his neck and he moaned.

'They're mostly five stars,' Sarah continued, caressing Roshan's neck as she spoke. 'Only one three star and that was because of the cost and not the treatment she received. Whatever you may think of Austin, he's helping people.'

Roshan put down his phone and turned to face Sarah.

'Enough of Austin and his therapy,' he said, his voice now heavy with emotion. 'I can think of a better way of getting five-star reviews.'

'Me too,' Sarah giggled, and began undoing the buttons on his shirt.

EIGHTEEN

There was an hour to go: 3.30 would be the perfect time to strike. The staff at the bank would be winding down ready to close their doors at 4 p.m. Always exactly at four. They were very punctual at the small bank at the far end of the high street in the village of Maybury. It had only three staff: the manager, who was nearly always in his upstairs office, apart from when he left the bank at 3.20 p.m. to buy a cake, and the two women downstairs, one at the counter and the other working just behind her in the office. They rotated their roles as they were both trained cashiers. If the bank was busy, as it often was on a Saturday and weekday lunch-times, then they both worked at the counter for as long as necessary.

The building the bank was housed in was quaint, Chanel Woman thought as she continued to get ready. Pretty, with olde-worlde charm. It was a listed building with an entrance through a small Tudor-arched doorway. The timber cross-members of the red brickwork created a lattice effect around the four small casement windows that sat in two rows. The top two windows were just under the steeply sloping, hipped clay tile roof and were tiny. It was so dark inside that the electric lights were on all day. The main light switch for the downstairs was near the front door, and she'd switch it off as soon as she entered. Chanel Woman had done her homework and knew the bank well.

The residents of Maybury loved their bank and had fought to keep it open. It was now the only branch for miles as repeated cost-cutting measures had seen most village branches close. Maybury's bank was thriving and busy at peak times, but not at 3.30 p.m. Staff from local businesses who visited it during their lunchtime would be working again, and daytime shoppers had been and gone. The next wave wouldn't be until after 5 p.m., when only the supermarket was open.

Chanel Woman knew the movements of Maybury residents better than they knew themselves.

Yes, it was an audacious plan to rob a high street bank, she acknowledged as she dressed in the clothes she'd chosen to wear. It was only the third bank she'd robbed in the whole two years, but she was well prepared. She was familiar with the bank's routine, having spent over a month watching their comings and goings. There was a little coffee shop opposite where she'd sat nursing a coffee and croissant, but not for too long. She couldn't risk drawing attention to herself, so she'd walked up and down, casually looking in shop windows. As well as knowing the area and the bank's routine well, she was satisfied that the two middle-aged female staff, one of whom was part-time, wouldn't be interested in fending off a robber, especially if they thought their lives were at risk. They both had families; she'd seen them talking to them.

Now dressed in black slacks tucked into boots, a black jumper, and a dark grey jacket, Chanel Woman looked at the result in the full-length mirror of her bedroom. She was power-dressed and the scar on her cheek was as hidden as it could be by make-up. She checked the time again and ran through the sequence of events. She'd park on the patch of land at the side of the bank at 3.25. There was no CCTV there. There were cameras at the front and back of the building, but even if they captured her or her car, all the footage would show was a woman of average height and build with the features of the mask she'd chosen to wear, and the car's fake number plates she'd bought so easily online.

She scooped back her hair into a ponytail and secured it with a hairband so it would fit snugly under the mask when the time came. She put the mask and the gun into her shoulder bag, then picked up the perfume bottle of Chanel N°5. She squirted it on the inside of both wrists and behind her ears, and tucked the bottle into her bag too. Also in her bag were empty supermarket carrier bags that would shortly be filled with money. Satisfied she'd covered everything, she left her bedroom feeling slightly detached. She always felt like this as she prepared for and executed her crimes. Almost as if she was another person, which in a way she was. Chanel Woman – confident, assertive, a risk-taker, a femme fatale – was about to strike again.

Going downstairs she felt her pulse quicken as the adrenalin kicked in. She crossed the hall, her boots clipping the marble floor. She went through the integral door and into her car in the garage. She dropped her shoulder bag on the passenger seat and went to one of the cabinets on the wall, where she took out a screwdriver. Squatting down at the front of her car, she deftly removed the number plate, placing the two screws to one side, then did the same with the rear number plate. She placed both plates in a drawer, at the same time removing the fake plates. She screwed those into position and returned the screwdriver to the drawer.

Getting into the driver's seat, Chanel Woman pressed the fob to raise the garage doors, then started the engine and pulled out and along the drive. The garage doors closed automatically behind her. As she drove she concentrated on the practicalities of what lay ahead, trying not to think about the wider picture. In her heart of hearts she knew that one day she would have to stop this, but how and when she didn't know. She wasn't a bad person, she told herself. She didn't mug old ladies. And the businesses she robbed were covered by insurance, so didn't really lose out. She just had a compulsion to steal, an illness her husband said she needed help with.

She passed the signpost for Maybury and the narrow country lane widened a little, allowing two cars to pass more easily. Maybury was one of the larger villages in the area and had already had its fair share of headline news. A few years ago an elderly resident had been found unconscious in her cottage, and once she recovered enough to speak, she had claimed she'd been attacked and robbed of £20,000 and accused the vicar's son. But with no evidence, and as the woman was confused, the police had decided she'd more likely fallen and forgotten she'd spent the money. Chanel Woman smiled. Shortly they'd have a proper robbery to deal with!

The road ahead remained clear and, fifteen minutes later, at exactly 3.15 p.m. Chanel Woman entered the top end of Maybury High Street. As she had predicted, at this time on a weekday it was sparsely populated. The odd car and a few shoppers, but that was all. She slowed the car and drove past the baker's shop. The bank manager was sitting in his favourite place in the window, enjoying his cake and coffee. He never took a lunch break but waited until the afternoon. She continued until she was level with the bank and glanced up at his office window. The lights were off as they always were when the room was unoccupied. Keeping her face away from the CCTV camera she turned right and pulled onto the rough patch of land at the side of the bank. She did a three-point turn and parked close to the wall, ready to drive off. It was now 3.23, and she sat for a moment trying to calm herself. Corner shops, garages, and post offices were easy – the last had been child's play – but banks were a challenge. Even a small sleepy one like this. *Don't lose your nerve now*, she told herself. *That tingling fear is excitement and the reason you do this.*

She took a deep breath and reached into her bag for the prosthetic mask. It was now 3.25. She pulled on the mask and tucked her hair inside, then checked the result in the visor mirror. It still gave her a thrill – seeing that perfect face. If only real life was the same. Transformation complete, her pulse settled as she watched the clock on the dashboard: 3.27. She squirted on more perfume, her calling-card, and at 3.28 took the gun and carriers from her bag, and opened the car door.

Chanel Woman strode purposefully to the end of the piece of land where it joined the high street. She stepped onto the pavement and looked up and down. No one was approaching and no one was at the cash machine. Going left, she took the few steps to the first window of the bank and looked in. There were no customers inside and only one cashier was at the counter; the other was behind her in the office. Perfect. Just as it should be.

Another glance left and right, then she threw open the door to the bank and burst in, switching off the light and sliding the bolt on the inside of the door.

'Stay where you are! No one move!' she shouted, brandishing the gun. 'You won't get hurt if you do as you're told.'

The cashier at the counter screamed.

'Shut up!'

In the half-light she could see both women staring at her, petrified, but now standing still. She went to the counter and threw the carrier bags at the cashier. 'Put in the money you have within reach, then give the bags to your friend to fill, and return to your seat. One false move and you're both dead.'

The cashier stifled a cry but did as she was told.

'If you press the panic button, that's it,' Chanel Woman added. She kept the gun pointing at the cashier. Visibly shaking, she began putting the counter cash into the bag.

'Is that all of it?' she demanded when the cashier stopped. The woman nodded. 'Now take the bags to your colleague, then return to your seat.'

The cashier stood and Chanel Woman tracked her movements with the gun.

'We don't keep much cash in the safe,' the other woman said, trying to be a hero.

'Don't lie! I'm not stupid,' Chanel Woman shouted. 'Securicor don't collect your takings until tomorrow. Now fill those bloody bags! You, return to your seat,' she yelled at the cashier.

The poor woman looked like she might be sick, she'd gone so pale. Chanel Woman kept the gun pointing directly at her as the other woman in the office behind did as she'd been told. Safe open, she was stuffing the bundles of notes into the carrier bags. It was all going to plan. These little village banks didn't have the latest sophisticated security as the big town banks did. It wasn't cost-effective, and being a listed building, every time they wanted to make a change, no matter how small, they needed planning permission. It was more economical to close them.

'Faster!' Chanel Woman yelled, checking her watch. It was 3.35. One carrier bag was full and the woman was filling the other, but she seemed to be fumbling and wasting time. 'Hurry up!'

'The manager will be back soon,' the woman said, with another stab at heroism.

'No, he won't. Not for another ten minutes, when he's

finished his cake and coffee.' She saw the look of surprise and fear on their faces. 'You should know I'm not an opportunist. I plan my robberies before I strike.'

'Do you want the jewellery and valuables?' the woman now asked, her voice shaking.

'Yes, put them in,' she said. 'But what is jewellery doing in your safe? You don't have safe deposit boxes. I checked.'

'We're not supposed to, but we look after some of our clients' valuables if they wish.'

'Naughty, but good for me. A bonus. Put it all in, and get a move on!' She could feel herself sweating beneath the mask. 'Hurry!' she cried, waving the gun.

The woman quickly took the last of the items from the safe. 'That's it. It's empty,' she stammered, her voice catching.

'Do you have money or valuables anywhere else in the building?'

'No. Honestly.'

'Bring the bags here and put them on the counter.'

With trembling hands, the woman placed the bags on the counter not far from the cashier.

'Well done. Now you are both going upstairs to the manager's office. You will stay there until he returns. I will know you are there when you put the light on. If you call the police before he returns, I will shoot him on his way back from the coffee shop. Do you understand?'

They nodded mutely.

'Right, go now!' she cried.

She took the carrier bags from the counter as the women fled through the back office, disappearing through the door that led to the staircase. She heard their footsteps running up the wooden stairs, then the floorboards creaking in the room above – the manager's office. Good. They wouldn't call the police until the manager returned; they were too scared. Now to make her escape.

100

She was about to slide the bolt on the door when the handle turned. Shit! Someone was out there, trying to get in. *Stay calm*, she told herself, *you've dealt with situations like this before.*

She waited, hoping they would go away, but the handle rattled again. 'Hello? Is there anyone there?' a male voice asked.

'Sorry, we're closed,' she said from the other side of the door, keeping her voice steady. 'Power cut.'

'When will you reopen?' he asked.

'Tomorrow. Sorry.'

It went quiet. She listened. It was still quiet. She went to the windows, first one, then the other, tentatively peering through the glass. She couldn't see anyone on the pavement. Returning to the door, she listened again. Nothing. He would have gone by now, surely? She needed to go before the manager returned or another customer arrived. She slid the bolt, dropped the gun into one of the carrier bags and looped the bags over her arm as though they contained groceries. She stepped confidently out of the bank. The pavement was clear. Perfect. She walked to the right, heading to where she'd left her car. She turned the corner and stopped dead. A man was waiting part way down. *Keep walking*, she told herself, *your face is protected by the mask. Continue past him, your car isn't far behind him.*

Forcing herself to walk steadily, she continued along the unmade-up piece of land, trying to silence her racing heart. Nearly there now. But as she drew level with him, he suddenly stepped out in front of her.

'I thought so – it's you: Chanel Woman,' he said. It was the same male voice from outside the bank. 'I'm making a citizen's arrest.'

He went to grab her. She dodged out of his way and tried to run towards her car. But he was immediately behind her, grabbing her jacket. She lashed out, kicked his shin with the heel of her boot, causing him enough pain to momentarily let go. But only for a second. He was on her again now, tugging her hair. Her mask was slipping. She tried to hold it in place as well as fighting him off. But another hard jerk and it came off in his hand. She cried out in alarm, but as surprised as she was his grip had loosened on her which allowed her to run to her car. She jumped in and slammed the door. The internal locks automatically fell into place. He landed against her door, banged on the window, wrenched the door handle, trying to break in. She started the car, and, gripping the wheel for dear life, put her foot hard down on the accelerator. The engine roared, tyres screeched and grit flew. He jumped out of the way as she sped off down to the end of the road where it met the high street. She glanced in her rear-view mirror. He was on his phone now, presumably calling the police. Her stomach churned and she felt sick with fear. Not only had he seen her face, but he also had her mask. The game was over. Surely it was only a matter of time before the police came looking for her.

NINETEEN

'We'll get her this time!' DS Scrivener declared. News of the robbery at Maybury bank had just been phoned in. 'Uniformed officers are there now,' he said. 'Matt and Beth, I want you there on blue light. Don't let anyone touch anything, especially that mask. It will have her DNA all over it. Forensics are on their way. I'll join you once I've updated the DCI. Off you go. This is going to put Coleshaw CID on the map!'

'Let's hope it's for the right reason,' Matt said quietly to Beth as they both stood to leave.

She returned his smile.

Matt and Beth left the office and went hurriedly down the back staircase of the police station to the yard at the rear where the pool cars were kept. Two minutes later they left with the siren blaring and the blue light flashing. Matt was driving. If they were on an assignment together, they usually took it in turns to drive. Beth's phone rang and she let it go to voicemail. Caller ID said it was Danny Able, reporter from the *Coleshaw Times*, apparently already aware of the story breaking.

Ten minutes later they pulled into Maybury High Street.

A crowd had gathered outside the bank, grouping around two uniformed officers who appeared to be chatting and joking with them. As Matt parked the police car at the kerb, the crowd's attention turned to them.

'Have you caught Chanel Woman yet?' someone shouted as Matt and Beth got out.

'No, but we will,' Beth replied. Then to Matt, 'This area should have been cordoned off.'

She opened the boot of the car and took out cones and barrier tape as Matt addressed the crowd. 'Did anyone here actually witness the robbery?' he asked.

No one spoke, then a woman called out, 'It was definitely her though. I could smell her perfume. It lingers.' Others agreed.

'The only witness is the man who tried to apprehend her. He's waiting inside the bank with the staff,' one of the uniformed officers said.

'So no one here actually witnessed the robbery?' Matt checked.

It was clear from the silence no one had.

'In that case I need you all to go now. There could be valuable forensic evidence on the pavement that is being lost. Now, please!' he said, more forcefully. Spreading his arms, he began herding them away.

Once the pavement was clear, he and Beth quickly cordoned off the area with the cones and barrier tape, including stretching the tape across the entrance to the piece of land at the side of the bank. Forensics would do a better job when they arrived. Matt then asked the uniformed officers to make sure no one tried to cross the barrier.

'We'll be inside the bank,' he said. 'Shout if you need anything. The forensic team should be here soon.'

It was unlikely there'd be any fingerprints of use on the door, but even so, Matt and Beth put on disposable gloves before touching the door handle and going into the bank. It was dark inside, and the musty smell of an old building mingled with the lingering aroma of Chanel Woman's perfume.

'Can we have some lights on?' Beth asked.

'The switch is by the door,' the man in the suit said. 'We didn't like to touch anything.'

Beth flicked on the light switch. Four people stood grouped before them.

'I'm Aaron Head, the bank manager,' the man in the suit said, taking a step forward.

'And I'm the hero of the day, Gary Strong, living up to my name.'

Beth smiled weakly. 'You're the person who tried to stop Chanel Woman, and pulled off her mask?'

'Yes, that's me.'

Short and slender, he didn't look particularly strong.

'Here's the mask,' he said, standing aside to reveal the prosthetic mask lying on the counter. With its hair spread out behind, it looked very realistic.

'Don't touch it,' Beth said. 'We'll leave it there for Forensics.'

'I'm guessing you'll want my DNA to eliminate it from the mask,' Gary said, looking pleased with himself.

'Yes, and a statement,' Matt replied.

'You're bank employees?' Beth asked the two women. They looked very shaken.

'Yes,' was all one could say.

'She had a gun, so we did as we were told,' the other woman said.

'It's not your fault,' the bank manager reassured her. 'No one's blaming you. Your safety is paramount.'

The woman didn't look convinced.

A knock sounded on the door and Matt opened it to one of the uniformed officers. 'Forensics have just arrived,' he said. 'They want to speak to you.'

'Thank you,' Matt said. Then to Beth, 'I'll go.'

'I'll start taking statements in here,' she replied, and Matt left.

'Is there somewhere we can go rather than stand here?' Beth asked the manager.

'My office upstairs,' he suggested.

'Did Chanel Woman go up there?'

'No, from what my staff have told me, she stayed this side of the counter.' The women nodded confirmation.

'That's fine then. We can use your office, although I'll need to speak to you all separately,' Beth said.

'The room where my staff take their break is next door to my office,' the manager replied helpfully, 'we can use that too.'

He opened the gate that led from reception to the other side of the counter, and they followed him through, then crossed the back office and went up the wooden staircase. They arrived on a small landing with exposed wooden beams.

'My office is through here,' he said, pointing to a door bearing the nameplate *Mr Aaron Head. Bank Manager*. 'The break room is in there.'

'I'll speak to you first then,' Beth said to him.

'Make yourself a coffee,' the manager called as Gary and the two women went into the break room.

Aaron Head opened the door to his office and stood aside to let Beth in. The room was small with a low ceiling like the rest of the building. It looked out over the high street and his desk was positioned under the window. Beth crossed to the window. She could see the Forensics van parked behind their car. The team was busy in the street. Matt was talking to one of them.

'You've got a good view from up here,' Beth said, glancing at the manager. 'Did you see anything suspicious?'

'No, I was in the baker's shop just up the road when the

robbery took place. I don't take my lunch hour, it's our busiest time, so I have a break at three twenty.'

'You go at the same time every day?' Beth asked, trying to keep the criticism from her voice.

'Yes, I'm afraid so. Creature of habit. I guess Chanel Woman knew that?'

'I guess she did,' Beth said. 'Do you ever use that coffee shop across the road?' It was directly opposite and someone sitting in one of the window seats would have a pretty good view of the bank.

'No, I don't like their cakes,' he replied.

Beth tapped on the window to get Matt's attention. He looked up and she pointed to the coffee shop. He glanced over and, realizing what she meant, gave her the thumbs up. It was worth speaking to the customers and staff there. It was possible someone had seen something.

'Chanel Woman knew my movements,' he said, looking worried. 'She knew Securicor didn't collect our cash until tomorrow. She told my staff she planned her robberies and wasn't an opportunist.'

'That sounds like her,' Beth said, leaving the window and sitting in one of the chairs he'd pulled out. 'She does her homework. It's very likely she's been watching the bank for some time.'

'I've been going on at senior management to update our security system for ages,' he said with a sigh, running his fingers through his hair. 'They weren't interested. They said they couldn't justify the cost for such a small branch. They'll close us down for sure now. This is just the excuse they need.'

Beth nodded sympathetically but couldn't offer any re-assurance. He was probably right. From what she'd seen so far, their security was woefully inadequate. It was a wonder they hadn't been robbed before.

'There's a security camera at the front. Anywhere else?' Beth asked.

'At the back.'

'We'll need the footage from the cameras, and details of the company that maintains the system,' she said, going through a mental checklist. The manager picked up a pen and notepad from his desk and wrote. 'Also the details of any workers who have access to this building, including maintenance, electricians, cleaners, and so forth.'

'Do you think she had inside help then?' he asked.

'Not if she's following her usual modus operandi, but we need to cover all possibilities. I'll ask your staff this as well, but I'd like details of any new female customers fitting her description that have visited the bank in the last month or so. It's likely she came into the bank a number of times.'

His brow furrowed as he wrote.

'How many employees do you have, Mr Head?' Beth asked.

'Just the two, the women you met.'

'Have they been with you for long?'

'Yes, years, well before I joined this branch. I trust them implicitly.'

'Do either of them have any money worries you know of?'

'No, and I hope you're not suggesting they could be involved?' he said defensively.

'I'm not, but they need to be eliminated from our enquiries, just as you do.'

Beth's work phone vibrated with a text and, apologizing, she took it from her pocket and read the message. It was from Danny Able: *Outside now. Nationals not here yet. How soon will you be able to give me a statement?*

She returned the phone to her pocket.

'The press are here,' she said. 'But we'll wait for our DS to arrive before we issue a statement. Now, please tell me exactly what happened today from when you arrived here for work this morning.'

As Beth wrote, the traffic outside could be heard building, engines running and the occasional car horn tooting. By the time she'd finished, crews from national television news were outside, and DS Scrivener had arrived with their highest-ranking investigating officer, Detective Chief Inspector Aileen Peters. This was making headline news and they needed to get it right.

TWENTY

The television on the wall of the village pub was tuned to sport. The volume was low and a group of three elderly men, locals, sat at a table directly in front of the screen, nursing their beers. Austin, Sarah, Roshan, Brandon and Megan were at a table further away and glanced at the screen every so often to fill in the uncomfortable silences that had dogged their outing. They'd ordered their meals and were now sipping their drinks as they waited for the food to arrive. When Sarah had suggested they eat at the pub, everyone had agreed, but after a difficult afternoon, conversation had become awkward, and they seemed wary of each other. She and Megan were OK, Sarah thought, but the lads were taking every opportunity to spar with each other, even Austin. Smart quips and sharp retorts or stony silences, as though the three of them had locked antlers in some unspecified fight for male dominance. A couple of times Megan had sought eye contact with Sarah and raised her eyebrows in exasperation when Sarah had nodded. Whatever was going on was petty, but no one seemed able to stop it.

Their silence was interrupted by the landlady suddenly changing channels and raising the volume on the television.

'The news is on,' she called out from behind the bar. 'Chanel Woman has struck again and this time they have more evidence.'

The entire pub looked towards the screen where an outside reporter was speaking to camera:

'The Detective Chief Inspector attended the crime scene here this afternoon,' he said, 'underlining the seriousness the police are giving to this latest robbery by Chanel Woman.' The live broadcast was replaced with a video clip of DCI Aileen Peters outside Maybury bank. DS Scrivener could be seen talking to her, appearing to point out the good work they were doing. Blue and white *Police. Do Not Cross This Line* hazard tape blew in the wind, stopping pedestrians using the pavement. DCI Peters nodded thoughtfully as DS Scrivener spoke to her, then she addressed the waiting press.

'My team are doing an excellent job here,' she said with a professional smile. 'I have no doubt we will make an arrest before long.'

'How can you be so sure?' the reporter had asked. 'Chanel Woman has evaded capture for two years.'

'We'll issue a statement very soon,' the DCI replied, and, ignoring further questions, returned to her car.

The news went live again to outside the bank. It was 6 p.m.

'In another daring raid, Chanel Woman robbed this bank at gunpoint in broad daylight in the middle of the afternoon,' the reporter said. 'But unlike her previous heists where the only clue was her distinctive perfume, this time she was forced to leave behind her prosthetic mask. This is now being examined by Forensics, and the police have local have-a-go-hero, Mr Gary Strong, to thank for this vital piece of evidence.'

The camera drew back slightly and Gary Strong came into view.

'You were very brave,' the reporter began. 'Although we

should say that the police have warned against approaching a suspect who is armed.'

'I didn't stop to think about my own safety,' Gary said, drawing himself to his full height. 'I just did what I instinctively thought was right.'

The reporter nodded. 'I believe you were around the corner, lying in wait for her?'

'Sort of. I was pretty certain it was her, but I needed to be sure. I'd gone to the bank but the door was locked. A female voice, which I now know was Chanel Woman, told me through the door there was a power cut and to come back tomorrow. I was about to walk away when I caught a whiff of her perfume. These old buildings have a lot of draught-proofing issues – I know, because my parents live in one. I recognized the perfume because my wife uses it. I buy it for her sometimes, although personally I can't stand the smell.' He stopped, seeming to have lost his train of thought.

'Then what happened?' the reporter prompted. 'After you suspected Chanel Woman was in the bank.'

'I thought I'd better wait out of sight and see if I was right. So I went round the corner. There was a car parked there but at the time I didn't realize it was hers or I would have noted the registration. I've given a description of it to the police and I'm sure the registration began with TR6.'

The reporter nodded encouragingly.

'So I waited down the side of the bank. Of course I could have been wrong and it might not have been her, but as soon as she appeared I knew I was right. I grabbed hold of her and tried to make a citizen's arrest.'

'Did she have the gun?'

'I couldn't see it. It must have been in one of her bags.'

'Then what happened?'

'We struggled and I had hold of her hair. Suddenly her

112

face and hair came off in my hand. Although I knew it was a mask, it gave me quite a shock, I can tell you. She ran to her car and sped off. I had to jump out of her way or I would have been mincemeat, but I saw her face. She was a pretty lass apart from a bad scar on her cheek. I guess that's why she wears a mask.'

'Or it could be to hide her true identity,' the reporter suggested drily. 'Thank you, Mr Strong.'

The camera focused on the reporter again as he talked about the village of Maybury and its bank, which was one of the oldest in the country. The report ended with a photo of the prosthetic mask Chanel Woman had been wearing and an appeal that if anyone recognized it or remembered selling it, to contact the police. At the end a telephone number was displayed with an appeal for anyone who had information to call.

'Well, fancy that,' the landlady said, lowering the volume.

'Can we have the sport back on?' one of the locals called out.

She returned the television to the sport channel and went to serve a customer.

'I know Chanel Woman has done wrong, but you have to have a grudging respect for her,' Roshan said, and for the first time that evening Brandon agreed with him.

'That poor woman needs help,' Austin said.

Their food arrived, they ordered more drinks, and the evening improved. Talk and speculation about Chanel Woman dominated much of their conversation. It was neutral territory, and Austin took centre stage as he explained the psychology that could be responsible for her actions. Shortly after 9 p.m. he took a call from a patient and then apologized, saying he needed to leave to set up an emergency online therapy session with her. They'd come in his car, and he offered a lift to anyone who wanted to return now. No

113

one did; they could walk. It was only a couple of miles. Apologizing again, he left.

It was after 11 p.m. when Brandon, Roshan, Sarah and Megan decided it was time to leave. There were only a few customers left in the pub and the landlady was wiping tables in preparation for closing. As soon as Sarah stepped outside into the dark night she felt uncomfortable and regretted not accepting Austin's earlier offer of a lift. The lights of the pub quickly faded as soon as they left the car park, and there were no street lamps or a proper path on the route back to the church. They walked in single file along the makeshift trodden-down grass path. Brandon first, using the torch on his phone to show the way, followed by Sarah, Megan, and Roshan at the rear, who also had his phone torch concentrated on the ground. The moon was concealed behind thick cloud cover, and the only light apart from their phone torches came from the headlamps of the very occasional passing car.

'Perhaps we should phone for a cab?' Megan suggested after about ten minutes.

'We'd be waiting out here forever,' Roshan said. 'We'll be back before it arrives.'

Which was probably true, Sarah thought. She felt she was doing all right until a few moments later Brandon pointedly asked, 'Are *you* OK, Sarah?'

'Yes, why shouldn't I be?' she snapped.

'Just wondered because of your ghost thing.'

'I'm fine,' she said tersely.

But a short while later he asked, 'Did you ever complete Austin's target of walking alone in the graveyard after dark? If not, this could be your chance.'

He might have meant well, Sarah thought, but she didn't see it that way. 'Can you just shut up about that,' she retaliated. 'As if I need reminding of that now! And you and Austin have no business discussing it. That was supposed to be private between him and me.'

'Ouch. Sorry,' Brandon returned, in a tone suggesting he wasn't sorry and Sarah was overreacting.

She decided to let it go and continued in silence along the uneven makeshift path. The only sound came from the crunch of their footsteps and the occasional rustle of something moving in the hedgerow that separated the verge from the fields beyond. The hedge was thick and nearly as tall as them; very likely home to many small animals and birds. That's what the noise was, Sarah told herself, a small animal or large bird.

Yet it seemed to be keeping pace with them, moving parallel, just the other side of the hedge. She closed the gap between her and Brandon, then looked behind to make sure Megan and Roshan were keeping up. Megan was, but Roshan was a few steps further back.

'I'd have worn my boots if I'd known we were walking,' Megan grumbled. 'My shoes will be ruined.'

'Would you like a piggyback?' Roshan joked, and Megan laughed nervously.

A little further on, Sarah was sure she heard the noise again. Could it be something was stalking them? Did foxes hunt humans? She didn't know, and she supposed there could be any number of animals living out here in the middle of the country. The others weren't reacting and seemed oblivious to the noise. *Take a few deep breaths*, she told herself. *Stay calm. It's nothing. Coming after the scare you had this morning you're probably hypersensitive; that's what Austin would say.*

Head down, Sarah concentrated on the path and Brandon's heels. But the feeling that there was something there, another presence, grew, rising to fear. *Keep breathing*, she told herself. *There is nothing to worry about. You're not alone now as*

115

you were this morning. Brandon is in front and Megan and Roshan are just behind. Yet it seemed to be closer to her rather than them, as if it was singling her out. Anything could be concealed on the other side of the hedge.

A car could be heard approaching from behind, which was a relief. A car with people in it. It passed them, illuminating their outlines and the bank. A brief moment of light and normality before the darkness returned, even denser now. The car engine faded into the distance and the only sound was their footsteps, and the rustle of her jacket as she walked.

Then she heard the noise again, and this time so did Megan.

'What was that?' Megan asked, panic in her voice.

'I don't know,' Sarah said, relieved someone else had heard it. 'It's been on and off for a while.'

'I didn't hear anything,' Brandon said, but slowed his pace.

'I did; it came from the other side of the hedge,' Roshan said. 'Perhaps there are horses or cows in the field.' He shone his phone torch into the field as they continued walking, but nothing could be seen beyond fields and countryside.

'Perhaps it was a ghostie,' Brandon said.

'Shut up!' Sarah replied, and slapped his back harder than she'd intended.

'Ouch!' he said, and staggered forward pretending to lose his balance.

'You shouldn't take the piss,' Megan said. 'I heard something. It's probably an animal but our fears and phobias are real.'

'Point taken,' Brandon said easily. 'I'll behave. It's not far before we turn off.'

He picked up their previous walking pace and the others fell into step behind him. Nothing untoward happened for a few minutes, then suddenly the noise again, louder this time, just the other side of the hedge.

'What the hell!' Brandon exclaimed, having heard it too, and stopped.

Megan gave a small cry of alarm and Sarah froze. This wasn't just her fear now. It was real. The others had heard it too.

'Is there someone there?' Brandon called.

Megan clutched Sarah's arm as Brandon and Roshan shone their torches into the field.

'Who's there?' Roshan said.

Silence. But Sarah felt a presence just as she had that morning, as though someone or something was there, hiding in plain sight, maybe in another dimension.

'Show yourself,' Brandon demanded, but his voice shook.

Nothing. No movement, no sound. Yet they were all spooked, feeling it just as acutely as Sarah was.

'I think we need to get out of here,' Roshan said, the urgency in his voice adding to Sarah's fear.

'Let's walk in the road away from the hedge,' Brandon suggested. 'We'll be safer there, and we'll hear if a car comes.'

They scrambled down the grassy verge and onto the road and walked in single file as they had done before. Now their footsteps made a different sound on the tarmac surface compared to the muddy grass, an echo which to Sarah sounded as though there were more than four of them. Like the ghost of others could be walking with them.

Suddenly the noise again. Sarah screamed and instinctively looked towards the hedge. There, gliding through the hedge was a white, misty figure, almost transparent.

'My God!' Megan cried.

'What the fuck!' Brandon shouted, directing his torch at the apparition.

It shimmered and gradually disappeared as though absorbed into the light.

'You saw it too, Roshan, didn't you?' Sarah cried.

'Yes,' he replied, his voice slight. 'I saw something.'

He was shining his torch at the spot where the spectre had materialized, just as Brandon was.

'We need to get out of here,' Brandon said. 'Come on, let's go.'

He grabbed Megan's hand and began running down the centre of the road. She struggled to keep up. Sarah and Roshan followed, their shoes pounding the hard surface. She was panting and a pain had formed in her chest, but she kept going without looking back, just as she had that morning.

'There's our turning!' Brandon shouted.

They sprinted the last few hundred yards and stopped to catch their breath at the junction by the lane that would take them to the church. Sarah had her hand on her chest and the others were panting. The church was just visible through the trees, the downstairs light shining out.

'We're OK now,' Brandon said with relief.

Sarah finally looked back along the road and to the fields but there was nothing to be seen now, and the feeling she'd had of a presence had gone.

'Let's go,' Roshan said, and took her hand.

They continued at a walking pace along the lane. The church grew nearer with each step, and shortly they were there, passing their cars, and at the church gate. Brandon went to open it and stopped.

'I don't know what happened back there,' he said. 'But I don't think we should mention it to Austin.'

'No, I agree,' Roshan said. 'He'll think us barmy.'

'It was probably a trick of the light,' Brandon said.

'A trick of the light?' Megan asked, amazed. 'Of course it wasn't a trick of the light. I know what I saw.'

'So do I,' Sarah said quietly. And knowing it wasn't her imagination and the others had seen it made her even more afraid.

TWENTY-ONE

'Whatever happened to you lot?' Austin asked the moment he saw them. Having heard them enter, he'd come into the lobby.

'It was a longer walk than we thought,' Brandon said. They began taking off their shoes and jackets.

'Why didn't you phone me?' Austin asked. 'I could have collected you. I finished my online therapy session half an hour ago.'

Brandon shrugged. Sarah concentrated on hanging up her jacket, then followed Roshan into the living room and sat beside him on the sofa. Austin came in and returned to the chair where he'd left his laptop. An empty whisky glass was on the occasional table beside it. Brandon came in, followed by Megan. In the brighter light of the living room, Sarah could see how unsettled they looked. It was obvious something was wrong. Megan in particular looked deathly pale and was clearly very anxious.

'You look like you need a drink,' Austin said, surveying them all.

'I think I've had enough,' Megan replied.

'What about you, Sarah?' Austin asked. 'You don't look

so good. In fact, none of you do. Has something happened that I should know about?'

No one answered. They were like children caught in a misdemeanour, avoiding eye contact and saying nothing, having agreed in a loyalty pact not to tell. It was ridiculous, Sarah thought. Of course Austin would see through them. He was a psychologist and trained to read body language.

'Yes, something happened on our way back,' Sarah admitted. Brandon sighed and glared at her accusingly. 'What?' she asked. 'Why shouldn't Austin be told? It's obvious something is wrong and he knows about the other stuff with me.'

'But we don't know what we saw,' Roshan said.

'Or if we saw anything at all,' Brandon added.

'I suggest you let me be the judge of that,' Austin said in his calm, even voice.

How easy it was to dismiss what had happened now they were safely back, Sarah thought. Even Megan had gone quiet and was looking doubtful, apparently not wanting to commit. But Sarah had been in a similar position before and knew that hiding it away or denying the existence of the unexplainable made it worse, not better.

'I'll tell you what happened even if no one else will,' Sarah said.

Brandon huffed. 'I'm getting a drink and going to bed,' he said churlishly, and left the room.

For a second Megan looked like she might go too, but then decided against it and sat down.

'Well?' Austin asked, after a moment, looking at Sarah.

She took a breath. 'It was pitch black and a bit spooky walking back from the pub. I didn't say anything to begin with, but I started hearing noises coming from the fields we passed, just behind the hedge. I tried to persuade myself it was my imagination, but then the others heard it too.' She shivered at the recollection. 'There was nothing to see at that point, it was only a feeling that someone was there. The others felt it too because Brandon suggested we walked in the road. That was better for a while, then we heard the noise again, they did too, and it appeared – a ghostly apparition like I've seen before. The others saw it too, then a few seconds later it vanished.' She stopped, her heart pounding. She looked at Megan, who was concentrating on Austin, waiting for his reaction. Roshan, beside her, was looking at the floor. Was he embarrassed?

'So you all saw it?' Austin asked in the same even dispassionate tone.

'Yes, even Brandon,' Sarah said. 'Although he's now saying it could have been a trick of the light.'

'And could it have been?' Austin asked.

'No. There was no light, only the small torch beams from Brandon's and Roshan's phones.'

'Was the image the same as the previous ones you've seen in your nightmares?' Austin asked Sarah.

'Very similar,' she said, while thinking they weren't just nightmares. They were real sightings of the unexplained.

'The ones you have discussed with Roshan, and told Megan and Brandon about?' Austin asked.

'Well yes, of course Roshan knows. I told Megan, and Brandon seems to know too.'

Austin was starting to smile, not a derisive smile expressing contempt or ridicule, as if he was about to laugh at her. But one of satisfaction suggesting he knew the answer.

'What is it?' Sarah asked. Roshan and Megan were watching him closely too.

'If it wasn't a trick of the light – which I agree seems unlikely – then in my view it's a classic case of contagious dissociative phenomena, also known as mass hysteria. It can affect small or large groups when anxiety is present. It's like an instant chain reaction. It can be seen in "groupthink" where a group forms a consensus of opinion that they all feed into – reinforcing what they believe. You were all aware of Sarah's nightmares, which are real to her, then you found yourselves walking along an unfamiliar dark country lane. Suddenly you start to hear strange noises that were most likely badgers. Plenty live around here. But it was enough to feed into your fears. It was only a short step to actually seeing something, which disappeared very quickly in the light. Presumably before you were able to get a proper look at it or take a photo?'

'That's right,' Megan said, clearly relieved. 'That's exactly what happened.'

'I suppose it makes sense,' Roshan agreed.

Austin nodded sagely. 'I'm sure that's what happened. There are lots of well-documented cases of mass hysteria online if you want to have a look. It can happen in families and between close friends. They share common beliefs which can feed into the same hallucination. The mind is a weird and wonderful organ that we barely understand a fraction of. There's no other explanation, unless you believe in ghosts.' Drawing his fingers together, he sat back, satisfied.

Sarah stopped herself from saying she did believe in ghosts. It would have been a step too far. Megan and Roshan had accepted Austin's explanation and very likely Brandon would too.

'All right, Sarah?' Austin asked, searching for eye contact. 'You're happy with my explanation?'

She stood. 'I'm going to bed,' she said. 'See you in the morning.'

'I'll be up shortly,' Roshan said.

'Aren't you coming now?' Sarah asked.

'No, when I'm ready.'

'Suit yourself,' she muttered under her breath, and left

the room. She was close to tears. She really needed Roshan beside her now, not down there discussing what happened and very likely deciding, as Austin had, that her hysteria was to blame.

TWENTY-TWO

Chanel Woman looked at the pile of her belongings on the floor in the utility room ready to take outside and panic gripped her again. She felt hot and clammy. Her stomach was churning and her mind was racing, but she still wasn't thinking straight. Was this the best course of action? If so, how could she be sure she had everything here that could incriminate her? It was impossible to know. She should have thought of burning her belongings sooner. But having driven home that afternoon in blind panic, she'd then frozen like a rabbit caught in a car's headlight and hadn't been able to work out what to do for the best.

Now it was after midnight, and if she lit a bonfire in the garden a neighbour might spot it and call the emergency services. But then again, the other two houses along the lane were so far away they probably wouldn't see the flames, maybe just smell smoke, which hopefully they would ignore. Did she have any choice? She really needed to speak to her husband, but he wasn't answering his phone. She stared at the heap of her belongings. If she postponed burning them until the morning there was a good chance the police would have traced her by then and catch her in the act. It was only a matter of time. Her stomach churned again.

She checked the newsfeed on her phone as she'd been doing all evening. She knew the police were confident they would catch her quickly, and they were right. She'd grown complacent, overconfident, and should have been far more careful. Fuck that Gary Strong! she thought. Nasty little man. She'd seen him interviewed on the news, puffing himself up and making the most of his two minutes of fame. It was his fault the police had a description of her and her car, and, even more incriminatingly – the mask with her DNA and fingerprints on it. How long before the police matched them with those on their computer? Probably only a matter of hours, for she'd been caught before stealing. Nothing big like this; shoplifting, and years ago. But her fingerprints and DNA would be on the police database. She'd narrowly missed prison the last time and had received a community service order instead. The psychiatrist's report had helped, and she'd promised to get the help she needed. Which she had. And thanks to that and the continued support of her husband, as far as the police were concerned she'd kept out of trouble, until now.

No use having regrets, she told herself firmly. She needed to calm down and concentrate on the here and now. Get rid of as much of the evidence as possible, and with a good lawyer she should be in with a chance. If all else failed, she could plead a relapse of her condition, and with another psychiatric report get a reduced sentence. Although the thought of going to prison at all filled her with dread.

Perhaps she should just make a run for it while she had the chance, she wondered, glancing towards the door. Pack a bag and leave. She had her passport and plenty of cash, and the rest of the money she'd stolen was in offshore bank accounts in countries who didn't worry about money laundering. But then again, if she got caught trying to flee the country it would look bad and count against her. *Return to plan A*, she told herself. *It's come earlier than anticipated, thanks to that bloody Gary Strong, but it should still work. Stay calm, don't lose your nerve, and get rid of as much of the incriminating evidence as possible. You got greedy, that's all. Thought you could get away with it a few more times. Do as planned, and burn everything connected with Chanel Woman.*

Tucking a box of matches into her jacket pocket she switched on the outside lights and the patio lit up. So too did the fairy lights that zig-zagged above the garden and along the path. She opened the back door, then scooping up the first bundle of clothes went out. It was a chilly but thankfully dry autumn night. The garden looked pretty, as if they were hosting one of their summer parties. But this was no party. Her future hung in the balance. She followed the path to the end of the upper gardens and turned right. Out of sight of the house was the steel incinerator the gardener used for burning their garden rubbish. She'd never had reason to use it before but assumed it wasn't difficult – a metal bin with a chimney in the lid. How difficult could it be? She removed the lid and looked in. It was empty, just some ash lay in the bottom. She stuffed in the clothes, struck a match, and dropped it in. The flame went out. She tried again with the same result, then saw the row of holes around the base. She struck another match and poked it through a hole. That went out too. How could it be this difficult? Then she remembered the gardener asked for old newspaper to get the fire going.

She ran back into the house, grabbed the roll of kitchen towel and returned to the incinerator. Tearing off a strip, she rolled it up cigar-like and lit one end. It burnt and she poked it into a hole at the bottom of the incinerator, then did the same to the next hole, and the next, working her way around. The contents seemed to be catching fire. She could see smouldering, a little smoke, and then a small flame. Just to be sure, she struck another match, set fire to the rest of the roll of kitchen towel and dropped it into the incinerator, then put on the lid. After a few moments flames crackled and smoke billowed from the chimney.

She returned to the house and grabbed the next bundle of clothes, including two of the masks. She hoped they'd burn too. The hair was real, so that would catch fire easily. She knew from bitter experience. An image of being trapped in a burning car as a teenager flashed before her, and she forced it away. Going down the path she could smell smoke and burning, but not enough to worry a distant neighbour.

She went to lift the lid on the incinerator but drew back in pain. She should have realized the lid would be hot. The gardener always wore thick gloves. She wrapped one of the jerseys she was about to burn around her hand, took off the lid and set it on the grass. Best leave it off for now, she thought. Flames were dancing and crackling inside the incinerator. She fed in the clothes one at a time and watched them disappear into the fire. Then she dropped in a mask. She could barely look as the hair caught fire and the mask began to shrivel, the latex melting, much as her face had done. Steeling herself, she dropped in the other mask, and immediately returned to the house for the next bundle. One more to go after this and that should do it, all the clothes she'd worn as Chanel Woman. But as she came out the air had changed. It was no longer the faint whiff of smoke, but something more pungent, noxious, like rubber burning. It must be the latex masks.

She turned the corner at the bottom of the garden and saw there was more smoke than before coming from the incinerator and it was darker and thicker. The smell was getting worse. She covered her mouth and peered in. The flames weren't as strong. She remembered the gardener poking a rod into the holes at the bottom to keep the air flowing. She looked around and spotted the metal rod he used on the ground nearby. Picking it up, she poked it through the holes. Some ash fell out and then the fire rekindled. She needed to get a move on. She quickly fed in the clothes and masks, then ran back to the house for more, hoping the toxic fumes would disperse into the night air.

She was about to scoop up the last bundle when she remembered the gun was still in her bag. She went into the living room and, taking the replica gun from her bag, returned to the utility room. The gun was made of plastic, so hopefully would melt. Gathering up the last of the clothes and masks, she returned outside. The pungent smell had intensified. The air smelled toxic, of chemicals, presumably from the latex. She could see the smoke rising as she approached. It was thick black now. Rounding the corner, she tried not to breathe it in as she quickly fed in the last of the clothes, masks, and the gun. Thank goodness. She rammed on the lid and began up the path, but before she got to the back door a siren could be heard in the distance. Police, ambulance or fire brigade, she wasn't sure. Heart racing, she went in and closed the back door. All she could do now was hope for the best and not lose her nerve. Plan A should still work.

TWENTY-THREE

'I promised the DCI we'd have Chanel Woman in custody by the morning,' DS Scrivener said as he handed out more coffee to the four officers working through the night. 'We've had a good response following the news bulletin. However, based on Gary Strong's description, and the waitress in the coffee shop across the road from the bank, she's been sighted all over the country. I still think she's local. Matt, how's the number plate tracing going?'

'Still working on it, sir,' he said, glancing up from his computer screen, and taking a sip of the coffee. 'None of the cars so far beginning with the registration TR6 match the make and model Mr Strong gave us. It's all we've got, because you can't see the full registration on the bank's CCTV. I'm still checking, but I think we need to consider the possibility that she could be using false number plates, in which case this will go nowhere.'

DS Scrivener nodded thoughtfully. 'Thanks, keep going for now. I've heard from Forensics,' he said, addressing them all. 'They're confident they can retrieve a useful DNA sample from the mask, but as usual it could take weeks to analyse and check against our records. The fingerprint match – if there is one – should be back in a couple of hours. Beth, anything on the mask? Where it was made, sold, etc.'

'Nothing from the suppliers I've spoken to so far, sir, although they all seem to agree that looking at the photo it appears to be of a decent quality and professionally made. Film standard, one of them said. But they've also said a lot are imported now as it's cheaper.'

'OK.' Returning to his desk, DS Scrivener added, 'If anyone needs to take a break do so, but remember all eyes are on us.'

'No pressure then, sir,' Matt said.

For nearly an hour all that could be heard was the tapping of computer keys, occasional huffs of frustration, quiet exchanges of conversation, and the sound of a chair moving if someone left the room to use the bathroom, make a drink, or buy something from the vending machine. They'd had pizza delivered earlier and the empty boxes were in the kitchen ready to be taken out.

It was a little after 2 a.m. when DS Scrivener finished a phone call and, standing, approached Matt and Beth.

'Do you two want a change of scenery?' he asked them.

'Wouldn't mind, sir,' Matt replied.

Beth nodded, and clicked 'save' on the computer file she was working on.

'I've just heard from a friend in the fire service,' DS Scrivener continued. 'They received a 999 call to what was originally thought to be a house fire, but when they arrived it was a woman burning rubbish in her garden.'

'Bit late for that, sir, isn't it?' Matt said.

'The householder said the fire must have rekindled during the night. It was nearly out by the time the fire brigade got there, but they were concerned about a noxious chemical smell, and asked what she'd been burning. They looked in the incinerator she'd used and found plastic and latex. A member of the fire crew talked to her about what you are legally allowed to burn in a garden. She apologized and said she'd been burning old dressing-up clothes as her children no longer used them and they weren't good enough to give to a charity shop.'

Beth and Matt nodded.

'They accepted her explanation, but on their way back to the fire station one of the crew remarked on the resemblance between the woman and the description we've put out on Chanel Woman. My friend thought they were getting a bit carried away, but one of the lads said she was wearing a lot of make-up which could have been hiding a scar on her cheek. They persuaded him to phone me – off the record. I know it's a long shot, but the address is local.' He gave Beth the piece of paper he was holding. 'Just have a chat with her. Find out where she was yesterday. Routine enquiry.'

'Now, sir?' Matt asked, checking the time.

'Yes. Obviously, apologize for waking her.'

'Very good, sir.'

TWENTY-FOUR

She should have left earlier instead of trying to burn the evidence, Chanel Woman thought as she crammed more clothes into the suitcase that lay open on her bed. She should have gone that afternoon as soon as she'd returned from Maybury, instead of dithering indecisively, then wasting valuable time on that bloody incinerator. Had she gone then she'd be on a plane by now, before the police had time to alert the airports and ferries. Now she wasn't sure what her plans were other than to get out of here. Maybe lie low for a while and then leave the country. Hide in the city, London, a long way from here? Her hands shook as she picked up the tube of make-up, dabbed more onto her cheek, then slipped it into the cosmetic bag and added it to her hand luggage.

Of course, it was possible she'd got away with her bluff to the fire brigade and they hadn't informed the police. The lead fire officer had accepted her explanation of burning old dressing-up clothes, but that young lad with him had kept looking at her quizzically, as if he might have recognized her. The facial composite image the police had released was all over the internet. No, best to leave now while she had the chance and go into hiding, she decided.

Suitcases full, she closed them and checked her face in the mirror again. She'd arranged her hair as she often wore it, hanging over her damaged cheek. She looked longingly at the bottle of Chanel N°5 that had been her accomplice, ally, and friend for so long. No. Better not take it with her; that life had to end now. She heaved both cases off the bed and dragged them to the door then downstairs, parking them in the hall. The cab should be here soon. She'd made the decision not to take her car. It was too risky. Although the number plates wouldn't be recognized, the description of her car might. It was all over the news. She'd told the cab firm her mother was critically ill in hospital.

She just needed her passport. She went into the study, took the picture that concealed the safe off the wall, and keyed in the code. Removing her passport, she tucked it into her shoulder bag. The cash was already in her suitcase. She returned to the living room to wait for the cab. The curtains were slightly parted as they always were. She could see the drive with its ornamental trees lit up by the lanterns. In some ways she'd be sorry to leave.

She paced the room and checked the cab's progress on her phone using the web link the cab firm had sent. It was only a few minutes away now. She watched and waited, then saw headlights flickering through the trees as the cab entered the far end of the drive. Thank goodness. She waited until it pulled up outside and, trying to calm her nerves, went into the hall.

She had everything she needed, didn't she? She checked her shoulder bag again then opened the front door.

'Morning,' the driver said.

'Morning, just these two cases, please.'

He took them from the hall and she followed him out, closing and locking the door behind her.

'Do you know you've left all your lights on?' he asked helpfully.

'Yes, for security, to give the appearance of someone being in,' she replied, and got into the back of the car.

Having loaded the cases, he got in. 'University College Hospital in London,' he checked.

'Yes, please.'

He concentrated on the satnav and was about to start the engine when a set of headlights suddenly appeared at the end of the drive. Her stomach churned.

'Looks like you've got visitors,' he said.

'I'm not expecting anyone, so go.'

'Are you sure?' he asked, glancing at her in the rear-view mirror. 'There's only your house down here, they must be coming to see you.'

'It could be a wrong address. It happens a lot,' she said, trying to keep her voice even. 'Go please. My mother is very ill. I need to see her quickly.'

'All right, your call.'

He started the engine. The headlights continued to gain ground, drawing nearer by the second.

'Please, go quickly,' she said again, and heard the panic in her voice.

But as he began to pull away the approaching car suddenly gained speed, came onto their side of the drive and pulled up directly in front of them, blocking their route.

'What the hell!' the driver exclaimed.

Immediately a man and woman jumped out of the car and appeared at their windows. The man opened the driver's door. 'Police officers, get out of the vehicle, please,' he said to the driver, and flashed his ID.

The female police officer opened her door and two years of being Chanel Woman kicked in. 'What is the problem, officer?' she asked in an authoritative tone. 'Has this man done something wrong? My mother is very sick in hospital and I need to get to her quickly.'

She saw the flash of uncertainty on the female officer's face.

'Can I see your driving licence, please?' the male officer said to the driver while the female officer went on staring at her. She adjusted her hair further over her cheek.

'Here we are,' the cab driver said, producing his licence.

'Thank you.' The officer checked it and handed it back.

'Are you Leslie Chambers?' the female officer now asked.

'Yes.'

'Could you get out of the car, please?'

'Why? My mother is ill.'

Another look of uncertainty.

'It won't take long, but we need to talk to you.'

'About what?' She stayed where she was.

'There was a fire here earlier.'

'Yes, and it was dealt with.'

More uncertainty. She saw them exchange a look.

'We do need to speak to you, either here or at the police station,' the male officer said. 'The cab can wait, if you like.'

'This better be good!' she said in the same tone. 'If I don't get to see my mother before she dies, I'll make sure you lose your jobs.'

'Do you want me to wait?' the cab driver asked uncertainly.

'Yes, of course,' she snapped. 'I'm not going to be long.'

He cut the car's engine and turned off its lights as she got out.

'I'm DC Beth Mayes and this is DC Matt Davis,' the female officer said as they returned to the house. 'Thank you for your cooperation.'

She opened the front door and led the way into the living room, dimming the lights as she went.

'Is anyone else home?' DC Beth Mayes asked.

'No.'

'But you live here with Mr Chambers?'

'Yes, my husband. What's this all about?' She didn't ask them to sit down. She needed them gone as quickly as possible.

'Where were you this afternoon?' Beth asked.

'Mainly home, apart from popping out to do some shopping.'

'Can anyone confirm that?'

'I doubt it. I always shop alone.'

'Your husband?'

'He phoned me, but he's away.'

'Where were you going just now?' Beth asked.

'I told you, to see my mother in hospital. She's very ill.'

'I'm sorry,' Beth said. 'Which hospital is she in?'

'A London hospital – UCH. Can I go now?'

'Not just yet,' Matt said. 'The fire that the officers attended earlier – can we have a look at it, please?'

'Why? It's out,' she said, trying to keep her voice even.

'There are some concerns about what you were burning,' Matt said.

'Yes, I know. The fire officers explained, and I promise I won't do it again.'

'We'd still like to take a look,' Beth said.

'Very well, but there's nothing to see!'

Clinging to the last vestige of her composure, she led the way out of the living room, down the hall, and through the back door. She didn't switch on the patio or garden lights, so it was very dark outside without the moon. She led the way down the path to the end of the garden and behind the tall hedge.

'That's the incinerator I used,' she said as they rounded the corner.

She watched as Matt switched on his phone torch and then took the lid off the incinerator and looked in. Then, picking up the metal rod she'd left on the ground, he began poking around inside the bin.

'It still smells bad,' Beth said. 'What did you burn?'

'As I explained to the fire officers, dressing-up clothes. It must have been the Halloween masks.'

Matt continued prodding more thoroughly than the fire officers had done. Their main concern had been that the fire was safely out, but he was definitely looking for something. Her mouth was dry and she swallowed hard. The rod could be heard tapping against the sides and bottom of the metal bin as he dug around. Then he hooked up the remains of something plastic. Her heart stopped. Mangled and melted by the heat it was still recognizable.

'It looks like the handle of a gun,' Matt Davis said. 'It's the right shape.'

'Yes, a toy gun,' she said. 'It was broken so I burnt it, or tried to.'

He took an evidence bag from his pocket and dropped it in, prodded around a bit more, then replaced the lid on the incinerator.

'Finished?' she asked hopefully.

'For now, yes.'

She retraced her footsteps up the path. They followed until they drew level with the door that led into the back of the garage.

'Is there a car in the garage?' Beth asked.

'Yes.'

'Can we take a look at it, please?'

She could hardly refuse. Trying to retain a calm, indignant manner, she let them into the garage. Matt Davis switched on the light, illuminating her car. She saw their looks of surprise and little-concealed delight.

'Is this your car?' Beth asked, going to it.

She nodded.

'It matches the description of the car seen in the vicinity of Maybury bank yesterday afternoon during a robbery.'

'That doesn't surprise me. I was there. I told you I went out to do some shopping. I also got some cash out. I parked beside the bank while I went to the cash machine at the front, but I certainly didn't rob it.'

'Can we have a look inside?' Beth asked.

'It's unlocked.'

As Beth opened the driver's door the unmistakable smell of perfume wafted out. It always lingered in a confined space. If she could smell it, then so could they. But Matt appeared more interested in the number plates. 'Have you taken the plates off recently?' he asked. 'One of the screws is very loose.'

'I used to have personalized plates on the car, but decided to put the originals back on.'

'So these are the original number plates?' he checked.

She nodded.

'That's strange, because I've been trying to match a plate beginning with TR6 with a car like this all afternoon, but couldn't. I'll check again.'

At that point she knew it was just a matter of time, and the game was over. It briefly crossed her mind to make a run for it, but she knew she wouldn't get far. So she waited with as much pride and dignity as was possible while Matt checked the registration number on their database, aware the inevitable was approaching like a runaway train but unable to stop it.

He ended the call and looked at her. 'This isn't the original registration plate for this car.'

'No?'

Beth straightened as she finished checking the inside of the car. A moment's hesitation when they exchanged looks, and then he began arresting her by reading her her rights . . . *Anything you say can and will be used against you in a court of law* . . .

*   *   *

'Out of interest,' Beth said as they accompanied her through the house, 'why did you choose Chanel N°5.'

'My husband likes it. It's labelled as the "sweet smell of success".'

'Fair enough.'

'Can I phone him?' she asked.

'Yes, once we've got you processed at the police station you're allowed to make a call,' Beth replied.

'Then what?'

'You'll be interviewed, with a solicitor present if you wish.'

'I'd better let the cab go then,' she said. 'I don't suppose I'll be needing that for a while.'

'No, I don't suppose you will,' Beth said.

Don't lose your nerve, just keep to your plan, she thought.

TWENTY-FIVE

Megan could always sense when there was a spider close by. She didn't need to see it, or even catch a glimpse of its shadow or slight movement as it scuttled across the room. She just knew. Like a sixth sense. And she knew there was a spider in her room now.

She forced herself to open her eyes. Her heart was racing as her skin crawled with fear. She felt hot and clammy all over. Oh no. Please no. Could she possibly be wrong? She was alone with no one to help her.

'Confront your fear,' she heard Austin say. 'Don't let it control you and ruin your life.'

She'd been doing so well until now using the techniques Austin had taught her. *Meet and greet your fear*, he'd said, which had made her smile then, but not now.

First she forced herself to look at the ceiling directly above her – over her bed – one of the worst places to spot a spider as it was sure to drop before she was able to move out of its way. Thankfully the ceiling above was clear. She moved her gaze and slowly scanned the rest of the ceiling, concentrating on the dark wooden beams where a spider could easily hide and blend in. Thankfully, that seemed clear too.

She allowed herself to breathe again and then turned her head slightly so she had a better view of the window. The sun was shining through the stained glass, casting patterns onto the floor, making it more difficult to spot a spider. She watched and waited, her heart drumming loudly. But there was no movement, nothing running out of the shadows and across the floor. So where was it?

The speed at which they could run was one of their most frightening features, together with their abnormal shape: eight hair-encrusted arched legs, which were disproportionately long for their small round bodies. She shivered at the thought. She'd read once it was their hairy legs that allowed them to climb walls and run effortlessly upside down across ceilings. The sticky web they produced was disgusting and cruel, designed to catch helpless prey and render them immobile until they died and could be eaten. Surely not one of God's creatures.

Megan looked at her phone on the bedside cabinet. Perhaps she could call one of the others to come and deal with the spider, because there was definitely one here, although she couldn't see it. Not Austin, he would be disappointed in her. Her thoughts flipped back to the discussion they'd had last night about Sarah's ghost and how Austin had said she was doing much better confronting her fears, compared to Sarah. Perhaps it was talking about it that had rekindled her phobia? *So deal with it*, she told herself firmly.

She eased herself further up the pillow, watching the walls, ceiling and floor for any movement. Perhaps it was *on* the bed, she thought with a stab of horror, and threw back the duvet. She frantically checked the bed, but it was all clear. She sat for a moment trying to catch her breath and let her pulse settle, then reached for her phone. It was 9.45 a.m. She needed to deal with this so she could get up, use the bathroom, shower and dress and try to make the most of her last three days here before they all went home. It certainly hadn't been the holiday reunion she'd expected, and in many ways she'd be pleased to be home again. She was missing Ella, and this place was really making her feel uncomfortable. If she thought too much about it she could believe in ghosts just as Sarah did, despite what Austin had said.

'Get up,' she told herself forcefully. The spider had probably gone by now, disappearing out of the room the same way it came in. There was a small gap under the door, but big enough for a spider. These old buildings were full of crevices where spiders could get in. She'd stuff a towel under the door tonight.

She checked the floor again, then gingerly lowered her feet into her slippers. She never went barefoot, even at home, just in case there was a spider on the floor. She paused and looked around for any sign of movement, got to her feet and headed towards the bathroom. She took a few steps and froze. Fear gripped her. Something was tickling her back, between her shoulder blades. *It's your hair, pull yourself together*, she told herself. But it moved; she could feel it running across her back. She screamed, tore at her nightshirt, struggling to get it off over her head. The worst terror ever. All her fears had come together. A spider was on her! Wrenching off her nightshirt, she threw it on the floor and turned her back to the mirror. She sobbed and cried out in pain. There it was, in the middle of her back, just below her neck. It stayed still for a second and then ran into her hair.

'No, no!' she cried hysterically, pulling at her hair. 'Help, someone help me. Please!' She was sure the shock would kill her.

Clutching her head, she dropped to her knees, trying to pull out the spider. Then through her sobs came the sound of a door opening behind her, and a voice.

'Megan?'

'It's in my hair. Get it off of me!' she cried, pulling harder at her hair.

Strong hands clasped hers and, taking control, eased her hands away from her head.

'Megan, open your eyes. You're safe. It's Roshan. Nothing can harm you.'

'Roshan?' she asked, and opened her eyes. 'Has it gone? The spider. It was on me, it was in my hair.'

'There's nothing there,' he said gently.

'Can you look?'

'Yes, if it helps.'

She didn't feel embarrassed by her nakedness as he leaned over her and his firm hands gently parted her hair, just relief that someone was helping her, and the need to know the spider had gone.

'There's nothing here,' Roshan confirmed tenderly. 'I promise you. You were having a nightmare. I've seen it in Sarah. Come on, stand up.'

'No, it was real.'

She allowed him to help her to her feet. He picked up her towelling bathrobe and, shaking it out, wrapped it around her. He led her to the bed and sat her on the edge. She couldn't feel it moving any more, but that didn't mean it wasn't there.

'Can you get my hairbrush, please? It's in the bathroom.'

'Yes, of course.'

She sat very still, rigid, in case it was still in her hair and moving provoked it into running again. The terrifying tickle from its spindly furry legs. She'd never forget it.

'Would you like me to brush your hair?' Roshan asked.

'Yes please. Thank you so much. What must you think of me?'

'I think you were very scared from having a nightmare. Just like Sarah has been.'

'It was more than a nightmare.'

He didn't reply but sat beside her on the bed and began gently brushing her hair, long soothing strokes that helped calm and reassure her.

'I was awake,' she said after a few moments. 'I knew there was a spider in the room, but I couldn't find it. I got out of bed and felt it on my back. I tore off my nightshirt and saw it in the mirror. Then it ran into my hair. I could feel it moving around.' She trembled at the recollection.

'I know how real night terrors can be,' Roshan said reassuringly, keeping the rhythm of the brush going. 'I've lived with Sarah's nightmares for years, although she hadn't had one for a long time before we came here. And you seemed to be asleep when I first came in.'

'Was I?' she asked, confused. 'I think it's this place.'

'Just relax,' he told her. 'It's OK now.'

It was wonderful the way he was brushing her hair, comforting, soothing and, dare she say it, sensual. The feel of his hands, the motion. With each brushstroke the horror of the spider receded until she found herself in the moment, enjoying the closeness, the touch and feel of Roshan, of simply having him next to her. It was a long time since she'd been this close to a man, let alone having him brush her hair. Ella played with her hair sometimes but usually got it tangled. This was blissful. Roshan knew what to do, and briefly Megan wondered if he brushed Sarah's hair like this. If so, she was a lucky woman.

She was soon so relaxed that all thoughts of the spider had gone, her eyes closed, and she gave herself up to the sensation. It was only a small and very natural next step to rest her head on Roshan's shoulder. Then a few moments later to allow him to ease her onto the bed where he lay next to her. The hair-brushing had stopped and she nestled into the crook of his arm.

144

'You've got lovely hair,' he murmured, his voice thick with emotion.

'Thank you. I feel so much better now,' she said quietly. 'I hope the others didn't hear me crying.'

'They won't have. Brandon's still in bed and Sarah is out with Austin, retracing the route we took last night. He thought it would help her.'

Megan could feel the warmth of Roshan's breath on her cheek, his body pressed against hers, his arm around her, strong and reassuring. He was everything she could have wished for in a man. Why had she let him go?

'Do you remember we dated for a while at school?' she said dreamily, her voice far off and unreal.

'I do. I thought you'd forgotten. You never mention it.'

'No, I haven't forgotten,' Megan said.

He kissed her ear, then her cheek, and his lips sought hers. Kisses reminiscent of all those years ago, as exciting now as they had been then. Roshan had been her first proper boyfriend. The one she'd given herself to. Why hadn't it lasted? She couldn't remember, and it didn't matter. He was here with her now. She turned her head so his mouth met hers full on. The kiss lasted forever and made her tingle with desire. It took her to another place and time where only he mattered. She felt her body yearning for his in uncontrolled passion, and he was hard against her. She touched the zip at the front of his jeans.

'I feel a bit over-dressed,' he murmured.

'Yes, you are.'

She began undoing his zipper, then abruptly stopped, as though suddenly becoming aware.

'Roshan, we can't!' she said, shocked. 'You have Sarah.'

'Sarah!' he said with a jolt. 'Jesus. What are we doing? I'm so sorry, Megan.' He took his arm from under her and quickly moved away. 'Forgive me, please. I don't know what happened.'

'It's not your fault. We got carried away.' But was that what happened? she thought. Their bodies got the better of them? 'We stopped, didn't we? We haven't done anything wrong?' she asked, concerned.

'No but we nearly did. I don't know what came over me. I've never done anything like that before. I'm faithful to Sarah. I love her.'

'We weren't thinking straight,' Megan said. He looked as shocked and remorseful as she felt. 'You helped me, and I guess we just forgot ourselves and thought we were those teenagers again.'

He stood and zipped up his trousers as she pulled the bathrobe around her.

'Are you all right if I go?' he asked her, concerned.

'Yes. Thanks for helping me. You're a good friend.'

'We won't say anything about this to the others?' he checked, worried.

'No, of course not. You go. I'm going to get up now, see you later.'

He hesitated. 'There *was* a spider, wasn't there? I mean you didn't make it up?'

'No, of course not. Why would I do that?'

'To entice me in?'

'Roshan, no. How can you think that?'

He shrugged, confused, then tucking his shirt into his trousers, went to the door. As he opened it, Megan saw Brandon cross the landing. He looked straight at her.

'It's not what you think,' she heard Roshan say.

But any reply was lost as he closed the door, and Megan could have wept.

146

TWENTY-SIX

Chanel Woman was sitting in a cell at Coleshaw police station waiting for a solicitor to arrive before being interviewed. By the time she'd been checked in and processed, she was full of remorse and self-pity. The officers who'd dealt with her had been almost apologetic when they'd shown her into the cell and locked the door. Now she was fighting back tears. How had it come to this? All she'd ever wanted was some excitement, a few thrills to lift her from her humdrum life where there were no risks and everything was provided for. To be successful in her own right, just like the tag line of the advertising for the perfume she'd used stated – the sweet smell of success.

She drew her arm to her nose and smelled her wrist where she'd last dabbed on the perfume. But it had gone, faded beyond recognition, just like the persona of Chanel Woman. Obliterated in the moment of her discovery and arrest. All she could smell was smoke from the incinerator on her clothes, and, in the air, this awful cell. She raised her head and looked around again, at the scuffed emulsion grey walls, cold tiled stained floor, and the single window, high up, barred and closed. She was sitting on a narrow hard bed fixed to the wall behind her, and opposite the door. A coarse blanket was folded at one end. The cell was chilly, but she wouldn't use the blanket. It looked grubby, although they'd assured her it had been washed. In fact, the whole miserable cell looked like it needed a good scrub to eradicate the smell of damp sweaty bodies, decay, and something she didn't want to identify.

She'd been offered a sandwich a short while ago, but had refused, and had just accepted the water, which tasted of the plastic cup it had come in. Irritatingly, officers kept checking on her, either by opening the viewing hatch or the door. She thought it wasn't so much to check on her well-being, but for a glimpse of the fallen woman. Like a freak at a nineteenth-century peep show. She knew her arrest had made national news, and now the officers would be able to tell their friends and families they'd actually seen her. She'd experienced notoriety but could never have envisaged this. It felt surreal.

The viewing hatch clanked open again. 'Can I get you anything?' a young PC asked. She hadn't seen him before. Perhaps he'd just come on shift.

'No, thank you.' But he didn't immediately close the hatch. She thought that if he could have taken a photo he probably would. 'No, thank you,' she said more firmly, and he closed the hatch.

But ten minutes later another fresh-faced officer poked her head around the door and asked if she needed anything.

'How long will my solicitor be?'

'I understand he's on his way, but I'll check with DC Mayes.'

'Thank you.'

She tried to concentrate on what she should say to the solicitor when he arrived to make things easier for herself. That she suffered from an illness, kleptomania, and recognized she needed help. She thought that was her best line of defence as well as being true. Her husband would confirm it, but she should discuss it with the solicitor first and be guided by him in case he had other ideas.

Hopefully her husband would be here soon, she fretted. She couldn't understand what was taking him so long. She'd phoned him from the police station as soon as she'd been allowed, but that was hours ago and he should have been here by now. They'd taken her phone and other personal possessions, so it wasn't as though she could message him. He must appreciate the trouble she was in and that she needed his help and support. So where was he? It had crossed her mind that perhaps he was having doubts, and instead of supporting her he was trying to distance himself – to protect his reputation and career. It was possible. In which case she was completely alone. What would Chanel Woman have done? She honestly couldn't remember. That person seemed so distant now and had gone for good. She swallowed hard. A tear slipped from her eye and ran down her cheek, leaving a mark on the make-up that covered her scar. Before long there would be no make-up left and she'd be totally and brutally exposed. How would she cope?

TWENTY-SEVEN

Megan was still in her room trying to summon the courage to go downstairs and face everyone. Brandon had called up to say he was making brunch. She had showered, dressed, and phoned home – speaking to her mother and daughter, which had made her feel more guilty and ashamed. Her mother would have been appalled if she'd known she'd nearly made love to a married man – her friend's husband. And little Ella, so innocent and pure, Megan didn't feel she had the right to even talk to her for long, in case her grubbiness rubbed off and sullied her. She'd told Ella repeatedly how much she loved and missed her and would see her on Saturday – three more sleeps.

Megan was still struggling to come to terms with what had happened, what she and Roshan had nearly done. It could be explained by saying they were old friends, one-time lovers, caught in the moment, which Roshan had accepted. But then he'd asked if there really was a spider, suggesting she'd set a trap to lure him into her bed. She'd been shocked and upset, but now she wondered if he could be right. Had she dreamt it? Cried out in her sleep, and then when he'd come in pretended it was real to keep him there? It seemed plausible, and this explanation was preferable to having made it all up while awake. Even so, she'd acted badly and out of character.

She'd been doing that a lot since coming here, she thought as she looked at the door, preparing herself for going downstairs. Austin had said in one of their therapy sessions it was because she was free of the constraints she usually had of being a single mother and dutiful daughter. The freedom had allowed another side of her to come out, an alter ego – more risqué. Megan thought she didn't like this other person who stole wine, made nasty comments, and did things that were morally wrong. Sometimes she had to stop herself from saying something that was totally inappropriate or would have hurt the other person. That wasn't like her at all.

Brandon called up again, this time to say brunch was ready. She couldn't hide up here any longer. She had to go down and face them all. Austin and Sarah had returned from their walk, and she assumed Roshan was down there too. She prayed he hadn't told Sarah. She checked the room one last time for the spider, almost hoping it would materialize, thus proving it was real, but it didn't. Picking up her phone, she left and went down the spiral staircase, the smell of brunch and their voices drawing closer.

As she stepped into the kitchen-diner conversation stopped and they all looked at her. Brandon was at the range cooker, and the others were at the table already eating.

'There you are, good,' Brandon said, handing her a plate containing a vegetarian brunch.

'Thank you so much,' she said quietly, and joined the others at the table.

Conversation resumed. Sarah was talking to Roshan about her walk with Austin, retracing the route they'd taken last night. Austin was listening and occasionally nodding. Megan began to relax and eat. Perhaps they hadn't been talking about her.

'Thank you,' she said again to Brandon as he brought his breakfast to the table and sat down. 'It's nice of you to go to so much trouble for me.'

'You're welcome,' he said, then winked. A seductive, suggestive wink that made her feel cheap. Did he know?

She concentrated on her plate. The next time she was alone with Brandon she'd explain that Roshan had heard her cries for help and come into her room to deal with the spider, and that nothing had happened between them. She didn't want Brandon to think badly of her. It mattered what he thought.

'Yes, some of the early psychology experiments would be deemed cruel and unethical by present standards,' Austin was saying. The others were now watching him, intent on what he was telling them. He could easily capture an audience's interest; he was good at it. Megan too found herself wanting to hear more. You couldn't help it. When Austin spoke, others listened, they always had, even at school.

'Harlow's monkeys, for example – you may have heard of them?' Austin continued.

No one had.

'Harlow carried out psychological experiments on monkeys during the fifties, sixties and seventies. He took baby monkeys from their mothers and placed them in isolation in what became known as the pit of despair. He fed them, but that was all. They were denied physical contact, and within days they were incessantly rocking and clutching themselves, biting their skin, and ripping out their hair. He kept them there for up to a year, by which time they were so traumatized they barely moved. Some of them refused to eat and starved themselves to death.'

'That's absolutely shocking,' Megan gasped, appalled.

'It gets worse,' Austin said. 'To see what would happen if these traumatized monkeys gave birth and became mothers themselves, Harlow and a student created what they called a 'rape rack" where the monkeys were restrained and impregnated. They logged and photographed what happened as these mentally ill mothers abused and often killed their babies.'

'Unbelievable,' Roshan muttered. Megan thought she was going to be sick.

'It certainly is,' Austin said. 'But what interests me is how Harlow was able to persuade a student to be involved – that it was acceptable. The student continued the experiments long after Harlow had stopped. I find it fascinating that people can act against their morals and be able to justify it.' Austin glanced at Megan and she looked away.

Surely he didn't mean her, she thought, horrified. Had Roshan told him what had happened while she'd been upstairs? She looked at Roshan and their eyes met. She immediately looked away, but not quickly enough. She heard Sarah's chair scrape back a second before she was at her side and slapped her hard on the head.

'Find your own fucking husband!' she said, and stormed out of the room.

Megan would have liked to have fled too but to do so would have compounded her guilt. Roshan and Brandon were staring at her. Her cheeks burned from embarrassment and shame. Only Austin seemed unfazed.

'I'm assuming something has taken place that I don't know about,' he said dispassionately.

Megan gave a small nod.

'So tell me and perhaps I can help.'

Focusing solely on Austin, Megan began telling what had happened: that she'd seen the spider, cried out for help, and Roshan had come to her rescue. Then while comforting her they'd got a bit carried away but nothing had happened. Roshan remained quiet.

'I'm sorry I've let you down,' she finished. 'Your therapy seemed to be working, but I honestly believed there was a spider on my back. And all we did was kiss and cuddle, which I know was wrong.'

'It might have been "wrong" as you put it,' Austin said easily, 'given that Roshan is in a monogamous relationship, but it's understandable. We are only human, and you are an attractive woman, Megan, with natural desires. Don't beat yourself up about it. I am sure Roshan isn't.'

Roshan shook his head, confirming it wasn't a problem.

'And in respect of therapy and letting me down, you haven't,' Austin said. 'Everyone has setbacks in therapy. It's part of the journey.'

Relief flooded through her. 'But what about Sarah?' she asked.

'I think she needs to apologize for hitting you,' Austin said. 'That's not the way to address anger. It was out of character. I'm sure she's very remorseful now. Shall I have a talk with her?'

'Yes, please,' Megan said gratefully. 'If Roshan is happy with that. Tell her I'm sorry.'

Roshan nodded. 'Fine with me.'

Austin stood and left the room. Megan began clearing the dishes from the table as a distraction. Roshan and Brandon joined her. Working in silence, they loaded the dishwasher and cleared up the kitchen. As they finished, Austin and Sarah appeared.

'That was quick,' Roshan said. Sarah was smiling.

'Sorry I overreacted,' she said and, going to Megan, hugged her.

'I'm sorry for being such an idiot,' Megan replied. 'I value your and Roshan's friendship.'

'And we do yours,' Sarah said.

'All sorted then,' Austin said, satisfied.

'It would appear so,' Brandon said, with what could have been a touch of irony.

'Excellent. So, it's my turn to cook tonight,' Austin said. 'If I can trust you all not to get into trouble while I'm away, I'm going shopping. As it's the thirty-first of October, Halloween, I thought I'd make pumpkin pie.'

'Sounds good,' Megan said, relieved they were back to normal.

'And if you're up to it, once we've eaten we can play with the Ouija board just as we did as students.'

They fell silent and looked at him.

'You've never brought a Ouija board with you?' Sarah asked.

'Not just any board, but the one we used to play with. I found it packed away in my attic.'

'I don't think I will play,' Sarah said.

'Me neither,' Megan agreed.

'Count me in,' Roshan said. 'It will be fun.'

'And me,' Brandon said. 'If I can remember how to play.'

'Don't worry. I'll go through the rules before we begin,' Austin said. 'Strictly speaking, you're advised not to play in a cemetery, but as we will be inside I am sure it won't matter given that none of you believe in it anyway.'

TWENTY-EIGHT

DC Matt Davis and DC Beth Mayes sat at the table in the interview room at Coleshaw police station, opposite Chanel Woman and her solicitor, Mr Newby. He'd arrived half an hour earlier and asked for time alone with his client. Now she was ready to be interviewed. Beth still couldn't quite believe she was here, in police custody, the infamous Chanel Woman, although there was no sign of that person now.

DS Scrivener had asked Beth to lead the interview, feeling that Chanel Woman – or, rather, Leslie Chambers – might relate better to a female. However, they were all expecting a 'no comment' interview. Most solicitors advised their clients not to admit to anything at this stage.

Formalities over – Beth had stated their names, the time and date of the interview, and was about to ask her first question – when Mr Newby said, 'My client is willing to cooperate, but she has two requests.'

'Yes?' Beth asked, puzzled.

'She would like access to her skin camouflage products.'

Beth was trying to think what he meant when he clarified: 'The make-up she uses to cover the scar on her cheek. It's in her handbag.'

156

'Oh I see,' Beth said, and couldn't help but look at the scar. It was more visible now than when they'd first arrested her. Presumably because of all the crying and wiping her eyes.

'I'll speak to the duty sergeant after this interview,' Beth said. 'It will be with the other personal possessions your client arrived with.'

'She would like it now,' Mr Newby said. 'She feels very exposed and vulnerable without it.'

'I'll see what I can do,' Matt said, and stood.

'Also,' Mr Newby added. 'My client would like to know if her husband has been in touch yet.'

'I'll check,' Matt said, and left the room.

Beth paused the recording. Mr Newby checked his phone as Chanel Woman fiddled with the sleeve of her jersey, nervous and unsure. She was a poor replica of the woman who'd so audaciously committed those robberies with so much panache, Beth thought. It was almost impossible to reconcile this woman with that person, she seemed a shadow of her former self, and Beth wondered whether someone else could have been involved, someone who'd organized and controlled the operation – for surely Leslie hadn't.

Matt returned with a tube of make-up and passed it to Chanel Woman.

'Thank you,' she said in a small voice. 'And news from my husband?'

'No, nothing yet.'

She was clearly disappointed. Beth waited as she squeezed a little of the camouflage make-up onto her forefinger and rubbed it into her damaged cheek. She replaced the cap and put the tube on her lap. After the interview it would need to be returned to her other personal possessions until she was released, unless it was needed as evidence, when it would be kept.

Beth started the recording again and stated the time the interview was recommencing.

'Before the break your solicitor indicated you would be willing to cooperate and answer our questions,' Beth said. 'Did you commit all of these robberies?' She handed Leslie Chambers a printed sheet of paper showing the date, time and location of all the robberies they believed she had committed, stretching back two years. She gave another copy to Mr Newby.

Leslie looked down the list. 'Yes, all except that one,' she said, pointing. 'That was a copycat, I didn't do it.'

Beth nodded and made a note. They'd had doubts about that one.

'So you admit to all the others on the list?' Beth checked.

'Yes.'

'But there are mitigating circumstances,' Mr Newby said, looking pointedly at his client.

'Yes, I'll explain,' she said. 'It all started with the car accident I was involved in as a teenager where I nearly burnt to death.' Matt and Mr Newby began taking notes. 'I know I should have felt lucky to be alive, but once I'd recovered I couldn't see it that way. I was angry. I hated my face and the world. I felt ugly and started doing bad things to get my own back. I'm sure my previous convictions are on your police computer?'

'There's no need to go back over all of those,' Mr Newby told his client.

'Did you attend therapy after those convictions?' Beth asked. She'd read the court reports and the magistrates had recommended it.

'Yes, a little. Then later I met my husband and he helped me get out of that dark place. I began to feel attractive again, wanted, and that life was worth living. He saved me.'

'So why start stealing again, and on a much larger scale?

It was a big step up from your previous convictions for petty theft.'

Beth saw her uncertainty. Her gaze flickered around the room and she glanced at her solicitor.

'Why did you feel the need to create Chanel Woman?' Beth asked.

Leslie hesitated, then said, 'I really don't know now. I didn't mean to, it just seemed to happen. I think I wondered what it would feel like to have a new face, so I bought a mask. It gave me a new personality. Why I turned to crime, I honestly don't know. I feel like I was someone different then. I realize now it was wrong, but it's not as if I hurt anyone.'

'You committed armed robberies. You carried a gun!' Beth said incredulously. 'Those you terrorized didn't know it was a toy gun. It looked real enough.'

'I'm sorry, I didn't mean for them to be scared.'

'You have the replica gun?' Mr Newby asked as he wrote.

'The remains of it, and the other items your client tried to burn in the incinerator in her garden. They're with Forensics now.'

'I'm sorry,' Leslie said. 'Now it's all over I'm really struggling to remember what Chanel Woman was all about. She was another person, not me. I put on the mask and perfume and turned into her.'

'Where did you buy the perfume?' Beth asked.

'I didn't, my husband bought it for me. Could you check again to see if he's arrived?'

'When I got your make-up I asked the duty sergeant to let us know,' Matt said.

She looked sad and unsure.

'Did your husband know what you were using the perfume for?' Beth asked.

'I don't think so.'

159

'Did he know what you were doing? It must have been difficult to conceal it, living in the same house.'

'He's away a lot on business. Are you sure he hasn't phoned?'

'We'll be told if he does,' Matt said.

'What did you do with all the money you stole?' Beth asked.

'I don't know.'

Beth inwardly sighed and felt the cooperative nature of the interview had disappeared. 'How can you not know?' she asked. 'You stole millions of pounds. You must have done something with it.'

'I really can't remember,' Leslie replied.

'Your house is being thoroughly searched now and we'll check all your and your husband's bank accounts.'

She shook her head. 'Sorry, I can't remember.'

'Did you have an accomplice?' Beth asked.

'I think it was just me.'

'Think? Surely you must know.'

'My client has already answered your question,' Mr Newby said.

Beth changed the line of questioning. 'Where did you buy the masks?'

'A company that supplies theatrical costumes. I think they're made abroad. I don't know the details off-hand. But it's on my computer.'

'We're checking your computer and phone,' Beth said.

'Can I go now? I've told you everything,' Leslie asked naively, clearly unsettled.

'Not yet,' Beth said.

'In that case I would like to request a break,' Mr Newby said. 'My client is visibly upset and I need to speak to her alone.' Which he was entitled to do.

'Yes. Is fifteen minutes enough?' Beth asked.

Leslie nodded.

Beth paused the recording and she and Matt left the interview room. Recordings had to be stopped when a suspect was with their solicitor, but Beth would have loved to have been party to that conversation. Something wasn't right.

'Shall I tell you what I think?' Matt said as they made their way along the corridor towards the main office.

'Yes, please, do. There's something odd going on here.'

'I think she's going to plead diminished responsibility and say she can't be held accountable for her actions. The signs are there – the vagueness, claiming she can't remember and it was like another person took over. Her defence will be that due to her state of mind her judgement was impaired, so she couldn't form a rational judgement, thereby absolving her of responsibility.'

'You should be her barrister,' Beth said with a tight smile. 'But will that argument hold up, given that her crimes were so sophisticated she would need to have been thinking rationally to carry them out. She spent a long time planning and preparing for them. That isn't someone who isn't thinking logically. Unless someone else was behind it.'

'She's not trying to blame anyone else.'

'I know. She could be protecting them. I want to speak to her husband. At the very least, he must have had an idea something was going on. Perhaps he's our missing accomplice – we can but hope.'

TWENTY-NINE

Megan was alone in the living room, the television was on and she was vaguely watching the six o'clock news. It was the usual assortment of world events: heads of state and other dignitaries visiting, drought in one part of the world and floods in another, now attributed to climate change. It was raining outside but not heavily, more the drizzle of a damp autumn evening. Austin was in the kitchen preparing their Halloween dinner. She'd offered to help but he said he preferred to cook alone, and she should relax while she had the opportunity. She assumed Sarah and Roshan were still in their room and Brandon was in his. They'd decided to spend the rest of the afternoon 'doing their own thing', which had suited her. As well as giving her time and space to think, she'd taken the opportunity to catch up on her studying. She had a dissertation due in ten days' time.

The door from the kitchen-diner opened and Brandon came in. 'Can I join you?' he asked, almost sheepishly.

'Yes, of course.'

Unfolding her legs from under her, she made room for him on the sofa, and he sat a little way from her. His hair was damp, presumably from the shower. He looked well-scrubbed and his jeans were freshly pressed. She was reminded how attractive she found him.

'Sorry,' he said after a moment, turning to her.

'For what?' she asked, surprised, and lowered the volume on the television.

'For winding you up earlier, winking.'

'Nothing happened between Roshan and me, and I honestly thought there was a spider.'

'I know,' he said, and began to smile.

'You do?'

'I heard you cry out and was going to come to help, but Roshan got there first.' His smile deepened. 'I know nothing happened between you two. I just wish I'd have got there first.' His expression had become sensual and Megan didn't mind at all.

'Am I forgiven?' he asked.

'Yes, just don't do it again. I've got enough to deal with here, without you messing with my head.'

'What do you mean by that?' he asked, suddenly serious.

She silenced the television. 'I don't know,' she said with a sigh. 'But since I've been here, I've found myself acting really strangely at times. Not me at all. Austin says it's because I'm free of my usual responsibilities. But I don't think I like the person I've become. And to be honest, I'm not sure if that spider was real or not.'

'If it's any consolation, I've been having weird dreams here too, and some of them have been very real and quite terrifying.'

'Perhaps it's something in the water,' Megan half-joked. 'Like the Brontë sisters – you remember, from our English Literature classes? They were poisoned by the secretions from decomposing bodies in the cemetery seeping into the water supply.' She pulled a face.

'More like something seeping from Austin,' Brandon replied.

'What do you mean by that?'

'I think he's controlling and can be very manipulative at times.'

'He'd deny that vehemently,' Megan said. 'He claims his work is about guiding his patients to explore their problems and work through them and find their own solution. He says it has to come from them.'

'Maybe,' Brandon said dubiously. 'Anyway, enough of Austin. I'm glad I've found you alone. There's something I want to ask you.'

'Yes?'

'I was thinking that when we leave here it would be good if we kept in touch – maybe go out for a meal? I know we live some distance apart and you don't drive, but I drive. If you'd like to, that is.'

He looked so vulnerable and exposed; Megan was touched.

'Yes, I would like that,' she said.

'Good. It's a date!'

Then, not knowing what to say or do next, Megan looked at the television. The moving text at the foot of the news was showing *Breaking News: A woman is being questioned in connection with the Chanel Woman robberies.*

'Look at that!' Megan exclaimed, raising the volume.

'A woman was arrested earlier today in connection with what has become known as the Chanel Woman robberies,' said the presenter. 'She is being held at Coleshaw police station. Police have issued a short statement confirming that a woman is helping them with their enquiries.' And that was it.

'I wonder who she is?' Megan said as the news bulletin ended.

'Someone who's become very rich,' Brandon said. 'I wonder if they will recover any of the money she's stolen.'

As Megan silenced the television again, Roshan and Sarah's

voices could be heard in the kitchen, then a few moments later they came into the living room holding a glass of wine each.

'Looks like they've caught Chanel Woman,' Megan said.

'Yes, I saw it on the newsfeed on my phone,' Sarah said, phone in hand. 'Austin said to tell you dinner will be ready in half an hour.'

'Do you want a drink?' Brandon asked Megan.

'Yes, a juice, please. Doesn't matter which one.'

Brandon left the room to fetch their drinks and Roshan and Sarah settled into armchairs. Sarah began making small talk about the pumpkin pie and how Austin was making the pastry from scratch. Brandon returned with his and Megan's drinks, and conversation continued, light and easy. Megan thought their time apart had done them all some good. There was no uncomfortable atmosphere now.

'You know we're going to play with the Ouija board tonight,' Roshan said.

'I'm not,' Megan put in quickly.

'Me neither,' Sarah agreed.

'It'll be a laugh,' Brandon said.

'It was more than that when we used to play as students,' Megan reminded them. 'We scared ourselves silly and imagined all sorts of things.'

'It's different now. We've grown up,' Brandon said, sipping his drink. 'We can see it for what it was – hocus pocus. Even back then, Roshan and I used to make some of it up by moving the planchette and knocking on the table. Is there anyone there? Knock knock.' He was laughing, and Megan found herself laughing too.

'The girls don't have to join in, but how about doing that again?' Roshan suggested to Brandon, lowering his voice conspiratorially. 'We could pretend to see something.'

'I'm not sure that's wise,' Sarah said.

'It'll be fun to wind up Austin and see what he makes of it,' Brandon agreed.

'Perhaps we could see a green goblin with pointed ears,' Roshan suggested, falling about laughing. 'We'll have to agree on what we see to make it convincing.'

'How about a headless horseman cantering through the living room,' Brandon said. 'It could come through that wall there.' He pointed to the kitchen. 'Perhaps carrying a slice of Austin's pumpkin pie.' He was laughing so much he could barely talk.

'Coconut shells are good for making the sound of horses' hooves,' Roshan said. 'Pity we don't have any.'

As Brandon and Roshan continued to plot and laugh about possible manifestations, each suggestion more ludicrous than the last, Megan looked at Sarah. She wasn't joining in the fun and her expression was serious. Ghosts were real to her.

'You OK?' Megan asked.

'I guess so.'

THIRTY

Meanwhile at Coleshaw police station, DS Scrivener had gone to find Beth or Matt. They were both in the kitchen pouring themselves more coffee. It had been a long day and it wasn't over with yet.

'Leslie Chambers has asked to speak to you again,' DS Scrivener said.

'Her solicitor went over an hour ago, sir,' Beth said. 'Shall I see if he's free to come back?'

'No, she says there's no need for him to be there. It's her choice. But remind her of her rights before you begin.'

'Yes, sir,' Matt said. 'Did she say what she wants?'

'No. She asked again if her husband had been in touch, and when the officer told her he hadn't, she said she wanted to speak to you two.'

'Strange,' Beth said. 'After the break, she reverted to a no-comment interview.'

'Perhaps she's had time to reflect,' DS Scrivener said. 'Good luck.'

Quickly drinking their coffees, Beth and Matt went to the interview room where Leslie had been taken. She was sitting at the table, a beaker of untouched water in front of her.

'Any news from my husband?' she asked anxiously, rising slightly from her seat.

'No,' Matt said.

She sat down again, apparently defeated. Beth and Matt sat opposite. Beth went through the formalities, stating the date, time, those present, the place where the interview was taking place, and that it was being audio-visually recorded.

'You told the officer you spoke to you didn't want your solicitor present,' Beth said. 'Is that still your wish?'

'Yes. I just need to get this off my chest and tell you the truth.'

'So you weren't telling us the truth before?' Matt asked, assuming the role of 'bad cop' to balance Beth's 'good cop' approach – a tactic that sometimes produced results.

'Some of what I told you was true, but not all of it. I left bits out.' She stopped and Beth thought how nervous and out of her depth she looked.

'So what was true and what wasn't?' Matt asked when Leslie didn't continue.

'I committed the robberies but I didn't work alone.'

'So who was your accomplice?' Beth asked. It seemed she'd been right. It wasn't unusual for a suspect to suddenly start blaming someone else when they'd had time to think and realized how much trouble they were in.

'My husband, Austin Chambers. He knew all about the robberies and what the perfume and masks were for. He even helped me plan them.'

'So why not tell us this before?' Matt asked.

'Because I was scared and confused,' Chanel Woman said. 'He can be very controlling.'

'In what way?' Beth asked gently.

'Making me do things I don't want to.'

'You mean as in coercive control?'

'I'm not sure what that means.'

'It's when a person assaults, threatens or frightens their victim into doing what they want.'

'He didn't actually assault or threaten me,' Leslie replied. 'It was more like he got inside my head and controlled my mind. So I found myself doing things I wouldn't normally have done. He created Chanel Woman. She was a different person to me.'

That much at least was true, Beth thought. Chanel Woman was certainly a different person to the suspect that sat before them, but whether any of it could be attributed to or blamed on her husband was another matter. Clearly they needed to speak to him as soon as possible.

'Where is your husband now?' Matt asked.

'I'm not sure. He goes away when I'm due to commit a robbery and makes sure he's with others so he has an alibi. Usually I can contact him by phone, but not now. Either something terrible has happened to him or he has abandoned me.' Her face crumpled and she looked close to tears.

'Are you all right to continue?' Beth asked.

Leslie nodded.

'Given your husband must be aware you've been arrested, I think it's likely he has abandoned you,' Matt said bluntly.

Beth glanced at him.

'Yes, I know,' Leslie admitted lamely. 'I spoke to him yesterday before the robbery, but he hasn't answered his phone since or called. He always said if anything went wrong, he'd stand by me.'

'So when was the last time you saw him?' Beth asked.

'Saturday, before he left to meet with some friends. I suppose he could still be with them. I don't know.' She shrugged hopelessly.

'Do you have the address of where he's staying?' Beth asked.

'Yes. It's in one of the texts he sent me, but you have my phone. I was supposed to join them for part of the week.'

'I'll fetch your phone,' Matt said, getting to his feet and heading out of the interview room.

Leaving Beth wondering if any of this was true or if it was a ploy to deflect blame from herself to her husband.

THIRTY-ONE

Austin had turned off the lights in the living room and lit a candle which he'd placed on the coffee table beside the Ouija board. The flame allowed enough light to see the board while the rest of the room fell into the shadows that moved as the flame flickered. The atmosphere was perfect. He, Brandon and Roshan were grouped around the board. Megan and Sarah sat a little way from them, still refusing to join in but having agreed to be present. Now that Megan knew a lot of the weird stuff that happened when they'd played as students had not been from the spirit world, but instead had been Brandon and Roshan having a joke, she was a little more relaxed about the whole thing. Sarah, on the other hand, still had big misgivings, feeling that it was asking for trouble to play with a Ouija board, and something might happen that couldn't be explained.

In a low monotone voice, similar to the one he used with his patients, Austin began going through the rules for using the Ouija board, which spooked Sarah even more. He was taking it very seriously and kept referring to 'the spirit' as though it existed and might appear soon.

'Never taunt or make fun of a spirit trying to communicate

with us through the Ouija board,' he said. 'Be respectful and never ask when you are going to die.'

Sarah wondered why not, as it seemed an obvious question, but decided to let it go. Austin was talking and wouldn't appreciate being interrupted.

'There are good and bad spirits,' he went on sombrely. 'So be alert for any malevolent contact. If that happens, we end the session straightaway. One person in the group needs to be the leader, so I'll do that.'

Brandon glanced at Roshan but neither of them commented.

'A reminder,' Austin continued, completely engrossed in what he was saying. 'You need to keep your fingers on the planchette – the pointer – at all times, to build up the energy. Don't decipher the words until the planchette has finished moving. Just focus all your energy on the planchette. Megan, can you keep a note of the letters on your phone and then we'll work out what it means at the end.'

Sarah saw Megan smile to herself as she picked up her phone, for it would be Brandon and Roshan who formed the words, not a spirit.

'We end each session by saying goodbye to the spirit, and I will take the planchette off the board. If a spirit starts going through the alphabet or counting down, then we end the session immediately. It's a sign an evil spirit is present. Also, if the spirit makes a figure eight we immediately end the session as it's another sign of an evil spirit.'

'There's a lot of evil spirits about,' Brandon quipped.

'There can be,' Austin said seriously, unaware that Brandon was poking fun. 'If you suspect an evil spirit is trying to contact you, tell me and we end the session. Any questions?'

'It seems more sophisticated than when we used to play as students,' Megan said.

'That's because we're playing it properly now,' Austin

replied. 'Abiding by the rules. Not doing so back then was probably the reason we had some bad experiences.'

Sarah saw Brandon and Roshan exchange another glance, although Austin remained oblivious to any mischief-making.

'OK, let's begin,' he said.

Strangely, uncannily, just at that moment – as they placed their fingers on the planchette – the flame of the candle went out, plunging the room into darkness. Megan gasped and Sarah cried out in alarm.

'Don't panic,' Austin said, his voice slightly more intense. 'Stay where you are. Don't move.'

They could hear him opening the box of matches and then the match strike. He relit the candle and they were all visible again.

'It must have been a draught,' Austin said, although even he seemed to be a bit unsettled.

'Or a spirit is already making contact,' Brandon added.

And while Sarah knew Brandon was joking, she felt the temperature in the room drop. She curled her legs under her and tried to shake off the feeling that there was someone else in the room, other than them.

'Let's try again,' Austin said. 'Fingers lightly on the planchette.'

Roshan and Brandon each placed a finger on the planchette joining Austin's that was already there, and concentrated on the board. The light from the candle shimmered and gave their faces a slightly orange glow. For some time all that could be heard was the wind outside. Sarah thought it must have increased during the evening and was now finding its way in, under the doors and up through the floor. She could feel the chill rising and shivered.

They sat still and silent for what seemed like ages. Roshan cleared his throat, which made Sarah start, but the planchette didn't move. Austin had his eyes closed and a look of deep concentration on his face. Roshan and Brandon were gazing down, looking at the board, as though they too were concentrating hard. So the minutes passed and the silence continued, save for the wind outside. Megan stifled a yawn and Brandon flexed his shoulder; suggesting it was aching from holding his arm out in front of him for so long.

Sarah was hoping they'd give up and put the board away, because this wasn't a good idea. But then there was a small, almost imperceptible movement, which she might have missed, had it not been for the sound of the wooden planchette shifting its position slightly on the board. Sarah held her breath and looked at Brandon and Roshan, but they were still concentrating on the board, their expressions giving nothing away. She assumed one of them had nudged the planchette as they'd planned. All was still again and the minutes passed.

Megan stole a look at her phone and Sarah wondered, hoped, if perhaps that small movement was all that would happen and they could end the game soon. But suddenly, without warning, the planchette shot across the board, almost flying it went so fast. There were gasps, not just from her, but the others, and they were all looking at the board. The planchette had stopped and was pointing unmistakably to the letter L.

Had Brandon and Roshan done that? They weren't giving anything away. Austin had opened his eyes. 'L,' he said quietly to Megan, who made a note on her phone.

Their fingers were still on the planchette and as they watched it shot off again, this time to the letter E. 'E,' Austin announced, and Megan entered it on her phone.

Sarah folded herself further into her chair and looked again at Brandon and Roshan, hoping for a sign that they were making this happen, but there was nothing. All three of them were looking serious and concentrating on the board.

A few seconds passed, the wind outside howled, and the planchette was moving again, this time more steadily, to the letter A, which Austin repeated to Megan. Then it was off again, across the board, straight to the letter V. It immediately shot back to E before returning to the centre.

Sarah's heart was in her mouth as they waited, but the minutes passed and it didn't move again.

'The spirit must have gone, so we say goodbye,' Austin said quietly.

All three of them removed their fingers from the board and sat back. Roshan stretched.

'Well, Megan?' Austin asked. 'What was the word or words?'

The colour drained from her face.

'It spelt out leave,' she said, which Sarah had already worked out.

But at that moment the candle went out again, and the planchette was heard travelling across the board and then clattering to the floor.

Sarah screamed.

'Put the light on!' Megan shouted.

'I will, stay where you are,' Austin called.

Movement could be heard in the dark as Austin made his way gingerly to the light switch. He flicked it on and the room was bathed in light again. The planchette lay on the floor some distance from the board.

'What happened?' Brandon asked, straight-faced.

'No idea,' Roshan replied, equally serious.

Sarah looked from one to the other of them for any hint that might give them away, but there was nothing. They seemed as concerned and unsettled as she was.

'What the fuck!' Megan suddenly cried. Jumping up from her chair, she threw her phone away as if it was red hot.

'What is it? You're scaring me,' Sarah said.

Megan was visibly trembling and Brandon went to her. 'What's the matter?' he asked, taking her gently by the shoulders.

'Look at my phone,' she stammered, pointing to where it lay, barely able to get the words out.

Roshan picked up Megan's phone and read out the words she'd written: 'Leave now.'

'I didn't write "now",' Megan said, petrified. 'Just "leave" as you spelt it out.'

'It wants us to go,' Sarah said, terror-stricken.

'Calm down,' Austin said, and took the phone from Roshan. He studied the screen for a moment then looked at them. 'Yes, it says "leave now". Megan, if you don't remember writing "now" you must have done it subconsciously.'

'I didn't!' Megan shrieked hysterically. 'It appeared after the lights went out. I didn't touch my phone. There's someone in this room with us. Someone we can't see.'

'Roshan!' Sarah shouted. 'This has gone far enough. Did you put that on Megan's phone?'

'No, absolutely not. Nothing to do with me.'

Sarah glared at Brandon.

'Not me.'

'What about moving the planchette and the candle going out?' she asked, desperately searching for a rational explanation. 'Did you do that?'

'No,' Brandon said, while Roshan shook his head in complete denial.

Did she believe them? Yes. The temperature in the room had dropped further and the wind whistled at the windows as if trying to get in.

'We should leave while we can,' Sarah said, and stood.

A noise came from outside. They all looked towards the door that led from the living room to the lobby from where the sound had come. Sarah saw the looks on Brandon's and

Roshan's faces and knew they weren't responsible for this. Fear gripped her. Megan was right; there was a spirit in the room and it wanted them to leave now.

'I knew you shouldn't have played,' Sarah said, beside herself with fear.

'We should leave like it says,' Megan said. 'Out the back door.'

Another noise sounded out the front. 'No, there's someone knocking at the front door,' Roshan said.

They listened and it came again, then the doorbell rang.

'It could be trick-or-treaters calling on us for Halloween,' Austin said, recovering first.

'Right out here?' Megan asked.

'They may have come from the village.'

Another ring on the bell, more insistent this time.

'I'll go and see,' Brandon said.

'I'll come with you,' Roshan offered, following Brandon across the living room.

Megan and Sarah watched, hardly daring to breathe, as the wind howled outside and Brandon and Roshan disappeared into the lobby. The door swung shut behind them but didn't fully close. Another loud knock sounded on the front door before it was opened. Then voices, not children's but adults', and not trick or treaters, but the police.

'I'm DC Beth Mayes and this is my colleague DC Matt Davis,' they heard them say. 'Is Mr Austin Chambers here?'

'Yes,' Brandon replied.

'Can we come in? We need to speak to him.'

'It's the police,' Megan whispered. 'What have we done now?'

'Leave it to me,' Austin said.

THIRTY-TWO

Austin was good at taking control of difficult situations, but it was almost as if he'd been expecting their visit, Megan thought. Two police officers walked into the living room and Austin stepped forward, unfazed, to greet them.

'Good evening. I'm Austin Chambers. How can I help you?'

'Good evening, sir,' the female officer said. 'DC Beth Mayes and DC Matt Davis.' They showed their ID cards.

Megan's hands were shaking and her fists were knuckle-white with fear. She was convinced they were really here because of her – that she'd stolen something else but couldn't remember what.

'We need to speak to you, sir,' Beth Mayes said to Austin. But then she looked at each of them in turn. Megan shrank back. 'Who are all these people?'

'My friends,' Austin replied.

'We'll take their names and addresses. Is there anyone else here?'

'No, but why do you want our names and addresses?' Brandon asked. Megan moved closer to him.

'To eliminate you from our enquiries,' Matt Davis replied.

'My friends and I go back to our school days,' Austin said. 'We're here for a reunion, our first in ten years. I know they won't mind giving you their names and addresses. But what is all this about?'

'Let's establish who is here and then we can explain,' Beth said.

Matt took out a notepad and, beginning with Brandon, wrote down his name and address. Megan's voice caught in her throat as she spoke. Austin was the last to give his details.

'So none of you actually lives here?' Beth asked.

'That's correct,' Austin replied. 'We rented the place for the week for our reunion.'

'I see. Is everything all right?' Beth asked, looking directly at Megan.

'Yes, why shouldn't it be?' Roshan replied.

'When we first came in you looked unsettled, even frightened.'

'Probably by the police suddenly arriving,' Roshan said curtly.

Megan saw Beth's gaze go to the Ouija board lying open on the coffee table.

'We've been playing as it's Halloween,' she explained in a nervous rush. 'But we got ourselves in a bit of a state and thought there was a ghost in the room. That's why we looked scared. Silly really.' It was a reality check, having the main light on and two down-to-earth police officers in the room. Megan could see that very likely it had only been a game, and Austin could have been right when he'd said she'd added the word 'now'. But why were the police here?

Beth's gaze left Megan and returned to Austin. 'We need to ask you some questions. Would you like to go somewhere more private?'

'No, thank you,' he said. 'These are my friends. We've been

179

together all week. If there's a problem I'm sure they'll want to know so we can all support whoever is involved.'

Megan trembled and felt Brandon touch her arm reassuringly, but Beth was still looking at Austin, not her.

'Your wife is Leslie Chambers?' Beth asked.

'Yes, why?' Austin asked, immediately concerned. 'Has something happened to her? Don't tell me she's been taken to hospital.'

'No, nothing like that. Your wife is safe and well. She's at Coleshaw police station. Are you sure you wouldn't prefer to go somewhere more private?'

'Perfectly. I've got nothing to hide. Why is my wife at the police station?' he asked no less anxiously.

'She's being questioned in connection with a number of robberies in the area.'

'What?' Austin exclaimed. 'There must be some mistake. Leslie would never do anything like that. She wouldn't know how to, for one thing.'

'I'm afraid there's no mistake,' Matt said sombrely. 'She has admitted to the offences, but is claiming that you knew about them and were involved in their planning.'

'Ridiculous!' Austin said, finally losing some of his cool. 'She must be delusional again. You know I was her therapist?'

Megan felt Brandon touch her arm.

'I think it would be helpful if you came with us to Coleshaw police station to answer some questions,' Beth said. 'Voluntarily, of course.'

'If it helps my wife, yes. When?'

'Now please.'

'It's rather late,' Austin said.

'No one knows that better than us, sir,' Beth replied. 'We've been on a twelve-hour shift. But it's important we speak to you this evening. I'm afraid it can't wait.'

Austin sighed. 'All right, I'll follow in my car.'

'No need, sir, we'll take you in ours.'

Ruffled, and without his usual reserve, Austin turned to them. 'I'll be back later. Don't lock up.'

He tucked his phone into his trouser pocket and set off across the living room. He stopped where the planchette lay on the floor and picked it up. Closing the Ouija board, he placed it on top.

'Better you don't play while I'm not here,' he said to them, then followed the officers out of the room.

Megan tried to calm her racing heart. So it wasn't her they'd come for. She looked at the others, who appeared as confused and incredulous as she felt. No one spoke. They heard the outer door close, and then a few moments later a car started up and pulled away.

'The wind must have dropped,' Megan said. 'We didn't hear their car approaching as it was masked by the wind.'

'What just happened?' Sarah asked, bewildered.

'I'm not sure,' Roshan said.

'I think I need a drink,' Brandon said.

'Yes, me too,' Megan agreed. 'But let's go into the kitchen. It's cold in here.' Then she saw it and her hand shot to her mouth. 'The candle!' she cried, and pointed.

They all turned and stared in disbelief, unable to take in what they were seeing. The candle on the coffee table beside the Ouija board that had been extinguished earlier by a draught was now alight again, its orange shadow falling onto the board.

'But that's impossible,' Brandon said. 'Austin must have relit it. He was the one with the matches.'

'But when?' Sarah asked.

'On his way out?' Brandon suggested.

'We'd have seen him, surely, heard the match strike,' Roshan said.

'Not necessarily. We were preoccupied and concentrating

on other things – the police officers taking Austin away. He must have lit the candle at the same time he closed the board,' Brandon said.

'Why would he do that?' Roshan asked.

'I don't know, but it's the only explanation,' Brandon said.

Which they accepted as the safest, easiest and most rational option.

'Yes, Austin must have lit it,' Megan agreed.

THIRTY-THREE

'So you aren't arresting me?' Austin clarified from where he was sitting in the back of the police car.

'No, sir,' Beth said, turning her head towards him. 'You've agreed to come into the station voluntarily to help us with our enquiries.'

'Do you think you should be arrested?' Matt asked from the driver's seat.

Smart arse, Austin thought, cocky bugger. 'Of course not. Do I need a solicitor?'

'That's your decision, sir,' Beth replied. 'You have the right to independent legal advice if you wish. It's really up to you.'

'I will be able to leave the police station at any point?' Austin checked.

'Yes, sir,' Beth said.

'Unless you're arrested,' Matt put in.

Austin ignored it. 'But my wife is under arrest?'

'Yes, sir,' Beth confirmed. 'I understand she phoned and left a message on your voicemail.'

Austin saw Matt glance at him in the rear-view mirror, looking for his response.

'She phoned me a number of times over the last week. She always does when I'm away. She said she'd been arrested, but I thought she was delusional again, which I still do. Apart from her confessing to being Chanel Woman, what evidence do you have against her?'

He saw the look they exchanged, and it was a while before either of them replied.

'I'm afraid we can't discuss that now,' Beth said, looking straight ahead.

'What makes you think she has confessed to being Chanel Woman?' Matt asked, glancing at him again in the rear-view mirror.

'I assumed it,' he said. 'There can't be many women running around the Coleshaw area committing robberies.'

Beth nodded while Matt concentrated on driving.

'What evidence do you have against my wife?' Austin asked.

'I'm afraid we're not at liberty to discuss that with you, sir,' Beth replied.

'But she's had legal advice?'

'Yes, sir.'

'In that case I would like a solicitor.'

'Certainly. You can call the duty solicitor from the police station.'

'No, thank you,' Austin said tightly. 'I'll use my own.' He took out his phone and called his solicitor and long-time friend, James Branbury.

'James, it's Austin Chambers. Sorry I'm phoning so late but I'm in a spot of bother and need your advice.'

'Sure. What's the problem?'

'I'm in a police car with two officers who are taking me to Coleshaw police station.'

'Have you been arrested?'

'No, I've agreed to go, voluntarily, to be interviewed.

184

There's been a misunderstanding. They seem to think Leslie has been committing a string of robberies.'

'That's ridiculous!'

'I know, but she's confessed and also implicated me. She must be having one of her episodes.'

'Has she been seen by a doctor – a psychiatrist?' James asked.

'Just a minute, I'll find out.' Taking the phone from his ear, Austin said, 'Has my wife been seen by a psychiatrist?'

'Not as far as I know,' Beth said. 'When she was checked in at the police station she would have been asked if she had any medical conditions or needed to see a healthcare professional.'

'Did you hear that?' Austin asked James, returning the phone to his ear.

'Yes, but if she is having a psychotic episode she won't necessarily recognize she's ill and needs help. Her solicitor should have covered it. Who did she use? I don't think my office got a call from her.'

'Which solicitor did my wife use?' Austin asked.

'The duty solicitor who was on call at the time,' Beth replied.

Austin repeated what she'd said.

'Pity. They're generally overworked and don't have the time they need for each case. I can't represent both of you, so shall I attend the police station as your legal representative or hers?'

'Mine.'

'Very well. I'll get to the police station as soon as possible, but it's likely to be at least an hour. The firm usually sends the junior out at night but obviously I'll attend in person as you're an old friend.'

'Thank you, James, much appreciated.'

'Don't answer any questions until I'm with you. Have they charged Leslie?'

185

'Not yet.'

'Then get her seen by a psychiatrist before it goes any further. There will be one on call at the police station.'

'Thank you, James.'

They said goodbye.

'My wife needs to be seen by a psychiatrist,' Austin said as he returned his phone to his pocket.

'We can offer it again,' Beth said. 'But we can't insist. If she's charged, then the court might ask for a psychological assessment.'

'Well charge her then!' Austin snapped, finally losing his patience. 'Before this ridiculous charade goes any further. If this gets out it will ruin my reputation and career, and I'll sue the lot of you.'

THIRTY-FOUR

Brandon and Megan were sitting at one side of the table in the kitchen-diner, Roshan and Sarah at the other. All the lights in the converted church were on, and they'd turned up the thermostat. Even so it still seemed cold. The wind had got up again and was whistling at the windows. Every so often the back door rattled as a particularly strong gust hit it, as if someone was trying to get in. They'd opened a second bottle of wine and were trying to make sense of the police taking Austin away and his wife being accused of a string of robberies. This discussion had overridden further talk about the strange happenings with the Ouija board, the candle, and Megan's phone, for now at least. It seemed likely that Austin had relit the candle, although for what reason they couldn't say, and that Megan had added the word 'now' without realizing it.

'I'm going to say what we all must be thinking,' Brandon said, topping up his wine glass. 'It's too much of a coincidence that Leslie is being held at Coleshaw police station, the same as Chanel Woman, both accused of committing robberies in the area. Leslie and Chanel Woman must be the same person.'

'But we don't know what Leslie is accused of,' Sarah said.

'Robberies could mean anything from robbing a bank to a petty theft – shoplifting.'

'A big coincidence though,' Roshan agreed.

'It is, but I don't think we should jump to conclusions,' Sarah said. 'We spoke to Leslie on the phone on Tuesday.'

'Yes, Tuesday morning,' Brandon replied. 'The last robbery Chanel Woman committed was Tuesday afternoon. I know it sounds incredible, but think about it: none of us have ever seen Leslie. There are no photos of her online. She's not on any social media and Austin didn't include her in the WhatsApp group he set up. She was supposed to be coming here for the week but then fell ill at the last minute. Of course he couldn't allow us to see her. If Leslie Chambers and Chanel Woman are the same person then she'll have a scar on her cheek, just as the witness described.'

'But why would Austin be involved?' Sarah asked.

Brandon shrugged. 'Personal gain? Austin clearly has a very good lifestyle. Greed, power, control. Or maybe he's not directly involved but knew about the robberies, and has been protecting Leslie. That would make him an accomplice.'

'Or possibly it's a coincidence,' Megan said quietly. 'And Leslie isn't Chanel Woman. Do you think we should call the police and tell them we all spoke to Leslie on Tuesday? And that Austin has been with us the whole week.'

'If we're asked to,' Roshan said. 'The police have taken our contact details. Although we can't vouch for Austin the whole time. He hasn't been with us twenty-four seven. He went for walks by himself and spent time alone in his room giving his clients online therapy sessions – or so he told us.'

'But he wasn't gone long enough to play a part in committing the robbery on Tuesday,' Megan said. 'And I don't remember any witness in the past ever mentioning an accomplice to any of the robberies Chanel Woman committed.'

'We don't know exactly what part Austin played, if any,'

Roshan said. 'The police officer said Leslie was claiming he knew about them and was involved in their planning. Austin said Leslie was delusional, so maybe she's made it all up. Did we know he was her therapist?'

'I think he mentioned that was how they met,' Megan said.

'Is that allowed?' Sarah asked. 'Dating a patient doesn't seem very ethical.'

'Perhaps it was after the therapy ended,' Megan suggested. 'I think that's allowed.'

Sarah and Megan checked their phones again for any update on the Chanel Woman story, but there was nothing more after the statement the police had issued earlier that evening.

'Austin will be at Coleshaw police station by now,' Megan said. 'Do you think we should text him and make sure he's OK?'

'He can look after himself,' Brandon replied.

The wind rattled the back door, and Roshan got up and slid the bolt. 'We'll leave the front door unlocked for Austin,' he said. 'He seemed to think he'd be back tonight, so I'm guessing whatever has happened will be cleared up quickly.'

'It's probably just a misunderstanding,' Megan said. 'At least he'll have another good after-dinner story to tell us.'

Sarah smiled. 'Yes, I can imagine. Anyway, I'm going to bed now. It's late and I'm shattered. See you tomorrow.'

Roshan stood too. They put their wine glasses in the dishwasher, said goodnight and went up the spiral staircase. Their footsteps stopped as they crossed the carpeted landing and went into their bedroom.

'I should go up too,' Megan said, finishing the last of her wine.

'Are you OK?' Brandon asked, concerned. 'You still seem very anxious.'

'I'm slowly recovering,' she admitted. 'It was a shock when the police arrived. I was convinced they'd come for me, and that I'd done something else I couldn't remember. I seem to be doing that a lot recently. Sometimes I think I'm losing the plot here. I'm not like this at home, or rather I wasn't.'

'You're not losing the plot,' Brandon said gently, reaching out and placing his hand tenderly over hers. 'We can all be forgetful. You wouldn't believe the number of times I make myself a tea or coffee and then forget to drink it.'

Megan smiled. 'That's kind of you, but I seem to have taken forgetfulness to a whole new level. I mean how could I have typed "now" into my phone and not realized it?'

'Predictive text?' Brandon suggested. 'You just didn't notice. The room was dark and you were watching the planchette like the rest of us.'

'Except my phone isn't set on predictive text,' Megan said. 'And what about the wine I stole and the spider in my room? Did I really see it? I've been thinking a lot about that, and I honestly don't know any more, but I'm scared in case it reappears.'

'Would you like me to check your room?' Brandon asked.

'Yes, please.' Megan hesitated, not wanting to appear any more neurotic. 'Can I ask you something?'

'Sure, go ahead.'

'Did you and Roshan move that planchette tonight? I assumed you did, but you both seemed startled when it moved. Or was that part of the act?'

'It wasn't me,' Brandon said. 'I felt it moving and went with it, so I guess it was Roshan.'

'And he threw it on the floor too?'

'Must have been him or Austin.'

'If it was Austin that would explain a lot,' Megan said, a little relieved.

Her phone vibrated with a text message; Brandon checked his phone too.

'Talk about the devil!' he said.

'Yes, I'm reading his message now.'

It was from Austin to their WhatsApp group: *Interview postponed until tomorrow so I won't be back tonight.* With an emoji of an angry face.

'He'll be right pissed off with that,' Brandon said. 'He's a stickler for order and punctuality. I overheard him telling a client she was half an hour late and not to waste his time. Given that she was paying for the session anyway, I didn't see why he was so bothered.'

'I wonder where he's spending the night?' Megan said.

'Probably at home. He doesn't live far from Coleshaw,' Brandon said, and stood. 'I'll lock the front door as he's not coming back, and then check your room.'

'Thank you.' Megan smiled. 'I do appreciate it.'

'You're welcome.'

Brandon left the kitchen and went through the living room to the lobby to lock the outer door. Megan remained at the table waiting for his return. The wind kicked at the back door, making it rattle, even though it was bolted. She didn't like being by herself here any more, especially after what had happened tonight. It was thoughtful of Brandon to offer to check her room for spiders. He was such a nice guy. If he wanted to stay the night then she would agree, and be happy if he did. Not just because she didn't want to be alone; she liked him a lot and he'd already said he wanted to see her after they left here. She thought that if one good thing had come out of this gathering it was seeing Brandon again, and hopefully going on to have a relationship with him. She'd like that.

THIRTY-FIVE

Sarah was also pleased she didn't have to spend the night alone, and that she had Roshan beside her. Although they'd rationalized – most of – the strange happenings that night, now it was all playing on her mind again. Roshan was on his side, facing away from her, ready for sleep. But she needed to talk and work through what had happened. Not just about the Ouija board, but Austin and Leslie too. She lay on her back staring into space. With no moon the room was very dark. The only sound came from the occasional gust of wind against the leaded light window, and Roshan's slow rhythmic breathing.

'Are you still awake?' she whispered.

'Yes,' he replied, his voice heavy and close to sleep.

'You don't really think Austin and Leslie could be responsible for all those robberies, do you?' she asked. 'The more I think about it, the less likely it seems.'

'I don't know, love, but anything is possible when it comes to Austin.'

'What do you mean by that? You used to be friends.'

'He's not the person I knew at school.'

'None of us is,' Sarah replied, thinking back. 'We've all changed over the years.'

It was a moment before Roshan said, 'That's not what I meant.'

'No? What did you mean then?' She was wide awake now and propped herself on one elbow so she could better see Roshan's face, placing a hand on his back. 'What?'

'The idea of us getting together was to catch up and share what we've been doing,' Roshan said. 'We've been doing that, so have Brandon and Megan. But Austin, the one who organized it all, has given virtually nothing away. All we get is psychology theory and, as Megan put it, after-dinner stories. He spends a lot of time observing us, which can feel very uncomfortable.'

'I suppose you're right,' Sarah said, but she wondered why Roshan had quoted Megan. She reached out to the bedside cabinet for her phone and checked messages and newsfeeds. 'There's nothing more from Austin or on the news,' she said.

'OK, so go to sleep now, Sarah. It must be nearly 2 a.m.'

She returned her phone to the cabinet and lay on her back, trying to keep her eyes closed and will herself to sleep. But her mind was buzzing.

'I wonder where Austin is now?' she said, eyes open again and staring at the ceiling.

'I really don't know or care.'

'But we should care if we're his friends.'

'To be honest, Sarah, I'm sick of hearing about Austin,' Roshan said, turning onto his back. 'Can we just leave it for now? It's impossible to think rationally at this hour.'

'But I feel sorry for him,' Sarah persisted. 'I think we could be his only friends.'

'If so, he has only himself to blame.'

'What makes you say that?' She looked at him.

'He's arrogant and full of himself.'

'That seems a bit harsh.'

193

'Well, you asked me and that's how I feel. There's no way I'll be meeting up again every year like he suggested.'

'You might feel differently by then.'

'I doubt it.'

Roshan turned onto his side again, facing away from Sarah. She stared into the dark as her thoughts tumbled and somersaulted, mainly around their stay here. It was impossible to go to sleep feeling so unsettled. 'Roshan?'

'What?'

'You know when we played with the Ouija board tonight?'

'Yes.'

'It *was* you and Brandon who made the planchette move, wasn't it? You can tell me the truth now there's just us.'

'If I do, will you go to sleep?'

'Yes.'

'It wasn't me. I assume it was Brandon. I felt it begin to move and I followed it with my finger.'

'Does Megan know?'

'How the hell would I know!' Roshan snapped, losing patience.

'Well, you two are close.'

'Sarah!' Roshan cried, annoyed, sitting upright in bed. 'I'm not close to Megan, not in the way you're suggesting. I explained what happened when she called out having seen a spider, so please don't keep throwing that in my face. I've had more than enough of all of this. In fact, I'll sleep downstairs on the sofa.' He threw back the duvet, ready to get out of bed.

'No, don't do that,' Sarah cried, and grabbed his arm. 'Please don't go into the living room while it's dark.'

'Why ever not?' He stared at her with a mixture of anger and exasperation.

'It's not safe.'

'What are you talking about, it's not safe? Don't be ridiculous.'

'I'm sorry, but I think we released something bad in there tonight when we played with the Ouija board, an evil spirit, just like we did when we played as students. I think it could still be down there. I don't want you to get hurt. I couldn't bear to lose you.'

Roshan sighed and lay back down. 'I think you're being daft, but I'll stay as long as there's no more talk of Austin or Megan.'

'I promise. Can you put your arm around me please? It would help get me to sleep. I really don't like this place. It's got a bad feeling about it that seems to be getting worse.'

'We can leave early if you like. I'm not fussed about staying until Saturday. We could drive back tomorrow and then we'll have all of Friday and the weekend before school starts again on Monday. I've got some marking to do.'

'So have I. Thank you. Yes, please, let's go tomorrow.'

One more night and then home to the safety and normality of their flat, she thought. Where the occasional bad dream she had was no more than that and didn't intrude into the day. Where she wasn't continually looking over her shoulder, feeling she was being watched – haunted – and she knew what was real and what was imagination. Here the lines had become so blurred it was impossible to tell. They really shouldn't have played with the Ouija board, but it would have appeared churlish to insist they didn't. It was supposed to have been a bit of fun – a trick played by Brandon and Roshan on Austin. Perhaps Brandon had been responsible for moving the planchette, or it could have been Austin, although Sarah doubted that. Austin had never played a practical joke in his life, he was far too cerebral, and she'd seen the look on his face as the planchette had spelt out LEAVE.

'Yes, let's go tomorrow,' she said quietly, snuggling into Roshan's arms.

And a voice that sounded as though it came from inside the room added, 'Now.'

THIRTY-SIX

Brandon gradually surfaced from a very deep sleep. His left arm was uncomfortably numb, and it took him a moment to realize he'd fallen asleep with Megan in his arms. She was still lying on his left arm, cutting off the blood supply. Careful not to disturb her, he slowly slid it from under her. The blood rushed back, making it tingle. Megan stirred but didn't wake. He looked at her. What a beautiful woman she was. He felt the same joy at having her beside him as he'd felt last night. The warmth of her body, the gentle fragrance from her perfume, and her soft hair falling onto his shoulder.

He'd no idea what time it was, and he wasn't going to risk waking her by trying to find his watch or phone which were buried in the pile of his clothes on the floor by the bed. The time didn't matter. He was on holiday with Megan, and work and all that entailed lay a world away. He felt very lucky and contented, and a warm frisson of satisfaction ran through him as he thought back to last night. They had two whole days left when he felt sure they would spend every minute together, then after they left they'd date and see each other as often as possible.

It was a long time since he'd been this close to a woman, Brandon acknowledged, and it could have been awkward – the first time. But it hadn't, not at all. No embarrassment or nervous fumbling. It had been the natural next step, as if it was meant to be. Megan had said so too. He'd checked her room for spiders and then they'd sat on the bed and talked, about everything that mattered; including their likes and dislikes and hopes for the future. They had a lot in common, more than he'd realized. When they talked as a group she tended to blend in and not push herself forward, but one to one he could see the real Megan, and he liked her even more. She'd brought up the subject of Roshan again, although he'd said there was no need. But she'd wanted to explain exactly what had happened. How, in the moment, having had a dreadful fright believing a spider was on her, she'd let him get too close. She'd needed the comfort and reassurance Roshan had offered and had clung to him – a lifeline – but then she'd realized and stopped.

'I'd never do that with someone else's husband,' she said.

'I know,' he'd said, and held her close.

They'd kissed, lightly at first, then with mounting passion. They'd quickly removed their clothes, slid beneath the duvet and made love, before falling asleep in each other's arms.

Yes, life was good, Brandon thought. He lay awake thinking how good it was going to be dating Megan. They'd already talked about him coming to stay with her at the weekends, and she'd said her mother would babysit Ella sometimes so she could stay with him.

He lay in the dark with no sound but his thoughts. The wind had dropped and the house was silent, the like of which you only found in the country. You didn't get this depth of silence or darkness in the town. There was always a light on somewhere or a distant noise, a dog barking, a car or motor-bike engine. Here there was nothing. All right for a short stay, Brandon thought, but he liked town living and Megan did too. Something else they had in common.

Yes, so very quiet, except . . .

What was that?

Brandon was jolted from his thoughts and listened hard. He wasn't prone to fantasy, but he thought he'd heard something in the room. A noise he recognized and was afraid of. The sound of something that threatened his well-being and could even kill him. Senses on full alert, he listened. Megan slept on beside him, her lips slightly parted and her breathing shallow.

The noise again. No, not his imagination. How the hell had it got in? Not a spider, but the unmistakable sound of a wasp in flight. Its two sets of wings pulsating at over two hundred beats per second, which allowed it to keep up with a human running. The sound so slight it could be missed during the day or by another person not as vigilant as him. Brandon's heart was racing and he broke out in a cold sweat. Of all the nights! But he'd have to track it down and kill it. He didn't have a choice. He was badly allergic to wasp stings. If he waited until morning and it stung him in the night, Megan would wake up to find him struggling to breathe, his face swollen beyond recognition, or even dead. He needed to be very careful as he tracked it down and killed it.

His arm had fully recovered now and Brandon eased back the duvet and sat naked on the edge of the bed, listening, trying to work out where it was. It must have landed as the noise had stopped. He peered into the dark room and waited for the sound again. Nothing. It could be anywhere, watching and waiting, ready for him to make a move and then strike. First, he should cover his body and try to protect his skin. Although a wasp sting could go through clothing, it would offer some protection. He reached down in the dark and gingerly picked up his jeans, shook them, and put them on.

He picked up one shoe and then the other, tipping them upside down and shaking them. Satisfied they were empty, he put them on. Then his jersey. Still no buzzing sound. He stood by the bed, tense and vigilant, straining to listen for the sound that would give it away, its gossamer wings so delicate yet powerful and set on course for him.

Brandon knew a lot about wasps and was aware that all advice said not to swat them as it antagonized them. When provoked, they chased after their attacker and stung to protect themselves. And, unlike bees who lost their sting after one strike, rendering them impotent, wasps could sting the same person many times. But for Brandon and those like him, allergic to wasp stings, one sting would be enough to bring on anaphylactic shock and very likely prove fatal.

Stay in control, he told himself. *You've been in a room with a wasp before.* It would have helped to have been able to switch on the light, but then Megan would wake and have to watch him charging around like an idiot trying to hit a moving target. Each time he missed, the wasp would become angrier and more aggressive, but there was little alternative. The large stained-glass window didn't open. Only the small window in the bathroom opened, and it occurred to Brandon that that was probably how the wasp had come in. Silently, unseen, it must have crept or flown in during the night, maybe even while they'd been making love. He doubted he would have heard it then.

Suddenly the buzzing came at him again and he leapt away. It was close this time, nearly brushing his head. If he could waft it in the direction of the bathroom and close the door, he could deal with it in the morning. He needed something to bat in that direction and protect himself. His eyes were adjusting to the dark and he spotted some magazines of Megan's on the chair. Taking the top one, he quietly rolled it up and then opened the bathroom door as wide as it would

200

go, ready for the wasp. Megan stirred and turned over in her sleep, but didn't wake.

He stood very still and listened, sweat forming on his forehead and neck as he gripped the makeshift weapon tighter. Had it just been him in the room he wouldn't have risked getting stung, but would have left and returned in the morning, having bought a can of knock-down spray. But he couldn't leave Megan alone. What if it stung her? More people were stung by wasps in autumn than at any other time of the year. With the evening air cooling they were attracted into homes by the warmth and light, then unable to find a way out they panicked and, under threat, stung. And what could he have possibly said to Megan when she woke and found him gone? *Sorry, love, there was a wasp in the room and I didn't want to get stung.* He could imagine her response: 'Thanks a bunch! So you left it to sting me.'

Not an option.

Then he heard it again, coming straight for him. He batted the air with the rolled-up magazine and miraculously it made contact. He heard the ping of the wasp's hard body against the paper, and it went quiet. He doubted he'd killed it with one blow, but perhaps he'd stunned it. When it recovered, it was going to be even more threatening. He listened and heard a buzzing coming from the bathroom. Thank goodness! He quickly closed the door, trapping it inside. Hopefully once the sun rose it would be attracted to the light outside and exit the same way it had come in. If not, he'd deal with it then, in the daylight. Relief surged through him, and he felt pleased with himself. He hadn't panicked but had dealt with it in a manly and appropriate manner.

Going to the bed, Brandon took off his jersey and was about to take off his jeans when he heard the faintest noise. He froze. A buzzing, definitely a buzzing, and it wasn't coming from the bathroom but the other side of the bedroom.

Impossible that the wasp had escaped back into the room. There must be another one. Hardly daring to breathe, he grabbed the rolled-up magazine and waited.

An agonizing minute of silence, then it came at him out of the dark. He swiped at the air, while shielding his head with his free hand. He knew he hadn't hit it. It would return in a few seconds. He'd open the bathroom door again and hope it would follow its mate in there. If he switched on the light in there, hopefully this wasp would be enticed in. Yes, a plan.

But before he had a chance to put his plan into action the buzzing suddenly increased and intensified, as if it was coming after him from different directions. There wasn't just one, he realized, terrified, but many. Wasps didn't usually swarm, so had they disturbed a nest? Where, when, how? He hadn't time to think. They were coming for him from every angle, angry and ready to sting. He threw open the bathroom door, flicked on the light switch, and moved aside, expecting, hoping, praying, the wasps would fly into the bathroom. Nothing happened and it fell ominously, sinisterly quiet. Brandon realized that if they'd stopped flying, they must have landed en masse on something.

He looked into the room, followed the shaft of light that came from the bathroom and fell across the bed. He couldn't believe his eyes as he stared in horror. His worst nightmare ever. Hundreds of wasps were crawling over the bed, over Megan. He backed away. Wasps were crawling on her face, lips, nose, eyelids, through her hair. How was she still asleep? It was disgusting, abhorrent, unimaginable. If he didn't wake her, they would sting her to death. Not even a healthy adult could withstand the venom from all those wasps. Brandon knew what he should do. He should save Megan. Go to the bed, throw back the cover, brush off the wasps that were on her and then carry her from the room to safety. But in doing that he'd be putting his own life at risk. He froze in indecision. A dreadful, awful, untenable decision, unlike any he'd had to make before, and he knew he couldn't do it. He'd failed.

Slowly and quietly, so as not to disturb Megan or the wasps, he made his way across the bedroom towards the door, all the time watching the bed for any sign of movement. If they all took off, he'd make a run for it. Then, miraculously, he was at the door. He turned the key but the door wouldn't open. He rattled the key, turning it from left to right, but the door was jammed. He shook it hard, trying to force it. It wouldn't budge, and the noise had disturbed the wasps. They were buzzing more loudly, unsettled by the noise. He frantically pulled at the door, then kicked it. A moment's silence before the wasps rose from the bed; they were coming towards him, swarming as they weren't supposed to.

He backed against the door; there was no way out. The air around him filled with wasps, dots of black and yellow, all buzzing angrily. He tried to bat them away; two stung his hand, another his face, then more on his chest. The pain was like red-hot needles being driven into his flesh. He cried out for help, tried to protect himself, but it was impossible with so many attacking him at once. He felt the venom entering his bloodstream as his pulse slowed and weakened and his blood pressure dropped. His throat swelled and he collapsed in a heap on the floor, gasping for breath. This was the end. Not only had he failed to save himself, but Megan too.

THIRTY-SEVEN

At 10 a.m. the following morning, Austin was sitting in the interview room at Coleshaw police station with his solicitor and friend, James Branbury, at his side. Austin was uncharacteristically agitated and threatening to lodge a complaint. James was trying to calm him.

'I know it was inconvenient having the interview postponed at such short notice last night,' James said. 'I was halfway here before they called me, but it's not unheard of, and at least it gave you a chance to reflect on how you wish to proceed.'

'And that's supposed to make it all right?' Austin said, aggrieved.

'No, but I would advise you against making an official complaint. This sort of thing happens. There wasn't anyone available to interview you.'

'What about the two who brought me in?'

'They'd been on duty for over fourteen hours and needed some rest, which I think was explained to you.'

Austin huffed. 'And what about the state of my house?' he continued in the same disgruntled manner. 'I had to sleep in one of the spare bedrooms, the main bedroom was left in such a state from where the police searched it.'

'At least you were allowed home, and not held in police custody,' James Branbury said patiently. 'Forensics aren't required to clear up after themselves, but if anything has been damaged then you might have a case for compensation, although it will probably be easier to claim off your insurance.'

'Like I have time for all that,' Austin sneered. But he was stopped from complaining further as the door opened and DC Matt Davis and DC Beth Mayes came in.

'So you're back,' he said disparagingly. 'Hope you had a good night's sleep.'

'I wouldn't say that,' Beth replied convivially. She and Matt sat opposite him. 'Just a few hours. Thank you for your cooperation. Now we're all here, let's begin.'

Austin sighed as Beth went through the formalities, stating the time, date and who was present. 'Can we just get on with it?' he said.

'Of course, sir. A reminder that you are here voluntarily so can choose to terminate the interview at any time.'

'I know that, and I have to get back to my clients, so let's get it over with.'

Beth looked at him carefully. 'I thought you told us you were on holiday with old friends?'

'Yes, that's right, whatever,' Austin replied, less sure of himself. 'My solicitor has something to say to you.'

Matt and Beth looked at James Branbury, who was now taking two sheets of paper from his briefcase. He passed one across the table to Beth. 'My client has prepared a statement that he has asked me to read to you. I'll send you a digital copy as well.'

Beth nodded and took the statement as Matt toyed with the notepad on his lap. A prepared statement was an alternative to answering police questions, and one they were obliged to accept. Usually its contents were carefully prepared by the solicitor, controlling the amount of information disclosed, and closing any loopholes they might have explored in questioning.

'I, Austin Chambers,' James began solemnly, 'am attending Coleshaw police station of my own volition to clear up a misunderstanding in respect of my wife, Leslie Chambers, who is being held here on suspicion of committing a number of robberies. I doubt she was involved in any of them, but I am away from home on business a lot so can't vouch for her movements or give her an alibi during those periods. While at home I was never aware of any illegal activity, and I certainly played no part in it. As a result of childhood trauma, which resulted in Leslie's face being badly scarred, she can exhibit bizarre, even psychotic behaviour at times when she becomes delusional. What part that has played in her actions is a matter for her psychiatrist, but I want to reiterate most strongly that I was not involved in, or aware of, any crimes she may have committed.'

James stopped and put down the statement.

'Did you compose that?' Matt asked Austin.

'Yes,' he replied proudly.

'I thought so.'

'Will that be all?' James asked. 'My client has cooperated and now wishes to return to the holiday you interrupted.'

'Thank you for your cooperation,' Beth said, looking at Austin. 'It would be helpful if you could clarify a few points.'

'My client has nothing further to say,' his solicitor said.

But Austin was waving away his advice. 'Go ahead, ask. I have nothing to hide.'

James Branbury clearly disagreed with his client's decision but removed his laptop from his briefcase ready to take notes. Matt opened his notepad.

'Thank you,' Beth said. 'It shouldn't take long. Just now you mentioned your wife's psychiatrist. Is she seeing one?'

'Not as far as I know,' Austin replied as his solicitor typed. 'You or the court will have to appoint one.'

Beth nodded. 'Leslie told us that you fulfilled the role of her psychiatrist although you are not qualified to do so.'

Austin bristled. 'I'm qualified to give her counselling,' he replied stiffly. 'But I can't prescribe medication.'

'Is she taking medication now?' Beth asked.

'I don't know what she takes. You'll have to ask her.'

'We have,' Beth said, looking directly at Austin. 'Leslie told us she doesn't take any mediation and hasn't done so for a long time as she is in very good health.'

Austin snorted with derision. 'If you say so. Then why is she wearing masks and robbing banks brandishing a toy gun? That doesn't sound like normal behaviour to me.'

'So you knew she had a toy gun?' Beth said. 'Presumably from seeing it lying around your home.'

'No, of course not,' Austin scoffed. 'From the news.'

There was a short silence when James appeared to realize the slip his client had made before his client did.

'We haven't released the fact that the gun was a replica,' Matt said.

A brief hesitation from Austin before he said, 'I must have assumed it from the pictures you've released.'

'We could do with you on our team,' Matt said, with no hint of what was to follow. 'Because the gun was such a good replica no one here was able to say for certain from the CCTV footage that it was a toy.'

'You don't have to answer any more questions,' James quickly told his client.

'You made a good guess,' Beth said, throwing Austin an encouraging smile, and moved on. 'Your garage is very tidy, not at all like mine.'

'Of course it's tidy,' Austin replied haughtily, recovering his composure. 'Like my house and workspace. We all need order in our lives. Being organized allows us to prioritize, saves us time looking for things, maximizes our free time, and ultimately increases productivity and reduces stress. I always help my clients to organize their lives.'

'I get that,' Beth said. 'Knowing where everything is without having to search for it must be a real bonus. So you'll have known the false number plates that Leslie used on her car for the robberies were in the top drawer of the work bench in the garage.'

Austin stared at her while James asked, 'Are you arresting my client? If so, he will need to be formally cautioned and I will have time alone with him.'

'No, he's still voluntarily helping us with our enquires,' Beth clarified.

'I don't know anything about false number plates,' Austin put in before his solicitor could raise further objections. 'Like I said, I'm away from home a lot on business.'

'And what business is that?' Matt asked.

'Seeing my clients, writing research papers, giving lectures.'

'Thank you,' Beth said. 'Your wife's jewellery.'

'What about it?'

'We're having it examined at present, but some pieces appear to match items stolen in the Farthington Jewellery robbery last year. I expect you heard about that on the news too?'

'This is ludicrous,' Austin said. 'So some of Leslie's jewellery looks like pieces stolen last year. They could be replicas, like the gun. And what about all the money Chanel Woman has taken. If Leslie is Chanel Woman, where is it all? I certainly haven't seen any of it. I'm still working for a living.'

'We're looking into that now,' Beth said, maintaining eye contact. 'Leslie's laptop is with us and it would be helpful if we could have yours too, so we can eliminate your bank transactions from our enquiries.'

'Absolutely not!' Austin snapped. 'I never let my laptop out of my sight. It contains my client files with their personal information, which is highly confidential. Details of their illnesses, treatment plans, and so forth. I offer online counselling sessions and I keep the recordings of those. So no.'

'Where is your laptop now, sir?' Matt asked.

'Where I've been staying this week. It's password protected, so safe from prying eyes. Not that my friends would pry. They trust me.'

'You'll need a search warrant to take his laptop,' James Branbury pointed out.

'Yes,' Matt said. 'And if Mr Chambers doesn't agree voluntarily to handing over his laptop, then that will be our next step.'

The colour drained from Austin's face and it was a moment before he'd recovered sufficiently to reply. 'I am terminating this interview now and wish to speak to my solicitor in private.'

'Of course,' Beth said. 'That's your right.'

She switched off the recording equipment and she and Matt left the room. They headed for the main office to take advice from DS Scrivener, who'd been watching the interview on CCTV. Beth checked her phone as they went. Among her messages were two missed calls and a text from the reporter Danny Able. *Can you confirm Chanel Woman's husband is being questioned?*

Beth replied, *Yes.*

Has he been arrested? Came the instant response.

Not yet. Press release likely soon.

Thanks for the heads-up.

THIRTY-EIGHT

'Good morning,' Roshan said, entering the kitchen. 'Or rather, good afternoon.' He headed for the coffee. 'No more from Austin then?'

'No,' Megan replied, her voice flat.

Roshan looked over to where she and Brandon were sitting at the table. Something had happened. There was an atmosphere and no one had cooked breakfast, or rather brunch. Usually, whoever was up first began cooking. Had he walked in on an argument? Although he hadn't heard raised voices as he'd come downstairs.

'Everything OK?' he asked nonchalantly, pouring his coffee. At least that was ready.

Neither of them spoke.

'Sarah will be down soon,' he continued. 'I hope you guys don't mind, but we're going to head off home today. We've both got preparation to do for work on Monday.' He took his coffee to the table and sat down.

'We're going too,' Megan said, in the same dispirited tone. 'I need to get back to Ella, and Brandon . . .' She looked at him but left the sentence unfinished.

Roshan looked at Brandon too. He was slouched forward

over his mug of coffee, resting his weight on his forearms as if he had the problems of the world on his shoulders.

'Are you all right, mate?' Roshan asked.

'Yes, why shouldn't I be?'

Roshan shrugged and began drinking his coffee. The atmosphere continued deep and heavy, and he wished he'd waited for Sarah before coming down. Then Megan spoke. 'One of us better tell Austin we're all going. I feel bad. He arranged this and now we're just clearing off.'

'I'll text him,' Roshan offered. 'He might be on his way back now.'

Sarah's footsteps sounded on the spiral staircase and Roshan breathed a sigh of relief.

'Megan and Brandon are leaving today as well,' he said as she appeared.

'Really? Why?'

'I have to get back to Ella,' Megan said. Brandon remained quiet.

Sarah nodded, poured herself coffee and took it to the table.

'Late night?' she asked as she sat down. 'You don't look so good.'

'What the fuck!' Brandon exploded, and stood so abruptly his chair crashed back onto the floor, startling them all. Without righting it, he stormed off upstairs, his feet hammering on the metal staircase, then his bedroom door slammed shut.

'Something I said?' Sarah asked Megan. She was feeling much brighter at the prospect of returning home.

'Brandon stayed with me last night,' Megan said sombrely. 'Everything seemed fine to begin with, nice. But he must have had a really bad dream. When I woke, I found him slumped on the floor by the door. I thought he'd had a fit to begin with. His eyes were glazed and he could barely speak. I was going to call for you guys, but then he started to come round.

211

He was babbling about being stung by wasps and how he was allergic to them. It was really disturbing. It took him ages to come out of it and calm down, then he kept apologizing for not rescuing me. I've no idea what all that was about. He's a lot better now, but he's not right. I think he should see a doctor.'

'You're sure he hasn't been stung?' Roshan asked, concerned. 'I found a wasp down here yesterday but got rid of it. A sting can be very serious if you're allergic to them.'

'I know. I checked him all over a number of times,' Megan replied. 'I had to, to try to reassure him. He wouldn't believe me at first. There was no sign of a sting and he thought he'd been stung multiple times, and that they had stung me too. He just wants to go home now. I want to get going too, so he's going to drop me off at the station so I can catch the two thirty train.'

'Oh dear,' Sarah sympathized. 'I hope everything works out for you guys.'

'So do I.' Megan paused and concentrated on her mug of cooling coffee before speaking again. 'It was strange. Brandon's behaviour reminded me of when I thought a spider was on me. Real but then not real, if that doesn't sound barmy.'

Sarah nodded sympathetically. 'I'm sure you'll be fine once you're home with your family. It's a pity it's ending like this, but we'll keep in touch, won't we?'

'Yes, I'd like that,' Megan replied, and finished the last of her coffee. 'I think I'll check on Brandon now.'

'Shall I make us something to eat before we all leave?' Roshan offered. 'There's enough time.'

'I'm not really hungry,' Megan said. 'I'll get something on the train. Thanks anyway. I'll ask Brandon if he wants something.' She went upstairs.

'Are you OK with omelette?' Roshan asked Sarah, going to the fridge.

'Yes please.' She had an appetite. She would be on her way home soon.

Roshan took eggs, tomatoes, mushrooms and cheese from the fridge as Sarah checked her phone. Megan called down from upstairs, 'Brandon says he doesn't want anything.'

'OK,' Roshan replied, beating the eggs for the omelette.

'Brandon looked rough,' Sarah remarked, scrolling through her social media accounts. 'I was going to ask him if he moved the planchette last night, but obviously I won't now. Poor Megan, imagine your first night with someone and that happens. It would freak me out.'

'Megan is very understanding,' Roshan said.

'And I'm not?'

'No, I didn't mean that. Don't be so snappy.'

Sarah didn't reply; she was reading a newsfeed that had just arrived on her phone. 'Hey, listen to this: "A man thought to be Chanel Woman's husband is helping police with their enquiries. He was brought to Coleshaw police station late last night and is still there answering police questions. A statement is likely to follow soon."'

'That doesn't sound good,' Roshan said, pausing. 'It suggests Austin *was* involved or at least knew something about it.'

'That's what I thought,' Sarah agreed. 'I guess they'll say more in the statement.'

'It's just as well we're leaving, put some distance between us and Austin. We don't want to get caught up in all that.'

'Now who's not being understanding!' Sarah remarked.

'I'm just saying I can imagine the publicity that will follow if he is involved. The board of governors at our schools won't take kindly to us having spent our half-term holiday with Chanel Woman's husband, if he is her accomplice.'

'I'm still struggling to believe it. I'll send the link to Megan's phone in case she hasn't seen it.'

Roshan brought over the omelettes, cutlery, and bottles of sauces, and sat at the table. As they ate, Megan replied to Sarah's text with a shocked emoji expression; she hadn't seen the news. But there was no reply from Austin to Roshan's text.

'I guess he's still at the police station,' Roshan said.

An hour later, bags packed, the four of them stood in the lobby of the church with the front door open, saying their goodbyes.

'It seems ages since we arrived. So much has happened,' Megan mused.

'It certainly does,' Sarah agreed.

'Bye,' Brandon said, still very subdued, and took his and Megan's bags to his car.

'Is he OK?' Sarah quietly asked Megan.

She shook her head. 'Not really. But he doesn't want to talk about it. Hopefully he'll start to feel better once he's home.'

'I think we all will,' Sarah said. 'It's been a strange week.'

'It has. Did Austin reply to your text?' Megan asked Roshan.

'No. I'll text him again and let him know we've gone and left the key under the mat. Although I'm sure he has another key.'

'Give him my best wishes,' Megan said. 'I feel bad we're all going without saying goodbye.'

'You can message him,' Roshan pointed out. 'Or put something on our WhatsApp group.'

Sarah hugged Megan goodbye. Roshan closed and locked the front door, then slid the key under the mat. He kissed Megan goodbye and she got into the passenger seat of Brandon's car. As soon as she'd closed the door, he started the engine and quickly reversed off the hardstanding and pulled away. Only Megan was waving.

'We will keep in touch with them,' Sarah said as the car disappeared down the lane.

'Yes, I don't see why not.'

Roshan opened the boot of their car and put in their bags. Sarah paused for a last look at the surrounding countryside. It was a cool autumn day, overcast, a day that would never get properly light and not dissimilar to the day they'd arrived, although it had been nearly dark then. Her gaze returned to the church, and with a sinking feeling she remembered the shock of seeing it for the first time and realizing it was surrounded by a graveyard. Had her phobia improved with Austin's sessions? She wasn't sure; other events had taken over.

'I'll drive,' Roshan said. 'You can have a nap.'

'Suits me,' Sarah replied, and climbed into the passenger seat.

She closed her car door and gazed through the side window. The natural light was growing dimmer by the second. She was pleased she wouldn't be spending another night in the church. Tonight she'd be in her own bed in their small but comfortable flat, where, apart from the odd bad dream, nothing of concern happened. Where they went about their daily lives of work, weekends off, and school again on Monday, safe and reassuring in its familiarity.

Roshan set the satnav, started the car, and reversed off the hardstanding. Only Austin's car remained, abandoned, as he might feel when he returned. Perhaps one of them should have stayed at least until he got back, but none had been keen to make that offer. Sarah continued to gaze out of her side window as Roshan drove slowly along the lane. The graveyard was on her left, and as she looked her heart missed a beat as the spirit of a woman rose from between the graves. But there was no fear. It was a figure she recognized.

'Stop!' Sarah cried, and flung open her car door.

Roshan braked. 'Sarah?'

She got out and, flinging open the wooden gate, ran towards the spirit, but already it was fading.

'Stay, Mum, please!' she called, but even as she said it, she knew that wasn't possible. A second later it had disappeared. She felt tears on her cheeks and then Roshan's arms around her, leading her gently back to the car.

THIRTY-NINE

It was dark as the unmarked police car drove through the village.

'Church Lane comes upon you suddenly in about half a mile,' Austin said helpfully from the back seat. 'But you probably remember that from your last visit.'

'Thank you,' Matt said.

Since Austin had terminated the interview at Coleshaw police station to speak to his solicitor, he'd been far more cooperative. He'd said that as he had nothing to hide, the police could examine his laptop and search the holiday home where he'd been staying – with him present. They wouldn't need to apply for a warrant.

'What made you choose this place?' Matt asked, concentrating on the country road ahead. 'It's very remote.'

'It's a nice part of the country and the church has a lot of character. I didn't know about their phobias when I booked it.'

'Phobias?' Beth asked, from the front passenger seat.

'One of my guests had a phobia about graveyards and another about spiders.'

'Not the best location then?' Beth agreed.

'No, you can say that again. I spent a lot of time giving them therapy. Free of charge, of course.'

'A working holiday for you then?' Matt remarked.

'Yes, indeed.'

Matt spotted the turning, indicated, and turned left into Church Lane. Unlike their last visit, there were no lights shining through the trees from the church. It was in darkness.

'Are your friends out?' Matt asked as the tyres bumped over the uneven road surface.

'No. They've left,' Austin replied.

'I thought you were all here until Saturday?' Beth said.

'That was the plan, but they texted this afternoon to say they were all going. Perhaps it was something I said.'

Beth smiled weakly. Matt continued to the end of the lane and then parked beside Austin's car. As they got out something scuttled away in the undergrowth, but it was impossible to see what in the dark.

'This way,' Austin said, opening the wooden gate.

He went in first along the stone path, flanked on either side by tombstones.

Beth stumbled but caught herself. 'Watch your footing,' Austin said over his shoulder. 'It's very uneven.'

He retrieved the key from under the mat, opened the front door, and switched on the light for the porch and lobby. Beth and Matt followed him in.

'It feels like they turned off the heating before they left,' Austin remarked as he led the way through the living room. 'The boiler is in the kitchen. I'll switch it on.'

Beth and Matt went with Austin into the kitchen-diner where, like the living room, there wasn't much to see. All their personal possessions had gone and it had the feel of a rental between lets, tidy but impersonal. Matt opened some of the cupboard doors in the kitchen but all he came across was neatly stacked china, glasses and cookware ready for the next occupants.

'Will you stay on?' Matt asked, opening the fridge door.

'Probably for tonight, then I'll see,' Austin replied.

'They've left you some food,' Matt said, and closed the fridge door.

'Does this staircase lead up to the bedrooms?' Beth asked, looking into the alcove.

'Yes.'

'Any more rooms apart from those upstairs?' Matt asked.

'No, that's it.'

Beth took the handrail and began up the metal staircase. Austin went next, then Matt. Arriving on the landing, Beth stood aside. 'Can we see your room first?' she said to Austin.

'Sure.'

Austin crossed the landing and opened the door to his bedroom. Beth and Matt went in. It was meticulously tidy, the bed was made and there were no clothes or other belongings you'd expect to find in a holiday let where the occupant unpacked a little and then lived out of their suitcase.

'All right if we have a look around?' Matt said, opening the wardrobe.

'Help yourselves.'

'And your laptop?' Beth asked Austin.

'Yes, sure, it's here.'

He took it from a drawer and set it on the table beneath the stained-glass window. 'I'll remove the password,' he said.

Beth stood beside him, watching. They'd agreed with his solicitor before they'd left the police station that as Austin was voluntarily handing in his laptop, he could check his diary and emails first. He'd made a point of stating that he used his laptop rather than his phone for banking, emails and so on. He'd shown them his phone, which seemed to confirm this – just a contact list and text messages.

'I wish my wardrobe was as well organized as yours,' Matt said. Even Austin's underwear was folded in neat piles.

'Tidy house, tidy mind,' Austin said, without looking up from his laptop.

Having checked the bedroom, Matt went into the bathroom where a neat row of toiletries stood next to an electric toothbrush, mouthwash, and a roll of dental floss. His towels were folded over the towel rail, and a white bathrobe hung from the hook on the back of the door.

'I'm finished in here,' Matt said, coming out. 'Thank you. I'll take a look in the other rooms and then leave you in peace.'

'I'm finished here too,' Austin said, closing his laptop and handing it to Beth.

'All done?' she asked, surprised. 'That didn't take long.'

'I'll have it back as soon as you've finished.'

'Of course.'

They filed out of Austin's room and onto the landing. 'Do you want to know who had each room?' Austin asked.

'That would be helpful,' Beth replied.

'That was Megan's,' Austin said, pointing. 'Brandon's, and Roshan and Sarah's.'

Matt opened the door to what had been Megan's room and they went in. By contrast to Austin's, the bed was unmade, and strewn over the chair were discarded towels and a towelling robe similar to the one in Austin's room.

'The owner has the place cleaned between lets,' Austin said. 'The bed linen, towels and bathrobe come with it.'

Beth nodded and went into the bathroom, leaving Matt to check the bedroom. There was nothing to be seen in there beyond a vacated en suite waiting for the cleaner and next guest.

Leaving Megan's room, they went into Brandon's, which was much the same, although Matt found a sock beneath the bed. Roshan and Sarah's room gave no surprises either.

'Thank you,' Beth said as they came out. 'We'll just take a look outside and then we'll be off.'

Austin nodded stoically and went first down the staircase, their footsteps juddering the metal steps. Beth and Matt followed through the kitchen-diner where he unlocked the back door. 'You can go out this way,' he said. 'I'll put the outside lights on. The path runs all the way round to the front, so if you've finished, I'll lock up.'

'Certainly sir,' Beth said. 'Thank you for your cooperation. We'll get your laptop back to you as soon as possible.'

'Goodnight,' Matt said as they left.

The door closed behind them. The outside coach lamps gave just enough light to see the path. They followed it to the right, pausing at the bin. Matt lifted the lid and peered in.

'He's too smart to have thrown anything incriminating in there,' Beth said.

Matt poked around and then closed the lid. It was just domestic waste. They continued along the path around to the front of the building. The lights shone through the stained-glass windows of the living room.

'He was so cooperative it made me cringe,' Matt said, and opened the wooden gate.

'Yes, and I doubt we'll find anything on his laptop either,' Beth said. 'If there is anything incriminating to be found, it'll be on another device.'

'Or stored remotely on iCloud or similar,' Matt added.

Once in the car, Beth checked her phone messages. 'Excellent,' she said. 'Digital Forensics have done an initial check on Leslie's computer and the report is on its way. Once

221

we have that, we should be able to charge her and hopefully Austin too.'

Matt set the satnav for Coleshaw. It had been another long day.

FORTY

'Megan, what's going on, love?' her mother, Wendy, asked her quietly. 'I can't help you if you don't tell me. This isn't like you.'

Megan shrugged despondently.

'It's starting to affect Ella,' Wendy said, glancing at Ella, who was sitting on a beanbag watching the television. 'She was so looking forward to seeing you, but now you're worrying her. She was asking to come and stay with me again.'

'I'm sorry, Mum,' Megan said. 'Thanks for coming over. I saw something move out of the corner of my eye and panicked.'

'I understand that, and I've hoovered and checked every room as I used to when you were a child. There are no spiders here, trust me.' She paused and studied her daughter. 'Megan, this isn't just about spiders, is it? I feel something happened while you were away.'

'You mean beyond Austin's wife being a notorious criminal?' Megan said sarcastically, then apologized.

Her mother continued to look at her thoughtfully. 'That was pretty traumatic stuff, I agree. But you've never met

Leslie and there's a chance Austin might not be involved. The news said she's been charged but he's been released pending further investigation. I might be missing something here, love, but I don't understand why it's making you so depressed and anxious. Is it Brandon? While you were away you said how much you liked him and you were getting on well, but you haven't mentioned him since you've returned.'

'I texted him twice to make sure he got home OK, but he hasn't replied.'

'I see. Well, that's disappointing, but you can't force relationships.'

'I know that,' Megan said sharply, and took a breath as if she was about to say something else, but stopped.

'So what is it, love?' Wendy prompted, taking her daughter's hand between hers. 'Come on, love, tell me. We've always had such a close relationship and been able to share most things.'

Megan swallowed hard. 'You remember when Gran first got ill before she was diagnosed?'

'Yes.'

'She started behaving oddly, seeing things that weren't there, and doing things completely out of character. She could be rude and thoughtless sometimes too.'

'Yes, I remember. Then once she was diagnosed and we were told it was the start of Alzheimer's, we forgave her and made allowances.'

'Mum,' Megan said, turning to her mother with tears in her eyes. 'I think I might have it.'

'No, you haven't, don't be silly.'

'No, listen. While I was away, I started seeing things that weren't there and did some really awful things. I'm too embarrassed to tell you but it wasn't me. I kept having to apologize to my friends for my behaviour.' A tear slipped from her eye and ran down her cheek.

'Oh, love, come here,' Wendy said, taking her daughter in her arms.

Ella turned from the television. 'What's the matter with Mummy?' she asked her nana anxiously. 'She's crying again.'

'It's all right, pet,' Wendy said. 'Mummy is thinking about Gran and is a bit upset. Could you be a big girl and get me some tissues, please? I think there's a box in Mummy's bedroom.'

Ella left to fetch the tissues.

'Listen to me,' Wendy said firmly to her daughter. 'I don't think for one moment you're in the first stages of Alzheimer's. I think being with your old school friends for a week was too much, too intense, and from the sound of it you all had far too much to drink. But if you're worried then speak to the doctor. There are tests that can be done.'

'I'm not sure I want to know.'

'Then you will continue to worry unnecessarily. Did you discuss it with Austin? You said you had some therapy with him.'

'I'm not sure if I mentioned it. We talked about a lot of things, apart from my phobia of spiders.'

Ella returned carrying the box of tissues and placed them on her mother's lap.

'Thank you,' Megan said, taking a tissue and wiping her eyes.

'I don't like it when you cry, Mummy,' Ella said. 'It makes me upset and worried.'

'I'm sorry, darling. I'll try not to do it again, I promise.' Megan finished drying her eyes and kissed Ella. 'Now, it's getting late,' she said, glancing at the wall clock. 'You stayed up longer because of Nana coming, but you've got school tomorrow. We need to say goodnight to Nana and get you into bed.'

Ella's face fell. 'I want Nana to do it.'

'But Nana did it last night and all the nights I was away,' Megan said. 'I'd like to do it and read you a bedtime story.'

'No, I want Nana,' Ella said, her face setting. 'I feel safe with Nana. She's normal and not frightened of things like you are.'

More tears sprung to Megan's eyes.

'We'll do it together,' Wendy suggested, standing. 'Then I need to go home and feed my cat.'

'Can I come and stay at your house, please?' Ella asked.

'No, love. You'll be fine here with your mother.' Then quietly she said to Megan, 'Make that doctor's appointment tomorrow. This has got to stop.'

'I know, I will.'

FORTY-ONE

Not for the first time since he'd returned home, Brandon tried to imagine what he'd ever seen in Megan. She had so many issues, and a child. Also, she'd seen him at his most vulnerable, and he was still cringing at the thought of it. Crouched on the floor and snivelling like a baby, and all because of a dream about wasps.

As for the others, had they really been close friends as students? It was difficult to imagine. They were so different to him now. All that hocus pocus nonsense. Of course there were no such things as ghosts or candles relighting themselves. Mass hysteria, Austin had called it, probably triggered by them finding Sarah in the graveyard on their first night. Thank goodness he'd been able to leave early and return to the comforts of his house.

He'd done well for himself, he thought, taking another beer from the fridge. He opened his laptop. Time to find himself a woman. There were thousands of them online, many local. But first he'd have a warm-up. A practice run, to get some relief – a live online stream with a sex worker.

Having arrived home on Thursday feeling a complete idiot for imagining he was dying from wasp stings, he'd needed something to take his mind off it and had gone online. He'd no idea why he hadn't used these women before. It was better than watching television or Netflix. For as little as £10 you could watch; for £20 you watched each other masturbate; £30 and the session lasted longer and she introduced the sex toy of your choice; £40 and there were two of them doing things on screen Brandon had never dreamed possible. Just the thought of it!

He chose the website he'd been using over the weekend where his credit-card details were stored. Switching on his webcam he logged in. Sunday evening seemed to be a popular time, and the two women he'd been with previously were already busy. Lucky clients, Brandon thought. Never mind, there were plenty more, time for a change. He scrolled down the pages of women, all offering tantalizing glimpses so you could shop before you bought. Brandon didn't really have a favourite type. Bunny Diamond looked good and was available now. He clicked on her profile and there she was in real life, kneeling provocatively on her bed waiting to greet him, nipple tassels swinging, and the tiniest thong covering her pubes.

'Welcome,' she said, with a seductive smile. 'I don't think we've met before. How are you?'

'Ready for you,' he said brutishly. 'Slide your knickers down to your knees and part your legs.'

She did as he said. They all did what the client wanted and appeared to enjoy it, or they didn't get a tip.

His cock was hard and he lifted it from his open fly to show her.

'Hmmm,' she said, licking her lips lasciviously. 'You're making me wet already. If you're in a hurry, we'd better get started, big boy.' She began touching herself erotically, then slowly parted her labia and invited him in.

Brandon didn't say anything, he didn't like talking during

sex. She would know what to do, it was part of the package. Masturbate herself until he came. He watched her fingers moving as he rubbed his cock, up and down the shaft and over the tip. He needed the release, fast and urgent. He needed to come, but it seemed to be taking longer than usual. He rubbed harder and concentrated on her. The fifteen minutes he'd paid for came and went; he'd be automatically billed for more. He kept going, up and down, massaging his penis as hard as he could. He was breaking out in a sweat now. It never took this long. But rather than coming to orgasm the urgency seemed to be receding. He was losing his erection. Whatever was the matter? She was still rubbing herself and making noises of pleasure as if she was enjoying it, while watching him to see if he'd ejaculated yet. In truth, he thought she was looking bored.

'Do something different!' he cried.

He watched her as she followed his instructions.

'Harder!'

She did it again.

As he watched her, he suddenly felt fluid in his hand. Strange, as he hadn't been aware he'd ejaculated. He looked down and cried out in alarm. It wasn't semen coming out of his penis, but blood dripping from the tip. He clutched himself in horror and tried to stem the flow. But it was pumping out now, hot and sticky, running through his fingers, dripping onto the floor.

Panic gripped him.

He stood and, clutching himself, went as fast as he dared into the kitchen, where he grabbed the roll of kitchen towel. He tore off a wad and bound it around his penis. He felt sick and faint. He needed to call for an ambulance before he passed out and bled to death on the floor. Holding the makeshift bandage in place, Brandon hobbled back to the living room, picked up his phone, and collapsed onto the sofa. He pressed

999 for the emergency services. The image of Bunny had gone and the laptop screen was blank.

'Which service do you require?' the call handler at 999 asked. 'Police, fire or ambulance?'

'Ambulance,' he cried. 'Quickly!'

'I'm putting you through now.'

Another image was appearing on his laptop screen, not Bunny but Megan, laughing at him. He slammed the lid down.

'Ambulance. Is the patient breathing?' a voice on the other end of the phone asked.

'Yes. I'm bleeding to death,' he shouted, and looked down at his penis, expecting to see more blood.

But the kitchen towel was dry and there was no blood on it at all. His hands were free of blood too. He gingerly removed the wad of kitchen towel from his penis. No sign of blood. He looked at the carpet, there was no blood there either.

'Where are you bleeding from?' the voice on the phone was asking.

'I'm not, don't worry,' Brandon said, and cut the call.

He continued to stare at himself in horror and disbelief. His penis was flaccid but otherwise unhurt. What the hell was the matter with him? While away, he'd believed he'd been vomiting worms, then stung to death by wasps, and now this! There was something seriously wrong with him, and his first thought was how much he would have liked to have confided in Megan; feel her comforting arms around him. But that wasn't an option. He'd blown it by ignoring her texts, and what could he have said that would have made her think any better of him? He felt utterly wretched and scared, and not at all like the person he used to be.

FORTY-TWO

'Thank you so much for fitting me in,' Sarah said, following Katherine Fellows into her consulting room.

'You're welcome.'

The blinds were closed against the night, and two leather armchairs were positioned opposite each other in the centre of a comfortable-looking room. A couch was against one wall and a desk with a computer on it against another. A palm tree and soft lighting helped create a mood of tranquillity, which was just what Sarah needed.

'I always keep a couple of evening appointments free for clients who need to see me urgently,' Katherine explained. 'Do sit down, Sarah.'

Sarah hesitated, her gaze going from the chairs to the couch. 'Where do I sit?' she asked nervously. 'Sorry I've never been to a psychologist before.'

'It's up to you,' Katherine said with an encouraging smile. 'Wherever you feel most comfortable.'

Sarah chose the nearest chair and sat down. Katherine took a notepad and pen from her desk and sat opposite. She was in her late forties, Sarah guessed, of small build, with regular features and brown chin-length wavy hair. Someone who wouldn't stand out in a crowd, nondescript, yet giving off a quiet air that invited confidences.

'Just a few formalities before we begin,' Katherine said with another reassuring smile. 'Thank you for completing my online form with your details and the medical question-naire. You have no allergies or health conditions that you know of, and are not in treatment anywhere else?' she checked.

'That's correct.'

'You're married to Roshan, and he knows you're here, and you're self-funding?'

'Yes,' Sarah said.

'Have you ever seen a counsellor, therapist or psychologist before?'

'No – well, apart from Austin last week,' Sarah replied.

'Who's Austin?' Katherine asked, pen poised to make a note.

'The guy who organized a get-together for five of us last week. We knew him from school. He's some sort of therapist and gave those of us with phobias free counselling sessions – not that they did me any good.' Sarah decided not to tell her that Austin was the husband of the notorious Chanel Woman and had been questioned by the police. That would only confuse the issue, and she hadn't come here to talk about Austin.

'So, I'll tell you a bit about how I work,' Katherine said. 'Stop me if you have any questions. I'm a qualified psycholo-gist; you can see my certificates on the wall behind me.' She turned slightly and Sarah looked at the array of framed certificates and nodded.

'In line with most practising psychologists,' Katherine continued, 'I use talking therapies with my clients, including cognitive-behavioural therapy. Together we look at difficult situations in your life and identify negative or inaccurate thinking. I help you address these issues and change the way you view them, leading you to a happier, healthier life. I don't have all the answers, but I think you will see that within you lies the answer to many of them.'

'OK,' Sarah said.

'Any questions?'

Sarah's gaze went again to the framed certificates. 'So you've been practising a long time and have dealt with a lot of weird stuff before?'

'I've been practising for twenty years and yes, I have clients whose problems may be considered weird. How can I help you, Sarah?'

Sarah didn't know where to begin. She sighed and looked around the room for inspiration.

'You said on the phone you thought you'd been hallucinating, seeing things that weren't really there?' Katherine prompted.

'Yes.'

'Do you hear voices too?'

'Sometimes.'

'Can you tell me what you see?'

'Usually a spirit, a ghost which I'm now sure is my mother. I had a feeling it might be her when I first started having the dreams as a child, but I didn't know for certain until last Thursday when I saw her in the graveyard.'

'The graveyard where your mother is buried?' Katherine asked.

'No. The place where we stayed last week. Roshan and I were there with three old friends. It was a converted church, with a graveyard. It gave me the shivers when I first saw it, but I tried to believe it was going to be all right. It wasn't. The first night I was found sleepwalking, trying to follow a spirit. Then I began seeing it and feeling its presence. It was so real, scary. I didn't know it was my mother until last Thursday as we were leaving.'

'And when did your mother die?' Katherine asked gently.

'When I was six, nearly seven. Soon after her death I saw her spirit and began having nightmares. As I got older, it happened less frequently. I've only had a couple since I've been married. But then last week the nightmares returned. I must have freaked out the others, because they started seeing things too. Austin said it was mass hysteria.'

'Possible, but unlikely,' Katherine said. 'Getting back to you, Sarah. How did you feel when your mother died? You were very young.'

'I was devastated,' Sarah admitted. 'Upset, and angry that she'd left me, although I knew it wasn't her fault. She died of cancer. Even so, I felt abandoned. My father brought me up. I suppose he did his best, but he was grieving too. He remarried when I left home to go to college. I don't see much of him now.'

'Did your father ever talk with you about your mother dying?'

'No, he couldn't bring himself to talk about Mum so we never mentioned her. I remember he told me she was dying, and then she died, and that was it.'

'So nothing about the loss you were both experiencing?'

'No.'

'How did that make you feel?'

Sarah paused before replying, 'I sensed it was a taboo subject, so I steered clear of it. I would have liked to have talked about her, to keep her memory alive, but he couldn't. I had a photo of my mother in my bedroom and I used to talk to her every night.'

Katherine nodded thoughtfully. 'Sarah, you don't need me to tell you that losing your mother had a massive impact on you and your mental health. Not being able to talk about it compounded your feelings of loss.'

'Yes, but why am I frightened of her spirit? Shouldn't I be pleased to see her?'

'When someone dies, even from natural causes, we can be left with many conflicting emotions: – distress, anger, resentment as well as acute loss and abandonment. Sometimes we're just numb and it comes out later. Did you have a chance to say goodbye to your mother?'

'No, she died in hospital and my father said it was no place for a child, and I should remember her how she was. He told me she didn't look like my mother any more but was all skin and bones, like a ghost.'

Sarah's words hung in the air before Katherine said, 'That's a very frightening image for a young child to process. One you have carried with you all these years.'

'Yes, you're right. I hadn't really thought about it like that before,' Sarah said. 'But what about all the other weird stuff that happened last week? I haven't told you about that yet.'

'Go ahead.'

Sarah tried to keep her voice even as she described in detail that first night, then seeing the inscription on the memorial stone in the churchyard change to that of her mother, and hearing her voice. Going for a walk and feeling a presence so strong she ran all the way back to the church. Walking home with the others from the pub when they all saw a spirit. Playing with the Ouija board on Halloween when it spelt out 'leave', the candle going out and relighting, and 'now' appearing on Megan's phone.

'It wasn't just me who experienced bad stuff. Brandon thought he was vomiting green worms and was stung to death by wasps. He's allergic to wasp stings. And Megan kept seeing spiders, which freaked her out. To be honest, the week was a disaster. We weren't the people we used to be at school and there were a lot of snide remarks as well as all the weird things that kept happening.'

'Were you and your friends taking drugs, Sarah?' Katherine asked, without reproach.

'No.'

'You can tell me in confidence if you did. I ask because what you and your friends were experiencing has many traits of being under the influence of a hallucinogenic drug.'

'No. We didn't.'

'What about before you went? Did you take something then?'

Sarah shook her head.

'One of my clients is a businessman who spent a weekend at a rock music festival last year where he took a hallucinogenic drug, probably LSD. He had a bad trip and is still suffering from hallucinations and paranoia. He believes he is being haunted by the devil and sees him sometimes even at work.'

'How awful. But I don't do drugs, although we all drank too much alcohol last week. Far more than normal.'

'That in itself is unlikely to be responsible for what you are describing.' Katherine paused and looked carefully at Sarah. 'No one present could have given you a hallucinogenic drug without you realizing? The gentleman I'm seeing is adamant he didn't take so much as an aspirin. Someone must have spiked his drink. It was found in his blood.'

Sarah was about to say no, it wasn't possible, but stopped. 'We cooked for each other and poured each other drinks, so there was opportunity, but I can't believe any of my friends would do that. What would be the purpose?'

'I am not saying that's what happened, but it might be worth thinking about. Even a single dose of a hallucinogen can have a long-term effect on the brain. It distorts our perception of reality so we see and believe things that aren't real.'

Sarah didn't know what to say. She needed to think about it.

'It seems to me there could be two separate issues here,' Katherine continued. 'The unresolved emotions around your mother's death, and the hallucinations you and your friends experienced while staying together last week.'

'Can we talk more about my mother?' Sarah said.

'Of course. It would be useful if you told me what you remember of the time when your mother was alive, good and bad.'

Tears immediately welled in Sarah's eyes as she thought back and began telling Katherine what she remembered of her mother. The love and happiness, when her father was happy too; the family outings, her mother braiding her hair, making ice-cream even in winter, and then being told her mother was ill but believing she would get better. Followed quickly by the devastating news that her mother wouldn't be getting better and the doctors had done all they could. As eight o'clock approached, Katherine brought the hour's session to a close.

'We'll leave it there for now. How are you feeling, Sarah?'

'Sad but relieved,' she replied honestly. 'This is the first time ever I've been able to talk at length about my mother. Can I come and see you again?'

'Yes. I would suggest twice a week to begin with.' Katherine took a diary from her desk and opened it. 'Shall we say Thursday at seven o'clock?'

'That's fine with me.'

'I offer a payment plan for those who are self-funding that allows you to spread the cost if you wish.'

'No, it's OK,' Sarah replied. 'Roshan and I have savings and we've agreed to spend some of it on these sessions to get me the help I need.'

'Lovely to have such a supportive partner,' Katherine said.

237

She stood and returned her diary to the desk. 'I'll see you on Thursday then, but if anything urgent happens in the interim call my mobile.'

'Thank you, I will.'

FORTY-THREE

'Sarah, I don't believe that anyone spiked our drinks or food,' Roshan said, agitated. 'I've told you before it was most likely all the booze and mass hysteria, like Austin said. If you phone the others suggesting one of them put LSD in our food, they'll think you're trying to blame them for your problems. And while we're on the subject, are these therapy sessions really doing you any good? Because I have doubts. You've had three now and last night you were worse than ever, thrashing around in the bed, seeing things and crying out.' Roshan stopped and looked at her, waiting for a reply.

'She was here again,' Sarah said quietly.

'Your mother?'

'Yes. Not like I remembered her as a child, but the ghost that is haunting me, her face sunken – all skin and bones.'

Roshan sighed and ran his hands through his hair in frustration. 'Look, Sarah, I'm trying to be understanding and supportive but I just can't see where this is going. Some things are better left alone.'

'For you maybe,' Sarah said sharply. 'But not for me. I've left it alone all these years. Katherine warned me that exploring buried feelings often gets worse before it gets better.'

'She was certainly right there!' Roshan said caustically. 'Anyway, I've got some lesson plans and marking to do. I'll be in the spare room if you need me.'

Sarah watched him leave the living room. He really didn't understand. He hadn't had the experience of dealing with unresolved issues or phobias as she did. Katherine had said that often loved ones wanted to help the person in therapy but didn't appreciate how long it could take, as painful memories took time to surface and then work through. Therapy wasn't a quick fix, she said, and there were two issues here – her mother dying, and what had happened while they'd been away. There was some overlap, Katherine had explained – we don't leave our anxieties at home when we go on holiday – but that week had spawned new problems which she'd asked Sarah to think about. Sarah had thought about them and came to the conclusion that if their food or drink had been spiked then it would explain a lot, and she should contact the others.

Roshan had disagreed.

Sarah toyed with her phone. Roshan would be upstairs for the next couple of hours, working. Megan was the most approachable and they'd been very good friends once. She'd texted Brandon and Megan shortly after returning home, but only Megan had replied. It was now 8.30 p.m. Presumably Ella would be in bed and Megan was free to talk.

Sarah picked up her phone and pressed Megan's number. It rang for a while before a voice that wasn't Megan's answered. 'Hello. Sarah?'

'Yes, who's that?'

'Wendy, Megan's mother.'

'Oh, how are you?'

'All right, thank you. Long time no see. How are you?'

'Not so bad. Sorry to disturb you. I was hoping to speak to Megan. Is this a bad time to call?'

'She's having a lie-down on her bed. She'll get up later. She left her phone down here. I wouldn't have answered it, but I saw your name come up.'

'Is Megan not feeling well then?' Sarah asked.

'She's not herself. She's tired and anxious. She hasn't been sleeping well since she came back from holiday.'

'I'm sorry to hear that,' Sarah said, while thinking 'join the club'. 'What's causing the problem? Do you know?'

'I'm sure she won't mind me telling you as you're her friend. Megan is worried she has Alzheimer's like my mother did.'

'Why would she think that?' Sarah asked.

'She's having memory lapses, sometimes hallucinating, and experiencing personality changes like my mother did in the early stages. I understand that while you were all away she stole a bottle of wine, but she can't remember doing it. She also said she was flirting with your husband, which she feels bad about.'

'We all drank too much,' Sarah said, dismissing Megan's indiscreet behaviour with Roshan. She was more interested in Wendy's other comments. 'You say Megan's been hallucinating, so she's seeing things that aren't there?'

'Yes, love. It's very frightening for her. She mainly sees large spiders and believes they're hiding in the corners of every room. She phones me panic-stricken and I come straight over. Yesterday she locked herself in the bathroom. Little Ella was waiting outside, petrified.'

'How awful. Has Megan seen a doctor?'

'Yes. He did some basic memory tests which showed there was nothing wrong with her memory. He's given her some antidepressants, and has also referred her to a consultant.'

'I'm sorry. I hope she feels better soon. Do you know if she's seen Brandon at all?'

'She hasn't. She texted him but he didn't reply. From what

Megan's told me, he has a lot of issues too, so maybe it's for the best. To be honest, love, your get-together has done Megan more harm than good. I hope you're all right?'

'More or less,' Sarah said, feeling she didn't have the right to burden the poor woman more. She had enough to worry about and sounded at the end of her tether. 'Will you tell Megan I phoned her, please, and say I'd like to talk when she feels up to it. I'm sorry I didn't make more of an effort to renew our friendship while we were away. I've thought about it a lot and I feel bad about some of the things I said.'

'Megan does too. She said she felt she behaved very badly at times. I'll tell her you phoned.'

'Thank you. Take care.'

'And you, love.'

Sarah stayed where she was on the sofa toying with her phone. It was too much of a coincidence that Megan was still hallucinating too. Who else was affected? Roshan wasn't. What about Austin and Brandon? She scrolled through her contact list and called Brandon. His phone rang and then went through to voicemail, where she left a message.

'Brandon, it's Sarah, I hope you're OK. Could you give me a ring please when you have the chance? Thanks.'

She returned to the contact list: Austin. This was going to be a difficult conversation, and part of her hoped he wouldn't pick up.

One, two, three rings, then Austin's voice, 'Sarah, what a surprise.'

'I'm not interrupting anything, am I?' she asked.

'No. I'm just surprised to hear from you after the way you all disappeared.'

Sarah immediately felt guilty. 'I'm sorry, we thought we'd all be better off at home. Brandon had another bad night, and that place never really suited me. I hope you don't think we deserted you.'

'I didn't take it personally,' Austin replied.

Sarah had found it difficult to gauge Austin's mood when she could see him while on holiday, but now she found it impossible.

'So why are you phoning me, Sarah?'

'I need to ask you something.'

'Go ahead. I'm listening.'

'Have you been having hallucinations?' Sarah said, getting straight to the point. 'Either while you were away or since you got back?'

'No, but I assume you still are,' Austin said in the same even tone.

'Yes. And I've just spoken to Megan's mother and Megan is too.'

'What about Brandon?'

'I don't know. I haven't spoken to him yet. I've left a message on his voicemail.'

'And Roshan?'

'He's fine.'

Sarah was now expecting some further comment after his questions, but Austin remained silent.

'I know this might sound ridiculous, but I was wondering if someone could have spiked our drinks or food with a hallucinogenic drug while we were all together, you know like LSD.'

Austin laughed – and who could blame him, Sarah thought.

'Not ridiculous, Sarah, but very misguided, and a classic case of psychological projection – a way of dealing with unacceptable emotions by attributing them to others. I see it in my clients. You, Megan and Brandon all came to me with issues. I did what I could to help you, but clearly it wasn't enough. What's the matter with Brandon?'

'He's allergic to wasps, and the last night we were at the church he believed he'd been stung to death.'

'While saving Megan?' Austin asked.

'I don't know all the details.'

'And you're still seeing your ghosts, and Megan, her spiders?' he said with less compassion than Sarah would have hoped for.

'Yes.'

'I can't really offer anything, Sarah. I've got my own life to sort out.'

'Of course, I'm sorry. How are things?'

'*Things* are not good,' he replied, an edge to his voice. 'I'm sure you've seen the news. Leslie has been charged and refused bail, and I'm still under investigation.'

'I'm sorry,' Sarah said.

'Will that be everything?'

'Yes. Good luck. I hope things work out.'

But he'd ended the call and the line was dead.

Roshan had been right. She should never have phoned.

FORTY-FOUR

'Beth, I appreciate your frustration,' DS Scrivener said. 'We've done well to arrest and charge Chanel Woman and the charges are likely to stick. But there really isn't any evidence to charge her husband with being an accessory to her crimes.'

'Even though Leslie is insisting he made her do it? That he was controlling, manipulative, and she was in his power, so he forced her to act as she did?'

DS Scrivener was shaking his head.

'That's likely to be her defence, sir. She's pleading not guilty.'

'Whether the jury believes her is another matter,' DS Scrivener said sceptically. 'She'll evoke some sympathy for sure because of the trauma she suffered as a young person being trapped in a burning vehicle, but it's unlikely to get her off.'

'Austin Chambers's car was spotted in the vicinity of at least four of the robberies a week before they were committed,' Beth reminded her boss. 'Possibly gathering information.'

'I know, and he had legitimate reasons to be there. On one occasion he was in the barber's having his hair cut.'

Beth was trying to stay rational and objective, but it was difficult. She was convinced Austin was involved somehow.

'And the fact they lived together in the same house but apparently he had no suspicion at all? Then conveniently he managed to be away from home whenever a robbery was committed, giving himself an alibi.'

'Yes, and his alibis check out, Beth. You looked at them all. There were witnesses confirming Mr Chambers was where he said he was.'

'That's the point, sir. He's covered his back by creating these alibis in case Leslie was ever caught.'

'Beth, I've discussed all these points with DCI Peters and it's simply not enough; it's all circumstantial. There's nothing to directly link Austin Chambers to his wife's crimes. Forensics went through his laptop with a fine-tooth comb and found nothing. Unless you have fresh evidence, we can't bring him in again for questioning. His lawyer will accuse us of harassment.'

'Sir, could I at least speak to the friends he was staying with when Leslie was arrested?' Beth asked, in a final bid to keep the investigation into Austin Chambers live. 'They've all been friends since their school days so probably know him better than anyone. There was a strange atmosphere when Matt and I arrived that night. Almost as if we'd walked in on something. Matt felt it too.'

DS Scrivener sighed indulgently. 'All right, Beth, speak to them. I'll give you one day, then I need you back here on another case. Just you – I can't afford to let Matt go too.'

'Thank you, sir.'

Beth returned to the main office pleased, but with a feeling of trepidation. She'd been given twenty-four hours to find something substantial enough to give credence to Leslie's claims that Austin had forced her into being Chanel Woman, and link Austin to the planning and execution of her crimes. A day wasn't long, so she needed to make the most of it.

Beth sat at her desk and logged in to her computer. Matt's desk was empty. He was already out working on another case. She opened the file that contained the contact details of the friends Austin had been staying with that week – Brandon Edwards, Sarah Dara and her husband, Roshan, and Megan Hill. Megan first, Beth decided. She lived furthest away and had seemed the most jumpy of the group, claiming it was because of Halloween. Pity they hadn't questioned them further at the time, but there'd been no reason to.

Fifteen minutes later, Beth was in an unmarked police car with Megan's address in the satnav. If Megan worked, it was likely she wouldn't be at home, in which case Beth would phone her and arrange to return later. It was always preferable to arrive without warning if possible – the element of surprise left them with no time to prepare, or to confer with others.

It was 2.30 p.m. when Beth parked outside Megan's home, a Victorian townhouse converted into maisonettes. Beth walked up the path and pressed the bell for 11a. A moment later a silhouette appeared behind the leaded light glass in the door, but the door didn't open.

'Who is it?' Megan asked meekly from the other side.

'It's DC Beth Mayes. We met briefly on the evening of thirty-first October when you were on holiday with your friends. Can I come in? I need to ask you a few questions.'

'Why?' she asked, sounding as anxious as she had the last time they'd met.

'There's nothing for you to worry about. You haven't done anything wrong, but I'd like to ask you some questions. It won't take long.'

The door slowly opened and Megan looked at Beth nervously,

then at the ID she held out. 'You can come in, but I have to leave at three o'clock to collect my daughter from school.'

'That's fine, thank you.'

Beth went into the hall, which had retained many of its Victorian features, including a dado rail and ceiling cornices. She couldn't help but notice the sticky pads to capture insects dotted along both sides of the floor.

'You have a problem with insects?' Beth asked as Megan led the way into the living room.

'Spiders. I can't stand them,' she said with a shiver.

'You're not kidding,' Beth said drily as they entered the living room.

There were dozens of sticky pads all over the room – on the floor, chairs, table, bookshelves, in fact on every available surface. Although they all appeared to be empty.

'I have a phobia,' Megan admitted anxiously.

'I'm sorry. It must make life very difficult for you,' Beth said. 'I don't like moths, but I'm OK with spiders.'

'It's got worse,' Megan said, checking the chair before she sat down. 'I take it you're here because of Chanel Woman, but we never met her. She was supposed to come with us but didn't. She told us she was ill.' She appeared more nervous and agitated than when Beth had last seen her.

'So you spoke to Austin's wife?' Beth asked, taking out her notepad and pen.

'Only once. She was due to spend the week with us, but she didn't arrive. Austin told us she was sick but Roshan joked that perhaps she didn't exist, so Austin got her on the phone. We felt right fools.'

'When was this?'

Megan thought for a moment. 'On the Tuesday, in the afternoon.'

'What did you say to each other?' Beth asked, making a note.

248

'Austin put his phone on speaker so we could all hear, and we asked her how she was. She said she must have caught a stomach bug or had food poisoning as she'd been really sick. She said Austin hadn't wanted to leave her, but she'd told him to go as she knew how much he'd been looking forward to meeting with us after all that time. She was hoping to join us when she felt better, but she didn't.'

'Did she say anything else?'

'No, that was it. At the time we felt bad for doubting Austin. He'd gone to a lot of trouble to arrange our get-together.'

Beth nodded. 'Whose idea was it to get together?'

'Austin's.'

'I see. Can we go back a bit? I understand you were all good friends at school?'

'Yes, from infant school right through to when we left sixth form at eighteen. We went our separate ways then and lost contact. I kept in touch with Sarah a little and she came to see me when I had Ella.'

'That's your daughter?'

'Yes.'

'How old is she?'

'Five.'

'Do just the two of you live here?'

'Yes, my mother stays over sometimes.'

Beth noticed that as Megan spoke her gaze kept darting around the room, presumably looking for any sign of a spider. It must be awful to be at the mercy of an irrational fear, Beth thought.

'Did you keep in touch with Austin at all?'

'No.'

'What about the others in your friendship group – Brandon, Sarah and Roshan?'

'I don't think so. You'd have to ask them. We were on

social media, but Austin wasn't until he set up an account and contacted us to arrange the reunion.'

'So he contacted you all out of the blue to arrange your reunion?' Beth asked.

'Sort of. When we were eighteen and left school, we'd agreed to get together ten years later to see how we were all doing. I'd forgotten about it – I think the others had too. Only Austin remembered, but . . .'

'But what?' Beth asked, looking up from her notepad.

'It didn't work out. We argued a lot.'

'Ten years is a long time,' Beth said. 'How would you describe Austin?'

Megan's gaze swept the room again, before answering. 'He's intelligent, knows a lot of things. But he likes you to listen when he talks. That annoyed the lads, especially Roshan. I found what Austin had to say about psychology interesting, and he tried to help me with my phobia.'

'Have you spoken to any of the group since you left?'

'No, I texted Brandon but he didn't reply. Sarah phoned when I was having a lie-down and spoke to my mother. I haven't returned her call yet. I've been so busy with work, studying and looking after my daughter.' She rubbed her hands anxiously.

'I can imagine. What are you studying?' Beth asked. There were books and papers on the table beside a laptop.

'Occupational therapy, so I can help people, but it's difficult trying to fit it all in with working and Ella.'

'What is your work?'

'Cleaning,' Megan said, embarrassed. 'It's the only thing that fits in, and there's always work.'

'One last question and then I'll let you get on. Why did you all leave so abruptly? I believe you were due to stay until Saturday.'

Megan went quiet and took a moment before answering.

'Sarah and Roshan decided to leave. Brandon had a really bad nightmare and decided to go. I was missing Ella, and I didn't want to stay there by myself. It was too creepy.'

'The church is isolated,' Beth agreed.

'There was a lot of strange stuff going on,' Megan said nervily. 'Some of the time it was OK, but then we all seemed to be having really bad nightmares, and arguing. It was like that place magnified our fears and created tensions. I was sure I'd seen a spider on me. I thought I'd be all right once I got home, but to be honest my phobia seems to have got worse. I try to hide it from Ella, but that's not always possible.' Her gaze ran around the room again.

'It must be difficult,' Beth said. 'Have you thought about seeking professional help?'

'Yes, I'll have to. I'm sorry, is that everything? Only I need to be going soon.'

'Yes, thank you for answering my questions. I'll leave my business card.' Beth passed Megan a card. 'If you think of anything that might be relevant, perhaps you could phone me.'

'You mean about Austin?'

'Yes, or anything about your week away that might widen our investigation into the Chanel Woman robberies.'

'OK.'

'One last thing,' Beth said, putting away her notepad and pen, and standing. 'I'd appreciate it if you didn't contact the others until I've had a chance to talk to them.'

'Why? You don't think we're involved?'

'Were you?' Beth asked.

'No!'

'Then there's nothing for you to worry about. Thank you for your time,' Beth said, and headed for the front door.

So the reunion had been Austin's idea, thereby creating the perfect alibi to cover the last Chanel Woman robbery, Beth thought as she returned to her car. Too much of a coincidence. Megan had been tense and edgy, and Beth guessed it wasn't just about spiders, although clearly she had a real fear of them.

Roshan and Sarah Dara were next on her list to visit, but first she'd stop off on the way and get something to eat. She sat in her car and checked her phone for messages, then reprogrammed the satnav and pulled away.

Would Megan contact the others to warn them that the police were planning to pay them a visit? She would if she had something to hide. Did Megan know more than she was saying? Undoubtedly. And it crossed Beth's mind that arranging to meet that week might have provided more than an alibi. She still couldn't equate the daring, confident, charismatic Chanel Woman with Leslie Chambers; they were so far apart as to be two different people, so Beth couldn't accept she'd acted alone. Perhaps Austin had drafted in one or more of his old friends to help carry out the robberies.

FORTY-FIVE

It was 4.30 p.m. and already dark as Beth parked outside the block of flats where Sarah and Roshan Dara lived. She checked her phone for messages and was about to get out when a car pulled up directly in front of her. A man and woman got out, and by the light of the street lamp Beth could see it was Roshan and Sarah. Perfect timing, she thought. She waited until they'd retrieved laptops and other items from the back of the car and then approached them.

'Hello, Mr and Mrs Dara. DC Beth Mayes,' she said, showing her ID. 'We met—' But she didn't get any further.

'I know where we met,' Roshan said, closing the rear door. 'You came to see Austin when we were on holiday.'

'Yes, that's correct. I'm glad I've caught you. I'd like to ask you a few questions about that week.'

There was a moment's hesitation before Roshan said, 'Yes, come in. We've just got back from school.'

'You're teachers?' Beth asked, going with them to the main entrance.

'Yes,' Roshan replied.

'A very worthwhile profession, although I'm not sure I could do it,' Beth said.

'I couldn't do your job either,' Roshan replied, while Sarah smiled weakly.

He opened the main door and Beth followed them up a flight of stairs and then into their flat. They'd obviously left for work in a hurry. The sofa bed was still up and clothes were strewn everywhere.

'We're renting,' Roshan said, as if that explained it. 'Trying to save for a deposit on a place of our own.'

He removed a pile of exercise books from one of the two chairs so Beth could sit down. 'Do you want a drink?' he asked.

'No thank you.'

'I need a glass of water,' Sarah said, and disappeared into the kitchen at the far end of the room.

'Can you get me one too, love,' Roshan called.

Sarah returned with two glasses and, passing one to her husband, sat next to him on the end of the bed.

'We'd have cleared up if we'd known you were coming,' Roshan said.

'Don't worry. I won't keep you long.' Beth took out her notepad and pen. 'When we met last time, it was your ten-year reunion. How did it go?'

'Fine,' Roshan said.

Sarah remained silent and, Beth thought, watchful and on guard.

'What about you, Sarah?' Beth asked. 'Did you have a nice time while you were away?'

'It was all right,' she replied, and took a sip of water.

'You've all known each other since your schooldays. You must have a strong friendship bond to keep it going all these years.'

Roshan shrugged. 'Not really. We were close at school, but then most of us lost contact.'

'Until . . .?' Beth prompted.

'Austin got in touch to organize the reunion,' Roshan replied. 'Why exactly are you here?'

'I'm trying to fill in some gaps in our investigation into the Chanel Woman robberies. You are aware of Austin Chambers's connection with her?'

'Yes,' Roshan replied.

'You left in a hurry. Why was that?'

Beth saw Sarah's fingers tighten around her glass.

'Sarah and I had preparation to do for the start of term,' Roshan said. 'And to be honest, Sarah wasn't comfortable staying there.'

'It wasn't just me,' Sarah finally said, turning to Roshan. 'Megan and Brandon were going too.'

'So I understand,' Beth said. 'Leslie Chambers, Austin's wife, was supposed to be at your get-together. Why didn't she attend?'

'She said she was sick,' Roshan said flatly. 'We spoke to her on the phone.'

'Have you ever met her?' Beth asked.

'No, never,' Roshan replied.

'What about you, Sarah? Have you met Leslie?'

'No.'

'I believe Austin offered his counselling services to you all free of charge while you were there, to help with phobias?'

'Not me,' Roshan said. 'I don't have any phobias.'

'You're lucky,' Beth said with a smile. 'What about you, Sarah?'

'A few times, yes.'

'Helpful?'

She shrugged.

'It's sometimes difficult to judge the success of these things, but the week went well? You all enjoyed getting together again after so long? It would be something you'd do again?'

'Maybe,' Roshan said, and set his empty glass on the floor beside him.

Beth looked at them carefully. 'I don't think Megan would. She says there was a lot of arguing and, to use her words, "strange stuff" going on.'

She saw the look of surprise on their faces.

'You've spoken to her?' Sarah asked.

'Yes. She told me that all being together in that church seemed to magnify your fears and created tension within your group. She's not over it yet.'

'I know,' Sarah said quietly. 'I spoke to her mother.' Then looking at Roshan, she said, 'I'm going to tell her. We've got nothing to hide.'

Beth sat with her pen poised, looking at Sarah as she gathered her thoughts.

'I'm in therapy,' she said at last. 'Largely because of what happened that week. You see, my mother died when I was very young.'

'I'm sorry,' Beth said.

'Thank you. As a child I struggled to accept that she was gone and used to imagine she was still with me – in spirit form at least. Sometimes I had nightmares, but over the years they grew less, until that week in that church. Not only did I have nightmares but I saw spirits while I was awake. One of them was my mother. I thought I was losing my mind and yes, we were all arguing a lot. Brandon and Megan were having problems too. When I described what had happened to my therapist she asked if we'd taken hallucinogenic drugs like LSD. Roshan and I hadn't, we don't do drugs, and as far as we know the others don't either. But if she's right and my hallucinations are caused by drugs, then someone slipped it into our food or drink. I'm still seeing things, and from what Megan's mother said, she is too.'

Beth nodded thoughtfully. 'Thank you for your honesty,

Sarah. If your food or drinks were spiked, who do you think could be responsible?'

'*If*,' Roshan emphasized. 'I wasn't affected, and I ate the same food.'

'So it was in the drinks!' Sarah said, frustrated, and possibly continuing a previous argument, Beth thought.

'Who was affected?' Beth asked as she wrote.

'Me, Megan and Brandon,' Sarah said.

'Austin wasn't?'

'No,' Sarah said. 'I phoned him after I'd spoken to Megan's mother. He wasn't at all helpful and said he'd got his own life to sort out.'

'That's an understatement,' Beth said, more to herself than Sarah and Roshan.

'Austin never talks about himself,' Roshan said. 'He gets you talking about your problems, then changes the subject if you ask about him. I don't like that; it's a way of gaining the advantage over people.'

'How is Brandon?' Beth asked. 'Have you heard from him?'

'No. Neither of us has,' Sarah said, talking more freely now. 'I left a message on his voicemail after I'd spoken to Megan, but he hasn't got back to me.'

'What does Brandon do for a living?' Beth asked.

'He's a civil engineer,' Sarah said. 'He's done well for himself, owns his own house. He used to be a nice guy.'

'Used to be?'

'I'm not sure any more.'

'Thank you,' Beth said. 'Anything else you think I should know?'

Sarah shook her head.

'One last question. Why did you choose that particular week to meet?'

'We're teachers so we can't take holidays during term time,'

Roshan said. 'We left it too late to book something for the summer, so half-term was the next option.'

'I see,' Beth said, and closed her notepad.

'Are you going to see Brandon?' Sarah asked as they all stood.

'I hope to.'

'I'm worried about him,' Sarah said. 'He lives by himself. Will you ask him to phone or text just to let us know he's OK?'

'Will do.'

Beth returned to her car, mulling over what she'd learned so far. One thing was for certain, Sarah and Megan hadn't played any part in the Chanel Woman robberies. They didn't have what it took and would have been more of a hindrance than a help. They were bad liars, and were clearly struggling with issues of their own. The robberies had been expertly timed and coolly executed – more Austin Chambers's style. Roshan? Beth thought as she got into the car. She wasn't sure. He'd been cooperative just now but had been a bit confrontational when she and Matt had arrived at the church to speak to Austin. So that left Brandon. He'd hardly said a word before, apart from asking why they needed to give their names and contact details. Could he be the missing piece of the jigsaw? Hopefully she'd find out soon and have something positive to tell DS Scrivener.

FORTY-SIX

It was a little before 6 p.m. when Beth arrived at Brandon's address, a detached house on a newish private housing estate. Sarah had said he'd done well for himself, and being able to afford this seemed to confirm it, unless he had money coming from another source. How much did civil engineers earn? Beth didn't know.

Before getting out of the car, she checked her phone. There was a message from DS Scrivener asking her what time he could expect her back in the office tomorrow. She'd reply once she'd seen Brandon. If Brandon was at home, she would be in the office at 8 a.m., if not and she had to return to interview him, it would be later in the morning.

Beth walked up the drive flanked by a lawn in need of a good cut, and at odds with the other gardens in the road. There was no car on the drive so it was either in the garage or Brandon wasn't home yet. The blinds were closed and a light was on in the hall, which gave some hope he was in. Beth pressed the doorbell and waited. No one answered. She pressed it again and was about to walk away when she heard a key turn in the lock. The door slowly opened and a man looked at her questioningly. Bearded, dressed in crumpled jeans and a shirt that looked as though they'd been slept in, he was thinner than when she'd last seen him. It took her a moment to realize it was Brandon.

'Brandon Edwards?' she said, showing her ID. 'Detective Constable Beth Mayes.'

He had dark circles under his eyes, and a distant look suggesting he didn't remember her.

'From Coleshaw CID,' she added. 'We met three weeks ago when you were on holiday with your friends.'

Brandon looked back, nonplussed.

'Can I come in and ask you a few questions about your holiday?'

He continued to stare at her.

'Are you all right, sir?'

'No, I haven't been sleeping,' he admitted. Turning, he went back into the house.

Beth followed, leaving the front door slightly open in case she needed to get out in a hurry. There was something seriously wrong here, and the place smelt stale, as if it had been shut up for weeks. She followed Brandon into the front room and saw the reason for the smell. There were takeaway containers of partially eaten food everywhere, some crusted over. A sleeping bag was on the sofa and a pile of dirty laundry on the floor. Her instinct was to open a window.

Brandon wandered around the room and then sat on the sofa, apparently exhausted. Beth remained standing, finger hovering near the panic button of her phone in case she needed emergency assistance. This wasn't the smartly dressed, confident young man she'd met before.

'Are you ill, sir?' she asked. 'Do you need medical help?'

'I don't know,' he muttered, bewildered, pushing his fingers through his matted hair.

'Do you live here alone?' Beth asked. A small draught of

welcome fresh air came from the open front door and into the living room.

'Yes. Apart from the wasps,' Brandon replied.

'You have wasps here?' Beth asked, concerned.

'Yes, and I'm allergic to wasp stings. I have to carry my EpiPen everywhere.' He took it from his trouser pocket to show her.

Beth looked around the room. 'I don't see any wasps in here,' she said.

'No, they're upstairs. There's a nest in my bedroom.'

'Really?'

'That's why I'm sleeping down here. I shut them in just in time before they swarmed.'

'Have you contacted a pest control service?' Beth asked. 'They'll remove them.'

'No point. They'd find me again.'

Beth looked at Brandon carefully. It was very unusual to have a wasp nest in a modern house like this. They were more likely to find their way under the eaves and into the loft space of an older house, and what he was saying seemed quite paranoid.

'How are you managing to go to work?' she asked, almost guessing the answer.

'I'm not. I've phoned in sick.'

'Have you seen a doctor?'

He shook his head.

'When did you start to feel like this?'

'While I was away, I think, but it's got worse since I've been back.'

'Brandon,' Beth said gently, going closer. 'Do you see things that might not be there?'

'Possibly. But the wasps are real.'

'Would you mind if I took a look upstairs?'

'If you want, but make sure you close my bedroom door.'

'I will.'

Very concerned for Brandon's well-being, Beth went into the hall. Before going upstairs, she closed the front door. He wasn't aggressive and she didn't want to make his paranoia worse. Was he suffering from a phobia as Megan and Sarah were? Beth went up the plush, grey-carpeted stairs where four doors led off a landing. Three were slightly open. The first, on her left, led into the bathroom, very stylish and tiled in light grey marble. She looked in the second room, a guest bedroom, spacious, tastefully furnished and with the bed made up ready for guests. She wondered why Brandon wasn't sleeping in there rather than downstairs. The third was a slightly smaller room that was being used as a study. One wall was lined with books and beneath the window was a large, double-pedestal, inlaid wooden desk with a leather swivel chair. This room smelt stale like the others and Beth guessed it hadn't been used for some time. She came out and approached the closed door – Brandon's bedroom – where he said the wasps' nest was. She opened it a few inches. No buzzing noise.

She pushed the door open wider and flicked on the light switch, half-expecting a swarm of wasps to rise into the air, preparing herself to quickly close the door again. But the room remained quiet. She gingerly went in. The room was stylish, bespoke, and furnished to the same high standard as the other rooms. It had the same stale smell and looked like the *Marie Celeste*, abandoned without warning. The duvet had been hastily thrown back, exposing a crumpled bottom sheet, and discarded paperwork that presumably Brandon had been reading in bed. A half-drunk glass of water and an iPad still plugged into the charger were on the bedside cabinet. But there was no sign of even a single wasp.

Beth raised the blinds slightly. No dead wasps on the window-sill where you would expect to find them. She looked up at the ceiling and then under the bed. She opened the bedside cabinets, and one of the doors to the built-in wardrobe. Nothing flew out. She began moving the hangers containing Brandon's clothes, good quality suits, shirts, and smart casual. His jumpers were neatly folded on the inbuilt shelf, and his shoes and trainers paired on the shoe racks in the bottom. She checked the rest of the wardrobe and drawers. Nothing, not so much as a single dead wasp, let alone a nest. There was nowhere else for the wasps to go in this room and she came out.

'Don't forget to close the door!' Brandon called from the floor below.

'I won't.' She returned downstairs.

'You'll be relieved to know I couldn't find any wasps,' she said, going into the front room.

'They'll be back later,' Brandon said, frightened.

Beth's heart went out to him. He clearly needed help. 'Brandon,' she said, going to him. 'You said you started to feel unwell while you were away.' He nodded. 'Did you and your friends take drugs?'

'No.'

'Do you ever use drugs? That's not the reason I'm here.'

'I smoked a bit of cannabis at uni, but that was all.'

'Nothing recently?'

'No.'

'I really think you need to see your doctor. Can I phone your practice for you?'

'If you want to,' he said despondently, as if he hadn't the energy to do it.

'Is the number in your phone?'

'Yes.' She picked it up from the coffee table and found the number under D for doctor and sent it to her phone.

'I'll phone the practice as soon as I leave here,' she said. 'Your friends are worried about you. I've just seen Megan, Sarah and Roshan. Would you like me to call one of them?'

'I need to think about that,' Brandon replied.

'Of course. What are you going to do now?' Beth asked.

'Watch television.' The standby light was on and the remote was within his reach on the sofa.

'I'll go now and call your doctor.'

'Don't forget to close the front door when you go so more wasps can't get in.'

'I won't,' Beth said, and left.

It was heartbreaking to see the shell of a person he'd become. She hadn't bothered to ask him any questions about Austin or Chanel Woman, as anything he said would be unreliable and not admissible in evidence. He was confused, irrational, and struggling to take care of himself. If it wasn't drugs, what on earth was it? Megan, Sarah, and now Brandon, all paranoid as a result of their phobias. And what, if anything, did it have to do with Austin Chambers and his wife? Beth had nothing to offer DS Scrivener and time was running out. If she went back empty-handed she'd be assigned to another case. Perhaps her boss was right after all and there was nothing on Austin and he was innocent of his wife's crimes as he maintained.

And yet . . .

FORTY-SEVEN

It was nearly 9.30 p.m. when Beth arrived home. She went straight to the shower and then put on fresh pyjamas. Still deep in thought, she took a portion of bolognaise sauce from the freezer and pinged it in the microwave as the spaghetti cooked in boiling water. As with other meals, she made them in batches for evenings like this when she arrived home late and hungry. She'd phoned Brandon's doctor from her car and he'd promised to send a community nurse to assess him. He was clearly worse than Megan and Sarah. Perhaps because he lived alone? Sarah had Roshan to keep her grounded and she was seeing a therapist. Megan had her daughter to look after and her mother for support.

Beth drained the spaghetti and, placing it in a bowl, poured on the heated sauce and added parmesan cheese. She set the bowl on a tray with a glass of water and carried it into the living room. She intended to work as she ate dinner. If she didn't come up with something tonight, she'd be back at her desk in the morning and there'd be no case against Austin Chambers. She hadn't messaged DS Scrivener yet.

Careful not to let her meal drip onto her laptop as she

ate, she googled for Austin's website. The home page was sparse: *Austin Chambers, therapist and counsellor* was the heading, and below a picture of the sun rising over the sea beneath which was the motto: *Every new day is a new beginning*.

She'd taken a quick look at Austin's website earlier in the investigation but now intended to read it all. His laptop hadn't yielded anything of interest and contained mainly client files, as he'd said, and articles on psychology, some of which he'd written and were on his website. He'd used his laptop for banking, but those accounts were clean with payments from clients and lectures he'd given going in and bills going out. Leslie's laptop by comparison had been incriminating and shown large sums being paid into various accounts (that she'd claimed to have no knowledge of) then disappearing into cryptocurrency which had become impossible to trace. Digital Forensics were still working on it, but cryptocurrency enabled money laundering and other criminal activity on a massive scale. It needed proper regulation, as it was hampering police work.

Beth took another mouthful of her dinner and clicked on the link to Austin's *About Me* page. This gave his name, mobile number, email address, and a brief description of his work. It referred to him as 'highly experienced', although there were no professional qualifications listed and no photo of him as one might expect to find on a biography page. Next was the *Services Offered* page. It said Austin successfully treated anxiety, stress, depression, eating disorders, phobias, and emotional difficulties. Beth clicked through to the next page, which listed organizations offering support and also further reading. On the following page Austin had set up a question-and-answer forum where members of the public posted questions about their mental health and Austin gave a therapeutic reply, approximately a paragraph in length. All his replies ended by saying he felt that the person would benefit from a more detailed and personalized response that could only be achieved through a one-to-one therapy session. There were no new postings since Leslie's arrest. Beth wondered if he was still seeing clients.

Beth finished her dinner, made herself a mug of tea, and continued with some of the articles he'd written. She learned a lot about therapy, but nothing relevant to their investigation. Having exhausted Austin's website, she began to follow links to other websites, many with forums. Some mentioned him by name. It was shocking what some people had been through, and many still suffered with post-traumatic stress. She read until her eyes ached, scanning the webpages, without knowing exactly what she was looking for. At 11.30 she made the decision she'd give herself another half an hour then admit defeat. No one could accuse her of not being thorough!

Five minutes later she was reading yet another discussion forum about phobias and treatments when she saw it. Her heart missed a beat. Someone calling themselves Jay, no photo, had posted: *Don't go near Austin Chambers. He messes with your head. My phobias became worse after I'd seen him, and I developed new triggers and delusions.*

There was no way of telling who Jay was and the thread had ended, so it wasn't possible to post further comments now. This forum was a long way from Austin's website and presumably he hadn't seen it, for surely he would have replied defending his reputation, as she'd seen other therapists do on these forums. Someone had 'liked' the post and someone else had posted, *Thanks for the warning.*

Of course Jay could be wrong and his condition might have deteriorated without Austin's intervention, but it was a damning indictment of the treatment he'd received. Beth reread the comment and then searched for any other comments about Austin, but nothing appeared. She looked back at an article she'd read earlier on phobia, triggers and delusions.

. . . a trigger in this context refers to something that affects the person emotionally often causing them deep distress, feelings of helplessness, loss of control . . . It affects the person's ability to remain in the present . . .

Beth followed links to articles on therapies that were thought to help phobias, including exposure therapy, hypno-therapy, behaviour therapy and coping strategies, some of which Austin offered. She pondered; read some more, and then went back to one of Austin's articles and stopped. Her pulse quickened. Surely not? Could it really be hiding in plain sight? She sat back and tried to think objectively about what she'd read. It was a hell of a long shot and somehow she'd have to prove it. If she was wrong, she'd be a laughing stock and also in trouble. But if she was right? Well, then Leslie, still being held on remand in prison, could be telling the truth.

FORTY-EIGHT

'Unconventional isn't the word, Beth! It's highly irregular,' DS Scrivener said, astounded. 'I've never heard of anything like it before. And yes, it is a long shot!'

'I appreciate it needs a leap of faith, sir, but if I'm right it could change the course of our investigation into the Chanel Woman robberies.'

'And if you're wrong it will end my chance of promotion. Is it even ethical to set up such an experiment?'

It was just the two of them, using an empty office to talk in private.

'We won't call it an experiment, sir. It's an interview to clarify a few points. Leslie and her solicitor shouldn't have any objection to that, and I'll keep it short.'

DS Scrivener paused in thought, then asked, 'When were you thinking of bringing her in? Her solicitor will need to be notified, and so will the prison.'

'Tomorrow, sir, if her solicitor is able to attend and the prison has an officer free to escort Leslie here.'

DS Scrivener thought some more, considering all Beth had said.

'Highly unusual,' he said again. 'But then I suppose it's

not so far from the element of surprise when a suspect is interviewed and we suddenly produce a new piece of incriminating evidence that they were unaware of.'

'Exactly, sir,' Beth said, and waited on tenterhooks for her boss's decision.

'All right,' he said at length. 'Go ahead and set it up for tomorrow. But once you've done that I want you to go with Matt and bring in Charlie Bates for questioning. He was only released from prison forty-eight hours ago and appears to have been involved in a fight last night.'

'Certainly, sir,' Beth said. Charlie Bates was a member of a notorious local family of hardened criminals. The police always went in pairs to their house.

'And Beth?'

'Yes, sir?'

'Don't let on to anyone in the office what you are planning to do. If it turns out you're wrong, we'll try to pass it off as the police showing consideration for those being held on remand.'

'Very good, sir.'

Beth returned to the main office with a mixture of elation and apprehension. A lot rested on this. Without a major incident inquiry in progress the office was relatively empty at 8.30 a.m. Matt was due in at 9 a.m. when they'd go straight out again to bring in Charlie Bates. Beth logged in to her computer and filled in the relevant prison request form to have Leslie Chambers escorted to Coleshaw police station at 10.30 a.m. the following morning. She then sent an email to Leslie's solicitor, Mr Newby, informing him of the interview. He was a duty solicitor, part of a large legal firm they used, so if he wasn't available, they'd presumably send someone else. Lastly, she filled in the necessary form to remove what she needed from the evidence room, marking it *Confidential*.

FORTY-NINE

Beth didn't sleep well that night and the following morning she was at her desk early again, checking she had everything she needed. She'd spent most of the night visualizing the interview with its various possible scenarios. Not only did she need to prove her theory, but it would have to stand up in court. One slip, one overlooked protocol, and it could be inadmissible as evidence, and Austin Chambers would walk free.

As she worked, Beth thought it was rather ironic that here she was trying to prove a suspect innocent when normally she would be gathering evidence to prove them guilty. But in this case one person's innocence was another's guilt. She concentrated on her computer monitor as Matt concentrated on his. At 10.25 her desk phone rang. 'DC Beth Mayes.'

'Leslie Chambers has arrived,' the duty officer said.

'Thank you. Please show her into Interview Room 2 and I'll be down. Is her solicitor here yet?'

'Not yet.'

Avoiding Matt's questioning glance, Beth picked up the file she had ready on her desk and crossed the office to DS Scrivener.

'Leslie Chambers has just arrived, sir,' she said quietly. 'I've asked her to be taken to Interview Room 2. We're waiting for her solicitor.'

DS Scrivener nodded and tuned his monitor to the CCTV in Interview Room 2. To begin with the room was empty, but as they watched, the door opened and Leslie was shown in.

'Take a seat, DC Beth Mayes will be here soon,' they heard the duty officer say. 'Is there anything you need?'

'No, thank you,' Leslie replied in a small voice, and sat at the table.

The door closed.

Beth and DS Scrivener continued to watch the monitor. With her shoulders hunched forward and lank hair falling over her damaged cheek, she looked a pitiful sight. Nervous and unsure, she seemed smaller than Beth remembered: insignificant, and a far cry from the confident, charismatic Chanel Woman who'd evaded police arrest and had kept the public entertained with her daring, well-planned robberies for over two years.

'I'd better go down,' Beth said. 'Wish me luck.' DS Scrivener would be watching the interview on the monitor.

Beth left the office and went down two flights of stairs to the evidence room, where she signed out the item she needed, tucking it into her folder. She returned up one flight of stairs to reception level.

'Has Mrs Chambers's solicitor arrived yet?' she asked the duty sergeant.

'Just now. I was going to buzz you.'

Beth went into reception, where she saw Mr Newby. 'Good morning. Thank you for coming at such short notice. Your client is already here so we can begin straight away.'

'I may need to speak to her alone first,' Mr Newby said, which he was entitled to do.

'Of course.'

Beth led the way through the security door at the back of reception, down the corridor and to Interview Room 2.

'Hello, Leslie,' her solicitor said as he went in. He sat on the chair beside her and took his laptop from his briefcase, while Beth stood to one side waiting for him to inform his client of her rights. 'The police have requested this interview. I understand it is to clarify some points. Shall we discuss this in private first?'

'No need,' Leslie replied dejectedly. 'I've told them all I know.'

'It's your decision. I can stop the interview at any time and request a break.'

'All right,' Leslie said in the same dispirited tone.

She looked wretched, and Beth felt sorry for her as she sat opposite, placing her folder on the table.

'Thank you for agreeing to see me,' Beth began, then went through the formalities. 'How are you, Leslie?'

She shrugged.

'Do you have everything you need? I understand you have access to your make-up?'

'Yes. What will happen when it runs out?'

'The prison service should be able to arrange for you to have more brought in. It comes under your health needs.'

'Thank you.'

'Leslie, I'd like to start by going over how you first met your husband, Austin Chambers. Could you tell me how you met?'

'I believe my client has already told you,' her solicitor said.

'Yes, but I'd like to be very clear on this point,' Beth said, and looked at Leslie.

'He was my therapist,' she said, her voice flat. 'Once I was better, we started seeing each other, going out.'

'How would you describe your relationship then?'

'Good. He was nice to me, looked after me, made sure I

had everything I needed. He was in charge, which I quite liked. He knew so much more than me.'

'You said in your statement he was controlling. When did that start?'

Leslie thought for a moment. 'Once we were married, I guess. He was still helping me and knew everything about me. He said it would be best if I gave up my job. He provided for everything. I suppose I should have been grateful that I didn't have to worry about money or anything, but I was bored and I didn't have any friends.'

'So there was a power imbalance from the start?'

'What do you mean?' Leslie asked, the frown lines in her forehead deepening.

'Therapist and client, like a doctor and patient, lecturer and student, a police officer and a suspect – where one person has power and control over the other. That's why some relationships are not permitted.'

'I was in awe of him right from the start,' Leslie admitted hopelessly.

Beth made a note as Mr Newby watched her curiously.

'How would you describe your marriage?' Beth asked.

'As I said, I had everything I needed.'

'Were you happy, fulfilled?'

'Sometimes. It's difficult to know. I mean, I'm damaged goods.'

'Did Austin continue to give you therapy after your initial treatment had finished?'

'Yes.'

'How often?'

'Every week; more if I needed it.'

'What sort of therapy did he use?' Beth asked as Mr Newby typed on his laptop.

'I'm not sure what you'd call it,' Leslie said after a moment. 'He used to make me feel very relaxed by talking to me in a low tone and counting down, then I'd drift off and when I woke I felt a bit better about myself.'

Beth nodded. 'You said in your statement that not only did Austin know of your crimes but he helped in their planning and to dispose of the money and jewellery you'd stolen.'

'Yes. I know you don't believe me but it's true,' Leslie replied.

'The problem is that so far we haven't been able to find any evidence to support what you're claiming. And there is no paper trail of the money in any of his accounts, only yours.'

'I told you before, I don't remember doing all that banking,' Leslie said, desperation in her voice, and looking close to tears. 'Austin took care of all our finances as he did everything else. I've no idea about money laundering.'

'I understand,' Beth said. 'I'd now like to show you what we are calling exhibit A.' She took the evidence bag from her folder and placed it squarely on the table in front of Leslie and her solicitor. 'For the benefit of the recording I am showing Leslie exhibit A, a perfume bottle.'

'Do you recognize it?' Beth asked Leslie.

'Yes, it's my perfume, the one I used when I committed the robberies, that made me Chanel Woman.'

'I have an identical one that I bought yesterday,' Beth continued. She took the new perfume bottle from her jacket pocket and placed it beside the evidence bag. 'Do you agree they are the same?'

'They look it,' Leslie said, peering closer. 'But I'd need to smell it to be sure.'

'That's why I bought it, for you to smell. I can't open the evidence bag so I would like you to smell the perfume from this bottle which is exactly the same.'

'I don't see how this is relevant . . .' Mr Newby began, but it was too late.

Beth had squirted a little of the perfume in Leslie's direction and the effect was instant and dramatic. Her eyes widened, her pupils dilated, as she drew herself upright and looked at them haughtily. She wasn't so much smiling but had assumed an expression of self-assured confidence – someone who was at ease with themselves and could conquer the world. Mr Newby was staring at her dumbfounded; her whole demeanour had changed. When she spoke her voice was firm and authoritative, completely at odds with the meek, timorous and hesitant Leslie. 'What are you staring at? Where's my mask?'

'Leslie?' Mr Newby asked anxiously, staring uncomprehendingly at his client.

'What is it?' she demanded.

'Are you all right? Do you need a break?'

'Don't be silly. Of course I'm all right. I'm in charge here. Do you have any more questions?' she asked Beth haughtily. Mr Newby looked at Beth nervously.

'Just a few,' Beth said.

'Hurry up, then,' Chanel Woman replied. 'Then I want a decent cup of coffee before I'm escorted back to that godawful prison.'

'Of course,' Beth said. 'For the sake of the recording, could you state your name, please.'

'You know who I am! Everyone does. I'm the infamous Chanel Woman.'

'Thank you. And when you are not Chanel Woman who are you?'

She had to think for a moment. 'Leslie Chambers maybe.'

'Can you describe Leslie?' Beth asked.

'From what I know she's a nobody. A wife who does what she's told.'

'And Chanel Woman? How would you describe her?'

Her face lit up. 'Superwoman. She is revered and respected,

someone who makes headline news and lives life on the edge.'

'Do you think Leslie Chambers would approve of Chanel Woman?'

'You must be joking! She would be appalled. She knows it's wrong to steal and frighten people, but . . .'

'But what?' Beth prompted.

'I don't know,' she faltered, unsure. Her shoulders had begun to hunch forward and her expression had changed. She looked insecure, dispirited, and out of her depth. Beth knew the effect was wearing off.

'Chanel Woman?' Beth asked, but she looked back, confused.

'Leslie?' she tried.

'Yes. Sorry, what were you saying?' she replied, coming to.

'Would you like that cup of coffee now?'

'How kind of you. Yes please, a coffee would be lovely.'

'Do you need a doctor?' Mr Newby asked his client.

'I don't think so, do I?' Leslie replied in the same self-effacing manner.

'What's the matter with her?' Mr Newby asked Beth.

'The perfume is a trigger,' Beth said, and glanced up at the CCTV camera where she knew DS Scrivener was watching. 'I believe it was planted by Austin Chambers during the therapy sessions he gave his wife when he hypnotized her. I'm not going to do your job for you, Mr Newby, but I think your case would be greatly helped if Leslie saw a psychologist who is a fully accredited hypnotist. Neither of us wants to see the wrong person go to prison.'

FIFTY

Leaving Leslie with her solicitor, Beth returned to the main office where DS Scrivener was waiting for her. He showed her into a side office where they could talk in private before he spoke. The look of astonishment on his face matched that of Leslie's solicitor.

'What exactly happened in there?' he asked, drawing up two chairs for them to sit down.

'It was pretty dramatic, wasn't it, sir?' Beth said, unable to hide her smile any longer. 'I'll tell you what I know. Leslie responded to a "trigger" which I believe was placed by Austin when he hypnotized her. Hypnotherapy is an acceptable treatment used by many psychologists as part of therapy, but Austin Chambers took it to a whole new level for his own ends. When someone is hypnotized they go into a deep trance-like state where they are very open to suggestion. Put to good use, this allows negative behaviour to be corrected. But Austin used it to plant "triggers" in Leslie so that she would act in a particular way when the time was right. The perfume was one trigger. There may have been others. Have you ever seen those stage shows, sir, that use hypnotism? There are some recordings on YouTube.'

278

'I've heard of them,' DS Scrivener replied.

'In those shows the hypnotist asks volunteers to go on stage where he hypnotizes them and plants a trigger word or action like snapping their fingers. When he invokes the trigger the person behaves in a particular way, often comically, acting like a child or animal. These stage shows are frowned upon by professional hypnotists but they prove the point that it is possible to dramatically change a person's behaviour and have control over them through hypnosis.'

DS Scrivener nodded. 'I'm with you.'

'Some people are more susceptible to being hypnotized than others. It would seem that Leslie was a good subject, but then Austin had been working on her for years and gave her at least one session a week.'

'So let me get this right,' DS Scrivener said. 'The smell of the perfume triggered Leslie to behave as Chanel Woman?'

'Yes, sir. Behaviour that Austin had complete control over.'

'And Leslie Chambers didn't know what she was doing when she was Chanel Woman?'

'Very likely not. The way hypnotherapy is normally used in therapy, it wouldn't be possible to make someone act against their will and do something they know to be wrong, like mugging or murdering someone. But by repeatedly implanting the same suggestion as Austin appears to have done, he could have overridden Leslie's conscience and literally brainwashed her.'

'If we take this to its logical conclusion then Austin Chambers is responsible for the crimes of Chanel Woman, not Leslie.'

'Yes, sir.'

'Is there any case law on this – where hypnotism was used as a defence?' DS Scrivener asked.

'There is. I researched online. There are a few here and in the US. I didn't have time to read all the case notes.'

'It doesn't matter. That's for Leslie's defence team to research,' DS Scrivener said.

'There's also a section on the Crown Prosecution's website about confessions and witness statements obtained under hypnosis,' Beth said. 'However, not about when it is used as a defence.'

'We'll need to refer this case back to the Crown Prosecution Service,' DS Scrivener ruminated. 'But, Beth, there seems to be a big flaw in your argument. The effect the perfume had on Leslie wore off after a few minutes. That wouldn't have been enough time for her to have committed the robberies.'

'The perfume I squirted just now was airborne. It wore off quickly as the particles dispersed. But perfumes are designed for the skin, where they can last for hours. Some reviews I've read of this brand claim the smell can last for six to eight hours. Austin didn't take any chances though, and he had Leslie programmed to top it up regularly. She always applied it just before she left the house and then took a bottle with her in the car to reapply before the actual robbery. That's why the smell was so strong at the scene of her crimes.'

'I'm impressed, Beth. But how did you ever consider this as a possibility?'

'Austin's friends, sir. You gave me permission to visit them all – Megan Hill, Brandon Edwards, Sarah and Roshan Dara. I was hoping they'd throw some light on Austin's character having known him since childhood. I also wondered if they'd been involved in the robberies as they'd provided his last alibi. But what I found took me completely by surprise and got me thinking. They're in a right state, paranoid, hallucinating, apart from Roshan. Megan has a phobia about spiders which has got a lot worse since returning from their reunion. Sarah has an irrational fear of ghosts that's got so bad she's started seeing a therapist, who suggested that she and her friends might have taken a hallucinogenic drug. Sarah is adamant they didn't. Brandon was worst of all. His paranoia about wasps has taken over his life to the extent he's not functioning. I phoned his doctor. I'll put it all in my report sir, but Roshan is the only one not affected and that's because he had no pre-existing phobias and therefore didn't have any need of therapy sessions with Austin.'

'You're saying Austin hypnotized them too?' DS Scrivener asked, astounded.

'I believe so, sir. While driving home from seeing them I remembered how Leslie had described Austin's controlling behaviour. She said it felt as if something came over her, like she was in a trance, and became another person. Of course she didn't know why. Once I got home I scoured Austin's website and found articles he'd written and links to other information about hypnotism and mind control. He's obsessed with it. The clues to what he'd done were there all along. We just didn't know what we were looking for. I suppose he arrogantly assumed no one would make the connection.'

'But you did. Well done, Beth,' DS Scrivener said admiringly.

'Thank you, sir. It was interviewing his friends that set me on the right path. They hadn't seen Austin since they left school and then he suddenly popped up on social media and reminded them of a get-together they'd promised themselves ten years before. None of the others had remembered, so they were touched Austin had. He arranged everything. It was his social experiment – to see how far he could control other people's behaviour. He's written articles on the subject. Though he'd told the others Leslie would be joining them, that had never been his plan. She says she was never asked to go but found herself talking to them on the phone. She had no idea why. Of course Austin couldn't let the others see her because of the scar on her cheek. One of them might have made the connection. He phoned her and doubtless said a trigger word so she played her part and told them she'd been ill.'

'Ingenious.'

'It was, sir. Austin had great success with Leslie and possibly some of his other clients – that's something we'll need to look into. He's a good listener and found the Achilles heel of each of his friends, then tapped into it. I think he intended to continue his experiment after they went home. He was already talking about another reunion, but he had to back off after Leslie got arrested. I know you won't want any of this released to the press while the investigation is ongoing, but I think I have a duty to warn Megan, Brandon and Sarah what might have happened to them so they can get help.'

'Yes, I agree. Do it subtly without giving too much away.'

'Yes, sir.'

'And Beth?'

'Sir?'

'The bottle of perfume you bought. Did you claim it on expenses?'

'No, sir.'

'Do so, and keep it as a thank you present. You've done well.'

FIFTY-ONE

'If what the police officer told you is accurate, then under hypnosis we should be able to find some trace of what Austin Chambers has been doing,' Katherine Fellows, Sarah's therapist, said. Sarah had made an extra appointment to see her after Beth Mayes had phoned. 'Now make yourself comfortable, Sarah.'

Sarah moved her legs and shoulders slightly, trying to feel more at ease on the couch. 'Do I have to close my eyes?'

'Only if it helps you to relax.' It was their first hypnotherapy session. 'Once I start talking to you, you'll find your eyes will close. Don't force it. Let it happen gradually.'

Sarah decided to keep her eyes open. She was on her back looking up at the ceiling. It was painted white and the plasterwork had a swirling pattern that reminded her of stirring jam into rice pudding – something she'd loved as a child and still did.

Katherine sat on a chair beside the couch, her voice low, even and soporific.

'I want you to take a deep breath in . . . then slowly let the air out. Nice and slowly . . . deep breaths . . . in . . . and . . . out. In . . . and out . . . in and out. Good. Now, keeping your breathing nice and easy, I want you to think about your feet.'

Sarah thought of her feet.

'Flex your toes then relax them . . . and again . . . all the while taking deep breaths. Feel how relaxed your feet are now. That feeling is going to slowly travel up your body. First your legs, flex and relax . . . then your thighs and lower body. Now your chest. You are feeling more and more relaxed with each breath.'

Sarah did.

'Your neck is relaxed too. Good. That feeling of being relaxed has spread throughout your body, so that your eyes are now growing very heavy, so heavy you can no longer keep them open.'

Sarah allowed her eyes to close and the ceiling disappeared from view. She did indeed feel relaxed just as Katherine was telling her.

'You are now so relaxed that you can't even raise your right arm. Try to raise your arm, Sarah.'

She tried to move her arm but couldn't. Her whole body felt pleasantly heavy as if she might never have to move again.

'Sarah, as I said at the beginning, although you are in a hypnotic trance you will still be in control at all times. I'm recording this session as I do all your others so there is nothing for you to worry about. All right?'

'Yes,' Sarah said, her voice far off and dream-like.

'I want you to think back to when you were a child. We've talked about your childhood in therapy. Now I want you to picture a time when you were happy. The happiest you've ever been.'

After a few moments Sarah began to smile, she couldn't help herself; not only could she visualize the happy scene but she could feel it too. It was so real, the colours, sounds, smells, the fresh air, she felt as if she was there again in the school playground, surrounded by her friends.

'Tell me what you're seeing,' Katherine prompted in her soft, encouraging tone.

'I'm at school. It's Friday afternoon playtime,' Sarah began, her voice higher than usual, childlike. 'It's my birthday party the next day and all my friends are coming. We're talking about the games we are going to play. I am so happy.'

'That's a lovely memory, Sarah. How old will you be?'

'Six.' She smiled again.

'Do you remember the party the next day, Sarah?'

'Yes. We had jelly and ice-cream, and Mummy and Daddy organized games, and we won prizes. I had a princess cake with pink icing. It was my best birthday ever.' Then her voice faltered and her smile faded.

'Sarah, you're looking unhappy. Can you tell me why?' Katherine asked gently.

'It was my last party ever. I didn't have another one. Mummy was dead by my next birthday so no more parties and fun.' A tear slipped from her eye and ran down her cheek.

'I'm sorry,' Katherine said gently. 'That was a very sad time for you. It was brave of you to tell me.' She paused, allowing Sarah time to recover. 'Sarah we've talked about your mother's death in our therapy sessions, and how that made you feel. Now you're in a very relaxed state I'd like to go back to that time again. Is that all right with you, Sarah? Remember you can stop any time you wish.'

'Yes.'

'You told me that shortly after your mother's death, when you were visiting her grave with your father for the first time, you thought you saw her spirit.'

'I did.'

'You told your father and he was angry with you.'

'Because it made him upset. I didn't tell him again when she came to me. Sometimes it was nice to see her, but at night it frightened me. Sometimes she didn't look like Mummy.'

'I understand. We've spoken about why this might have been. You were only young and found the concept of death frightening. Because your father couldn't talk to you about what had happened to your mother, your imagination conjured up all sorts of horrors. The nightmares faded with time as you began to accept your mother's death.'

'Yes, and after meeting Roshan I hardly had any nightmares, until . . .' Sarah stopped.

'What is it Sarah? What are you seeing now?'

'Is Austin here?' she asked anxiously, her eyes briefly flickering open.

'No, it's just me, Sarah – Katherine Fellows – your therapist.'

'But I can hear Austin's voice,' Sarah said.

'You're safe. I'm here. We can stop this session when you want.' Katherine paused, waiting for her client to recover.

'What is Austin saying? Can you hear him?'

'He's telling me to confront my fears and meet them head on,' Sarah replied, her brow creasing.

'Where are you now, Sarah? Do you know?'

'In the living room of the church where we stayed.'

'Is anyone else there?'

'No, just Austin and me. When one of us is having a session with Austin the others stay in another room. He's trying to teach me how to deal with my fear of ghosts. But it's not working. It's getting worse,' Sarah said, now clearly agitated.

'Take a few deep breaths . . . in . . . and . . . out. Good. Can you still hear Austin?'

'Yes, it's Monday. I'm trying to meet the targets he's set but I'm failing. I'm walking in the graveyard, trying to confront my fears like he said, but the memorial stone has changed again.'

'What memorial stone, Sarah?'

'It's in the graveyard by the church where we are staying. A married couple are buried here, Michael and Constance Wilson, but I see the name of my mother so I think it's her grave. I can't help it. It just happens. The words change.'

'You said "again", Sarah. Has it happened before?'

'Yes. But this time I can hear my mother's voice behind me. I turn and Austin is there. He's asking me if I've seen something, but I don't tell him. I feel foolish and I don't want him to know I'm not getting better.'

'I see. Were there any other times when Austin was there when you experienced something unexplained, like this?'

Sarah's breathing was becoming irregular again and her eyelids were fluttering.

'It's OK if you can't remember, Sarah. We can come back to this another time.'

'No! I do remember,' she gasped. 'It was the next day. My friends and I weren't getting on and I went for a walk. I walked to the top of the hill that overlooks the church. I can see it now. I'm sitting there gazing at the church and scenery. Austin comes out of the church. He's talking on his phone. He sees me and my mobile rings. It's him phoning to make sure I'm OK. I want to be left alone. The call ends and then I get scared. The ghost from my childhood is behind me and I run all the way back. Roshan is there waiting for me. He's very worried; he'd been trying to call me, but I haven't heard his calls, only Austin's. I tell him what happened. I feel like I'm losing my mind. I promise him I'll get help when we return.' Sarah stopped. She couldn't go on. Her breathing was fast and shallow. She was out of breath.

'It's all right, Sarah,' Katherine said soothingly. 'In a moment I'm going to end this session by counting backwards from five to one, and you will wake feeling calm and reassured. Austin has no control over you or how you feel. Five. Four. Three. Two. One. Open your eyes, Sarah.'

Sarah opened her eyes and looked at her therapist.

'How do you feel?' Katherine asked.

'OK, I think. I can remember what we said.'

'That's how it should be after hypnotherapy.'

Sarah pushed herself up so she was sitting on the couch.

'Take your time,' Katherine said.

'I'm sure Austin was there telling me things, planting thoughts I didn't want.'

'Yes. I'm going to listen to the tape and then we'll discuss it at our next session. If you think of anything else, write it down. But from what you've said so far that police officer was right. Austin has been "messing with your mind" as she put it. I believe when he gave you those sessions under hypnosis he planted triggers – words and actions that actually made your condition worse. For example, he was there when you saw the words change on the grave, and then he phoned you and you believed the ghost from your childhood was behind you. I suspect something similar happened to your friends Megan and Brandon. We'll do more in future sessions, but I hope this has been of some help.'

Sarah nodded. 'But that first night at the church when I was found wandering in the graveyard – I hadn't had a session with Austin then.'

'It might not have been obvious what he was doing. It's possible for an experienced hypnotist to move into someone's personal space, maintain eye contact, and talk in a monotone and plant suggestions. Or it could be that you were simply sleepwalking. It was your first night in that converted church where you didn't feel at all comfortable. It would have spooked me. But don't worry, we'll get to the bottom of it, Sarah.'

'Thank you so much. I do feel happier already.'

'Good. I'm sure I don't need to tell you that what Austin did was very wrong. I will report him when I have enough evidence. It gives hypnotherapy a bad name. Have your friends been told?'

'Yes, the police officer, Beth, contacted us all.'

'And it's important none of you talk to Austin until you have all been treated and are well again.'

'I don't want to talk to him ever again, but we can talk to each other, can't we? Megan, Brandon, Roshan and me?'

'Yes. In fact, I would recommend that you do. It can be cathartic talking about a shared experience. I'll see you again the same time next week?'

'Yes please.'

'And in the meantime, Sarah, if you need me, call.'

'I will. Thanks again, I do feel better, like I'm on the road to recovery. I can't wait to tell Megan and Brandon. It will give them hope.'

FIFTY-TWO

As soon as Sarah left her therapist's office, she phoned Roshan and told him of her session.

'So Beth was right. Austin did plant thoughts in your subconscious so he could manipulate your behaviour.'

'Yes, and very likely Megan's and Brandon's too. But Katherine says she should be able to undo the harm he's done. I'm so relieved. I'll phone Megan now, and tell you all about it when I get home. I love you, Roshan, very much.'

'I love you too. You sound more like your old self.'

'I feel it.'

Sarah got into her car but didn't start the engine. She needed to call Megan straight away. This was too important to wait. They'd texted since Beth had phoned them all, and Megan knew Sarah was seeing a therapist. Megan answered and Sarah now told her what Katherine had discovered, finishing with, 'You might find it helpful to see a therapist too.'

'Yes. When I told Mum what Beth had said, she suggested I see someone and offered to pay. I might do it, now that we know it's true. I can't believe Austin did that to us. It's so cruel.'

'It is.'

'Brandon phoned me, I'll call him.'

'Please do. How is he? He hasn't phoned me or Roshan.'

'He's trying to stay strong, but even after Beth told us what happened, he still feels embarrassed by the way he behaved. This should help him.'

'There's no need for him to feel embarrassed,' Sarah said. 'None of us were responsible for our actions. As well as making our phobias worse, Austin changed our behaviour. Katherine said that in the past behavioural scientists carried out experiments to see how far they could manipulate people to act against their conscience, but it's considered unethical now.'

'I'll tell Brandon. I'm sure all this will help. He's planning on working from home again and is hoping to return to the office before too long. He's also asked to see me in a few weeks – maybe over Christmas or New Year.'

'That's lovely, Megan. I'm sure you guys will get on. Give him my and Roshan's love. And when we all feel up to it in a few months it would be great if the four of us could get together. But not in a converted church!' she added, with a small laugh.

'Absolutely. Take care and give Roshan my best wishes.'

'I will.'

As it turned out, it was eight months before the four friends met again. It was the last weekend in July when the schools had broken up for the summer holidays. Sarah arranged it and booked three nights at a city centre hotel in the heart of Cambridge, with views of the university and the River Cam, and not a graveyard in sight. Not that it would have mattered to her, for after six months of therapy she'd come to terms with her mother's death and had laid to rest her ghost and other unhappiness from her past.

The reunion was a great success. During the day they strolled through the cobbled streets, punted down the River Cam, and in the evening over dinner talked tirelessly about what had happened, purging it from their systems. Megan's mother was looking after Ella, and Megan video-called her regularly, when they all waved and Brandon and Roshan pulled silly faces to make Ella laugh.

Megan had had ten sessions with a therapist near where she lived, who she felt had helped her come to terms with what had happened at the church. The therapist had also given her techniques for managing her arachnophobia. She'd seen a consultant who'd tested her for Alzheimer's and confirmed there was no sign of the illness, and that very likely the changes in her personality were due to Austin's manipulation, although it would be impossible to prove.

'I haven't felt this good for a long while,' Megan confided to the group over dinner one evening. 'I'm happy, comfortable with myself, and I'm teaching Ella to be less fearful of spiders. We can't pick them up yet, but at least we can shoo them out instead of phoning my mother for help.'

'You're both doing well,' Brandon said admiringly. He'd been seeing them regularly since their New Year together.

Brandon had decided not to have therapy, feeling that now he knew what had caused his bizarre and terrifying behaviour, he could deal with it himself.

'Obviously I'm still very wary of wasps and carry my EpiPen everywhere,' he said. 'But that's a sensible precaution, not paranoia. Megan knows which pocket I keep it in, just in case.' He smiled at her and took her hand. They were very touchy-feely and obviously in love.

'What really gets to me, though,' Brandon said after a moment, 'is that Austin's got away with it.'

Megan, Sarah and Roshan agreed.

The case had gone to court the previous month. Both Leslie and Austin were charged with the robberies, and both pleaded not guilty, blaming each other. The friends hadn't attended court, although Katherine had sent in a report on her findings. The case had lasted two weeks and had been widely reported in the press as it featured Chanel Woman and her defence was unusual: that she'd had no control over her actions as Austin had manipulated her while under hypnosis. Two psychologists gave conflicting reports on how far this was possible. The jury was unable to reach a verdict, so the judge had to discharge them, neither acquitting nor convicting the defendants. He explained to the court that the Crown Prosecution Service would now decide whether there was enough evidence for a retrial with a new jury, and until then Leslie and Austin were free.

Subsequently, both had disappeared.

'Beth phoned me last week and asked if I'd heard from either of them,' Sarah said. 'I told her I hadn't and would let her know if they tried to get in touch.'

'She phoned me too,' Megan said. 'You know he's deleted his website, the WhatsApp group he set up and all his social media accounts.'

'Yes,' Brandon said. 'I think he set those up purely to lure us in and find out as much as he could about us. I wouldn't mind seeing him again. I'd give him what for.'

'No, keep right away from him,' Sarah warned. 'He's dangerous. If he does phone, hang up and tell Beth. You don't know what he might be doing with your mind.'

'He won't get in contact,' Roshan said. 'He's probably in another country by now, living off the money he stole. They haven't recovered any of it, just some jewellery.'

'Beth was so disappointed the jury didn't convict him,' Sarah said. 'All that work and it's come to nothing. I have the feeling she'll keep looking for Austin, and try to find fresh evidence against him, even if the Crown Prosecution Service decide not to pursue it.'

'I hope so,' Brandon agreed. 'Austin needs to be punished for what he did to us.'

'And what he did to Leslie,' Megan said. 'I feel sorry for her. She suffered that horrific injury, and then when she was at her most vulnerable Austin preyed on her – pretending to help her in therapy while using her for his own evil ends. Little wonder she's disappeared and gone into hiding. She'll probably never be able to face the world again.'

'True,' Sarah said. 'At least one good thing came out of all of this, though – we're all in touch again.'

'Yes, and Megan and I have found each other,' Brandon added, and lovingly kissed her cheek.

FIFTY-THREE

The fiery crimson sun was setting over the perfectly calm azure sea, causing its surface to shimmer and sparkle like crystal. The soft white sand stretched leisurely to the water's edge, only a short walk away. The air was still, the temperature now gradually dropping after the heat of the day. It was truly paradise on this remote Caribbean island, Austin thought.

He reached for his glass of rum and coconut juice, took a leisurely sip, and without looking returned the glass to the table at his side. He opened his laptop and glanced up again at the view. From where he was sitting at the back of the beach bungalow, he had an uninterrupted view to the sea. Palm trees and other foliage either side of the property ensured privacy, but those living here respected privacy anyway. That was one of the reasons he'd chosen this island. As well as it being idyllic and outside the jurisdiction of the UK police, no one asked questions about why you'd left your homeland or how you'd made your money.

It didn't come cheap though, Austin acknowledged. In the four months he'd been here he'd got through a lot of money and now needed to access more. He'd closed his 'therapy' business straight after the court case, as continuing might have been a step too far. He'd seen the look on DC Beth Mayes's face when the jury had been unable to reach a verdict, and he'd walked free. He doubted she'd give up that easily. So best to lie low for a while, since he had plenty of money in the accounts he'd had Leslie unwittingly set up. Of course he knew the details; he'd committed them to memory. He'd always had a very good memory for people, places, and numbers.

Austin took another sip of his drink and, concentrating on his laptop, launched the websites for the bank accounts he needed. Another advantage of living here was that their money laundering laws were very relaxed – non-existent, some would say. As long as residents were spending money on the island and thereby helping their economy they didn't ask any questions. They had their own bank and residents were expected to use it. The manager, Mr Garcia, was a large man who was used to dealing with rich clients who liked their privacy. He offered an additional service for a not so modest fee whereby he let residents know if anyone was asking questions about them. It wasn't an option; it was part of the deal that allowed him to live here and kept him safe. Like the 'salary' he paid to Marsha, the young woman who took care of his needs. A salary that was substantial enough to help her extended family too. It all added up, and everyone here was friendly as long as you toed the line. But that was the price you paid for living in paradise rather than a UK prison.

Austin began inputting the login details for one of the cryptocurrency bank accounts. He was going to transfer money from that bank into the local bank where the balance was low. Leslie had told the truth in court when she'd said she'd no idea how cryptocurrency or money laundering worked, because he'd done it through her without her knowing, just as he'd made her steal the money in the first place. It was disappointing the jury hadn't convicted her, but more importantly they hadn't convicted him! If Beth Mayes did uncover enough for a retrial they would arrest Leslie, but not him. As long as he remained on the island and kept Garcia happy, he was safe. There was no extradition agreement between here and the UK, just the bank manager to contend with.

Too much rum, Austin thought as the error message appeared on screen. He must have made a mistake inputting the password, because the message said the login details he'd entered were incorrect. Not like him to make such a mistake. He sat more upright in his chair and concentrated. Glancing between the keyboard and the screen he carefully re-entered the login details, a digit at a time, and pressed enter. The same error message appeared.

What? His brain must have gone to seed. Too much sun, rum and sex. He needed to concentrate harder. He ran through the password for this account in his head, making sure he had it right, and tried again. The same result. Perhaps he was confusing the login details for this account with another – he had six in all. He couldn't think of another explanation.

He launched the website for his second cryptocurrency bank account and entered the same login details, carefully tapping each key. What the hell! Another error message telling him the password was incorrect. So he was right the first time and this must be the password for the previous account, so why hadn't it been recognized? He heard Marsha come out of the bungalow behind him, and then felt her hands on his shoulders.

'Are you ready for a massage?' she asked in a seductive voice.

'Not now!' he snapped. 'I'm busy.'

'Oh, someone is in a bad mood,' she said lightly, and returned indoors.

Austin stared at his laptop screen. The password must be right for the first account. But before he entered it again, he'd clear out the cookies and cache. Sometimes cached information confused websites, making it difficult to log in, especially if you made a mistake on the first attempt. That must be it.

He took a large sip of his drink and tapped the icon for *control panel*, and selected *privacy and safety*. He clicked on *tools* where a drop-down menu appeared and he was able to delete all the cookies, browsing history and website data. That should do it. He returned to the main menu and loaded the page for the first bank account again and inputted the login details. A few seconds as the website whirred trying to recognize his details now all the cookies had gone, but then the same error message appeared: *The password you entered didn't match our records*. What the fuck! The next message said they were going to send a *one-time verification code* to his phone. But he didn't have that phone; not the one he'd used for setting up this account two years ago. He'd thrown it in the river because the police had the number and if he turned it on he could be traced.

Feeling uncomfortably hot and clammy, he drained the last of his drink. He clicked on the option *don't have access to phone* and that told him he could have the verification code sent to another *trusted* phone number, but in order to do that – for his own protection – it said he needed to verify his identity first by answering the following questions. He began: full name, date of birth, mother's maiden name, then the answer to the questions he'd chosen when he'd had Leslie set up the accounts: town of birth, favourite book, pet's name and so on. Not a problem, but as he finished and submitted the form, another message told him the verification check could take up to twenty-four hours. Not the end of the world. In the meantime, he'd have to take money from one of the five other accounts. He launched the homepage for the second account again and entered the login details for this, which he now knew must be correct. An error message appeared – *wrong password*.

What the hell! He tried again, hitting the keys with far more force than was necessary. The result was the same – *wrong password*. Breaking out in a cold sweat, he launched the website for the third account. His mouth was dry and his glass was empty.

'Marsha! Get me another drink!' he shouted.

'Please,' she called from inside, 'don't be rude or I'll tell papa.'

Austin ignored the threat and concentrated on his laptop. He couldn't afford to get locked out of another account. He needed to transfer money tonight. Garcia's protection fee for next month was due and he didn't like to be kept waiting.

He waited for Marsha to place the fresh drink beside him before he entered the details.

'Thank you,' she said, when he didn't. 'I'm going for a walk.'

He didn't answer. He was staring in disbelief at the screen. He'd typed in the login details for the third crypto account and it had failed. *Incorrect password*, the error message said, just like the others. But it wasn't. It couldn't possibly be. This was too much of a coincidence. What the hell was going on? Only he knew the logins to these accounts. Hardly daring to breathe, he tried logging in to the fourth, fifth and the sixth account, all with the same results. Password not recognized. He felt a wave of panic. All the money from the burglaries was in these accounts, and only he knew about them. He'd put Leslie into a deep hypnotic trance when setting them up and managing the accounts on her laptop. She'd just followed his instructions; when he'd brought her out of the trance, she had no recollection of what she'd done. Was there a global problem on the internet, he wondered. An outage? A massive cyber-attack or hack? He googled the news, but no such attack had been reported, not on the scale that would be needed to affect all these accounts.

Austin felt his heart hammering in his chest as he sat there trying to make sense of what was happening. The sun continued to drop. It set quickly near the equator, and in a few more minutes it would be dark. His phone rang, making him start. He picked it up. Garcia's name showed on the display. The last thing he needed. He was tempted not to answer, but that would only postpone the inevitable, and antagonize him. Garcia wasn't a man who took kindly to being ignored, or getting his money late.

'Good evening,' Austin said, trying to keep his voice steady.

'How are you, Mr Chambers?' Garcia asked with exaggerated politeness. 'My good friend and business associate.'

'Fine, and you?' Austin replied, aware it was unlikely to just be a sociable call.

'I'm very well, thank you. You are still enjoying my beautiful island?'

'Yes.'

'That's what I like to hear. This is a courtesy call, Mr Chambers, just to remind you my fee to keep you safe and out of trouble is due by midnight.'

'Yes, I know.'

'Excellent. I was a little concerned because at present your account doesn't have the funds to cover it. That's not like you.'

'It will,' Austin said.

'As I thought. This was an oversight on your part and you will correct the matter now.'

'Yes.'

'Good. Have a pleasant evening, Mr Chambers.'

Fuck you! Austin thought as the call ended. He could feel sweat running down his neck. Since fleeing the UK he'd come to realize you were at the mercy of others if you didn't want to get caught. Until he could access the millions of pounds in his crypto accounts, he'd have to use the last of his savings in his British bank account to pay Garcia. He was reluctant to do this as it ran the risk of the activity on his bank account coming to the attention of the CID. But there was no alternative. If he didn't make Garcia's payment he could end up with a beating or worse.

FIFTY-FOUR

'I think you will be very pleased, Ms Osmond. The final stage in your transformation is complete. You have the face you wanted.'

The surgeon, Mr da Silva, stood back from the couch as the nurse removed the last of the bandages.

Leslie gasped with delight as she looked in the mirror the surgeon held. After six months of cosmetic surgery, she had been transformed. Not only had the scar gone, but now the bruising and swelling from the previous operations had faded and she could truly appreciate her new self. Her nose was more defined, her eyes wider, her jawline softened, and her cheeks enhanced. With her new hairstyle and colouring she was unrecognizable and ready to face the world in her new life as Leila Osmond. It was the name she'd chosen when she'd bought the fake documents online: birth certificate, passport, national insurance number and so forth. Money could buy you anything, she'd discovered, even a new face.

'You're a genius,' she told her surgeon, delighted. 'Thank you so much.'

Mr da Silva smiled, pleased. He knew he did an excellent

302

job, that's why his waiting list was long – but it was still good to hear. 'You are very welcome. What are your plans now?' he asked. 'Will you stay in Brazil?'

'I'm not sure yet,' Leslie replied truthfully. 'I was thinking about travelling to see the world.'

'I wish you all the best. Send me some postcards and remember to keep your face out of the sun and use the sunscreen I've prescribed. I don't want my good work being undone by the sun's rays.'

'I'll remember,' she said, and eased herself off the couch.

Coming to South America for the surgery had been her first trip abroad, and it had filled her with a sense of dread and exhilaration in equal parts. Six months in a hotel had loomed while her face was operated on, healed, operated on again, skin grafted, fat injected and whatever else Mr da Silva felt was necessary. But it had passed, and now here she was at the end of her treatment. She felt sadness and some trepidation at the prospect of leaving. Mr da Silva and his team had become part of her life as they'd nurtured and cared for her through all the procedures.

'My car is waiting outside to take you back to your hotel,' Mr da Silva said, kissing her hand. 'But please let me know if I can be of any further help.'

'Thank you.'

Leslie took the envelope bulging with cash from her handbag and handed it to the surgeon. It was the final instalment for his services, payable at the end of the treatment. All payments to him had to be in cash, money Leslie had had the foresight to put aside from each robbery instead of paying it all into the online accounts as Austin had told her to.

Mr da Silva was too much the gentleman to count the wad of notes in front of her and simply nodded. With a final goodbye the nurse went with her to reception.

303

'Take care. Enjoy your new life,' she said, hugging her as they parted.

'I will, thank you for everything. You've all been so kind.'

They cheek-kissed and then Leslie, or rather Leila Osmond, stepped from the hospital for the last time and into the heat of the afternoon. She quickly crossed the pavement to where the car was waiting with the driver holding open the rear door.

'Thank you, Carlos,' she said, getting in. She was on first-name terms with all of Mr da Silva's staff; they'd made her feel like part of an extended family. 'So this will be my last trip,' she said nostalgically as the car pulled away.

'I will miss you, madam,' Carlos replied.

Leila gazed out of the side window at the passing scenery. How many times had she made this journey between the hospital and the five-star boutique hotel where Mr da Silva's patients stayed during their recovery? She'd lost count, eighteen or more. But this would be her last. No patient had ever stayed as long as she had, but then no one before had had so much surgery in such a short space of time.

'My husband left me and I needed a new life,' was what she told them.

The car pulled on to the drive of the hotel and stopped close to the main entrance. She waited for Carlos to open her door before getting out.

'Goodbye, and thanks for everything,' she said, and gave him a tip that was close to a week's salary.

His eyes glistened as he thanked her, and, saying goodbye, he returned slightly embarrassed to his car. He'd talked about his family, shown her pictures of his five children – smiling despite their hand-to-mouth existence. She knew the difference her money would make, and was pleased she'd been able to help.

Inside the hotel air con hit her as it always did after the

heat outside. Francisca was on the reception desk, working at a computer, and glanced up. 'Good afternoon, Ms Osmond.'

'Good afternoon.'

'You are looking good, ma'am.'

'Thank you.'

Leila smiled as she took the lift to her room on the second floor. There were twenty rooms in all, ten on each floor, and all occupied by da Silva's patients. Plastic surgery was big business in Brazil, and Mr da Silva was one of the best.

Going into her room she adjusted the air con, which was always set too high for her liking, and looked in the mirror. She still couldn't quite believe it. Although her transformation had been gradual – each operation and procedure adding or taking away a little, now it was complete she could truly appreciate the wonderful work Mr da Silva had done, and embrace her new self. She was unrecognizable from down-trodden Leslie Chambers or Austin's arrogant creation, Chanel Woman.

Leila Osmond poured herself a gin and tonic, added ice and a cherry, and took it with her laptop onto the shaded balcony. She sat for a moment gazing out, enjoying the peace and calm of the luscious gardens – a contrast to the busy city outside. She breathed in the heady smell of sandalwood and jasmine that she'd come to love so much. A large Tabebuia tree, also known as a trumpet tree, brushed the side of the balcony, its huge white blooms hanging down in clusters. Passion flower, clematis and other tropical flowering climbers wrapped themselves around the trees. It was a wonderful place to heal and recover, and she'd miss it. But now that her treatment was complete, she needed to leave.

Leila took a sip of her drink and, setting down her glass, turned her attention to the emails that had been arriving all afternoon. As she read each one she saw they were from the crypto bank accounts Austin had had her set up, and all were saying similar: informing her there'd been multiple failed attempts to log into the accounts, and if it wasn't her she should reset her password. So Austin had finally run out of money, she thought. She couldn't help but smile and wondered what he was making of not being able to log in. He prided himself on having a very good memory. Had he worked it out yet? Perhaps not. Presumably he would at some point.

At last someone had got the better of Austin, for Leslie had realized when he'd first tried to hypnotize her that she wasn't a good subject. As hard as she'd tried to relax and concentrate on his voice, she couldn't go into the trance he'd assumed she would. They were newly married and, not wanting to disappoint him, she'd pretended to be in a trance. It wasn't difficult. She'd answered his questions, did what he'd asked of her, and used the techniques that were supposed to help her come to terms with her past and lead to a brighter future. She'd been confused, then upset, and finally angry, when Austin had started manipulating her for his own ends. When he'd told her to buy a prosthetic mask, a replica gun, and then plan and execute robberies, all the time assuming she was under his control, she'd become very angry indeed, but had gone along with it because she didn't know what else to do, until she'd formed a plan to take revenge.

Leila took another sip from her drink. She closed the emails and turned her attention to finding somewhere to go. The world and her new life beckoned. There was no need to reset the passwords on these accounts, for even if Austin did manage to access them, he'd find them empty. She'd transferred the money to other accounts long ago.

Now where to go? she wondered. The Caribbean looked lovely at this time of year and some of the islands were only a four-hour flight away from Brazil. A small island, unspoiled by tourists, she decided. There were plenty to choose from. One stood out; it looked idyllic, like paradise, with a population of only eight thousand, and with its own bank. *Overseas residents welcome* it announced on its website, and there was a paragraph about the island's government scheme to help the local economy. If a foreigner opened a bank account with a minimum deposit of £100,000 they were automatically granted right of residency for as long as they wanted. Perfect, Leila thought, that would make a good base, and she emailed the person responsible. It seemed not only did he run the bank but most of the businesses on the island.

He replied by return:

Dear Ms Osmond
I was delighted to receive your enquiry. Thank you for choosing my beautiful island to reside. I have pleasure in attaching a form to set up a bank account. Once I have received this with your initial deposit I will look forward to welcoming you.
    Warmest wishes
    A. Garcia

FIFTY-FIVE

'A wedding invitation?' Matt said, intrigued, referring to the fancy rose-gold card displayed on Beth's desk.

'Yes, it's from Megan and Brandon,' Beth replied, concentrating on her computer screen. 'Have a look, if you like.'

Matt picked up the card and read the message inside.

'That's nice of them,' he said. 'They say it's thanks to you they began dating. Will you go?'

Beth nodded. 'I'd like to see how they're all getting on. It's plus-one – you're welcome to come if you're free.'

'I'll put it in my diary,' Matt said, and returned the card to Beth's desk. 'Something interesting?' he asked. Beth hadn't taken her eyes from the computer screen.

'Very. There's been activity on Austin Chambers's bank account. The balance has been withdrawn and the account closed in an online transaction.'

'So he's not dead.'

'I never thought he was.'

'And I'm guessing you're going to try to trace where the money has gone?'

'Absolutely. But there's been another, equally interesting development,' Beth continued, still concentrating on the

308

screen. 'Money from one of the early Chanel Woman robberies has turned up in South America, deposited into a bank in Brazil, to be precise. Is that a coincidence or am I missing something?' She finally looked at Matt.

He shrugged. 'I've no idea, but the case is officially closed unless any more evidence turns up.'

'Possibly this is it,' Beth said, and continued to study the information on screen as Matt sat at his desk and worked on another case.

Twenty minutes later, Beth had learned that Austin's bank account had been closed by the account holder – namely Austin Chambers – and the balance transferred outside the UK. Not into cryptocurrency fortunately but into an account in his name at a bank on the Caribbean island of St Arie. Beth checked the time difference – it was 9.30 a.m. there – and phoned the bank. She explained who she was and that she was making enquiries into an account held by one of their clients. When she gave Austin's name, the assistant said it was one of the accounts personally managed by Mr Garcia, the bank manager. Beth asked to speak to him and was left on hold for some time before the assistant told her Mr Garcia was out of the office at present and would call her when he returned.

'Thank you,' Beth said, and took a sip of water from the bottle on her desk.

Next she phoned the bank in Brazil where the stolen money had been discovered. She had more luck there and when she explained who she was and the reason for her call, she was put straight through to the manager. She briefly repeated what she'd told the assistant, although there was no need as the manager was already aware.

'Money laundering is not unheard of here but I'm certain that isn't what happened in this case,' he said. 'The account the money was paid into belongs to Mr da Silva, an eminent plastic surgeon. Mr da Silva would never do anything to jeopardize his reputation. We went to school together and I have known him all my life. Mr da Silva's secretary often deposits cash into his account as his patients pay him in cash. He accepts all main currencies, but this is the first time we've ever had a problem. I . . .'

'Mr da Silva is a plastic surgeon, you said?' Beth interrupted, her thoughts working overtime.

'Yes, that's correct.'

'Was the payment made in pounds sterling?' Beth checked.

'Yes.'

'Does Mr da Silva know which patient gave him that money?'

'I believe so, but I don't know the details.'

'Do you know if it was a man or a woman?'

'A woman, but that's all I know. As soon as I was made aware the serial numbers on the notes matched those stolen, I passed the matter to the police.'

'I need to speak to Mr da Silva,' Beth said urgently. 'Do you have his number?'

'Naturally.'

Beth wrote down the number the bank manager read out. 'Thank you.'

'You're welcome. As I say, Mr da Silva is highly respected, so I am sure he acted in good faith, unaware the money he'd accepted was stolen.'

'I understand.'

Beth said goodbye and took another sip of water. This could still be coincidence, she cautioned herself as she called Mr da Silva's number. A woman answered. 'Prática do Senhor da Silva,' she said in Portuguese.

'I'd like to speak to Mr da Silva,' Beth said.

'Ah, English. I'm sorry, he is operating now.'

'Do you know when he will be finished?' Beth asked.

'Twelve o'clock. Then he will take his lunch before he starts his afternoon consultations. Can I help you by sending some of our literature?'

'I'm not looking for cosmetic surgery,' Beth said, then explained who she was, but not the reason for her call. 'I'll call back at twelve o'clock your time.'

'I'll tell him. Goodbye.'

Beth set down her phone, silenced her racing heart, and made a large note to call Mr da Silva at 5 p.m., which allowed for the five-hour time difference.

It was a long afternoon where Beth ate at her desk, tried to quell her rising sense of anticipation, and made little progress on the other cases she was supposed to be working on. Matt was busy and in and out of the office. At 4 p.m. when Mr Garcia still hadn't returned her call Beth phoned the bank in St Arie again, and was told that he hadn't returned to the office and wasn't expected back that day.

'Is there someone else there I can talk to?' Beth asked. 'An assistant manager, maybe?'

'No, only Mr Garcia handles this account.'

'Can I have Mr Garcia's mobile number then? It is important I speak to him as soon as possible.'

'I will ask him.'

Beth was then left hanging on until eventually the line went dead. She redialled straight away but a recorded message said that the bank was now closed and would open again at 8.30 a.m., which she supposed could be genuine.

At exactly 5 p.m. Beth called Mr da Silva's practice in Brazil. Matt's desk was empty again, as he was downstairs interviewing a suspect who had been brought in that afternoon.

The same assistant answered and remembered her. 'I'll see if Mr da Silva is free. Please hold the line.'

Silence, then a man's voice with only a slight accent: 'DC Beth Mayes, Dr da Silva here.'

'Good afternoon, Mr da Silva. Thank you for making the time to talk to me, I appreciate you are busy.'

'Very,' he said. 'I am pleased to say. I understand you wish to speak to me in connection with some money my secretary paid into my account. My friend the bank manager called me.'

'Yes, that's correct.'

'Let me assure you that when I accepted the payment I had no idea the money was stolen. I always ask for cash – dollars and sterling are fine – otherwise I might not get paid. Not everyone is as honest as you and me.'

'No indeed. The woman who passed you the cash was a patient?' Beth checked.

'Yes, a very good one. She was here a long time, six months, and had a lot of surgery.'

'Was her name Leslie Chambers?'

'No, Leila Osmond.'

Beth's heart fell. It had always been possible that the person who'd passed the money to Mr da Silva had received it innocently in payment for something else like the sale of a car. That was the nature of money laundering: it got passed on unwittingly, eventually disappearing into the banking system.

'What did she have done?' Beth asked.

'Rhinoplasty – nose reshaping. Blepharoplasty on her eyes. Orthognathic surgery to soften her jawline. Lipomodelling to enhance her cheeks, and skin grafts to treat the scar. She was always very pleasant and was pleased with the results.'

Beth's heart missed a beat. 'Where was the scar?' she asked.

'On her cheek. It was from a burn she received in her teens. It should have received more treatment at the time, but I am happy to say it has virtually gone now. You'd never be able to tell.'

'How old was she?'

'Twenty-eight.'

'Mr da Silva, if I send you a photo, could you tell me if it's the same person you treated?'

'Yes, I have a few minutes. Please send to my email, dasilva@dssliva.br. Then I need to have some lunch before I see my first patient.'

'Yes of course. Thank you.'

Beth quickly attached a photo of Leslie Chambers to an email and pressed send. She waited, senses tingling. It went quiet on the other end of the phone, then, 'Yes, this is the lady I treated. It took me a moment to recognize her, I did such a good job.'

'You're sure?' Beth asked.

'Positive. I have photographs of her transformation. I always take before and after photos. But she told me her name was Leila Osmond. That was on her passport too.'

'I assume you have her address there?'

'I did, while she was here. She stayed in a local hotel-cum-nursing home I use, but she left there the day after her treatment finished. There was no reason for her to stay. Everything had healed nicely.'

'Do you know where she's gone?' Beth asked, willing him to say yes.

'No, she was going to travel the world. She sent me a postcard shortly after she left, but that's all.'

'Where was the postcard from?' Beth asked, fingers crossed he remembered.

'A beautiful island in the Caribbean, not far from here. St Arie. I don't suppose you've heard of it.'

'Actually, I have,' Beth said. 'Can you send me a recent photo of Leila Osmond please.'

'Yes, I'll get my secretary to do it now.'

'Thank you. You've been very helpful, and if I ever need work doing, I'll know where to come.'

Beth quietly congratulated herself. All this time spent

313

looking and never giving up and finally a massive break-through. So Leslie and Austin were in it together after all, and now she had the proof she needed. She couldn't wait to tell Matt, but before that she needed to update DS Scrivener and ask to travel to St Arie with arrest warrants for them both.

Four months later at Megan and Brandon's wedding, Beth and Matt were able to tell them that Austin and Leslie Chambers were in custody facing a retrial, when they hoped justice would finally be done.

But there is one matter still outstanding that the friends discuss from time to time – a plausible explanation for the strange happenings at the converted church on Halloween. Who really did push the planchette, relight the candle, and add 'now' to the message on Megan's phone? Roshan and Brandon continue to deny it was their doing and have blamed Austin. From what is known, it seems highly unlikely it was him, but that's preferable to the alternative: that there really was a malevolent spirit released that night. One thing is for certain though – they won't play with a Ouija board again. Some things are better left alone.

While this story is fiction, phasmophobia –
a fear of ghosts – and hypnotism are real.

Acknowledgements

A big thank you to my readers for all your wonderful comments and reviews. They are much appreciated. Thank you to my editors Angel and Anne, and Holly, my literary agent, Andrew, and all the team at HarperCollins.

EXCLUSIVE ADDITIONAL CONTENT

Includes an author Q&A and details
of how to get involved in *Fern's Picks*

Dear lovely readers,

Brace yourself for an enthralling journey of reunion and revelations in *The Gathering* by Lisa Stone. You won't be able to look away from the pages of this captivating story!

Excitedly preparing to reunite with their close-knit group of old school friends, Sarah and Roshan head to a magnificent converted church, where they eagerly anticipate a week filled with nostalgia and laughter. However, their joyful reunion soon takes an unnerving turn.

When Sarah starts to feel the haunting presence of the church's surroundings, an eerie sense of fear begins to pervade the group, escalating as a masked marauder evades the police in a series of unsettling armed robberies nearby – and some of the group begin to have alarming visions. Soon, Sarah and her friends begin to question the nature of the reunion they were so keen on attending...

The Gathering will keep you on tenterhooks, combining friendship, mystery and unease into an unforgettable read. With its compelling characters and a mystery that unravels at an alarming pace, it's a thrilling experience.

I can't wait to hear what you think of this riveting tale of reunion, fear and hidden secrets.

With love
Fern x

Fern's Picks

Fern Britton
Picks

Exclusively for
TESCO

Look out for more books, coming soon!

For more information on the book club,
exclusive Q&As with the authors and
reading group questions, visit Fern's website

www.fern-britton.com/ferns-picks

We'd love you to join in the conversation,
so don't forget to share your thoughts using
#FernsPicks

Fern's
Picks

A Q&A with
Lisa Stone

Warning: contains spoilers

The Gathering **is set in a beautifully converted church that soon becomes eerie. What drew you to this particular setting?**

I chose a converted church as the setting because it's both beautiful and a little spooky. Churches are typically seen as tranquil, sacred spaces, but their history and architecture can sometimes make them eerie. That contrast between beauty and unease, between sanctuary and fear, felt like the perfect backdrop for a reunion that transforms into a nightmare.

How did you approach writing about the supernatural elements in the book? And how did you manage to keep the readers in suspense about the true nature of the visions the group experiences?

When writing about the supernatural elements, I wanted them to feel plausible and unsettling, just as psychological as they were fantastical. The supernatural is often portrayed as ambiguous and deeply connected with characters' emotional states. Is it real, or is it a manifestation of their fear and guilt?

It's this ambiguity that helps keep readers in suspense. Are they paranormal occurrences, or are they psychological in origin? This question is at the heart of the story, and I kept it alive by providing just enough hints to stoke speculation without confirming one way or the other. I wanted the readers to experience the same uncertainty and confusion that the characters do.

Can you share a bit about your daily writing routine? Does it involve any special rituals or habits?

I like to start my writing day early with a strong cup of coffee while the house is quiet. Mornings are when I'm most creative and least distracted. I always start by revisiting what I wrote the day before, making small edits and adjustments, which helps me get back into the flow. I don't really have any rituals as such, but I do find that a clean workspace and some soft music in the background help me focus.

Are there any personal experiences or insights that you imbued in your characters or the plot?

While *The Gathering* is not directly based on personal experiences, I believe every writer imbues their work with bits of themselves. Some of the group dynamics were inspired by my own school friendships and how they've evolved over the years. The sense of nostalgia, mixed with the realization that people change, is something I've personally experienced and tried to capture in the book.

Do you have any advice for aspiring writers who want to craft suspenseful thrillers like yours?

My main advice to aspiring thriller writers is to keep the reader in mind. Every twist, every revelation, every moment of suspense should serve to engage the reader more deeply. Don't lose sight of the human element amidst the suspense. Characters that readers can empathize with will make them more invested in the story. And lastly, don't shy away from revisions. The magic often happens in the rewrites!

Questions for your Book Club

Warning: contains spoilers

- How did you feel about the setting of the converted church for the reunion? Did it add an additional layer of tension to the story?

- What do you make of the relationship between Sarah and Roshan? How does their dynamic evolve as the eerie events unfold?

- The supernatural elements in *The Gathering* play a significant role. Did you find them believable? Did they enhance the suspense for you?

- How did the visions experienced by the group influence your understanding of the plot? At what point did you realize their significance?

- The story explores the tension between past friendships and present realities. How do the characters' relationships change over the course of the book?

- *The Gathering* is full of unexpected twists. Which one caught you by surprise the most?

- Discuss the role of Chanel Woman in the plot. How did your perception of her change as the story progressed?

- The narrative uses fear as a powerful motivator for the characters. How does this element drive the story forward?

- In the end, do you feel the reunion brought the friends closer or drove them further apart? Why?

- Would you recommend this book to a friend? What would be your main selling point?

An exclusive extract from Fern's new novel

The Good Servant

March 1932

Marion Crawford was not able to sleep on the train, or to eat the carefully packed sandwiches her mother had insisted on giving her. Anxiety, and a sudden bout of homesickness, prohibited both.

What on earth was she doing? Leaving Scotland, leaving everything she knew? And all on the whim of the Duchess of York, who had decided that her two girls needed a governess exactly like Miss Crawford.

Marion couldn't quite remember how or when she had agreed to the sudden change. Before she knew it, it was all arranged. The Duchess of York was hardly a woman you said no to.

Once her mother came round to the idea, she was in a state of high excitement and condemnation. 'Why would they want *you*?' she had asked, 'A girl from a good, working class family? What do you know about how these people live?' She had stared at Marion, almost in reverence. 'Working for the royal family . . . They must have seen something in you. My daughter.'

On arrival at King's Cross, Marion took the underground to Paddington. She found the right platform for the Windsor train and, as she had a little time to wait, ordered a cup of tea, a scone and a magazine from the station café.

She tried to imagine what her mother and stepfather were doing right now. They'd have eaten their tea and have the wireless on, tuned to news most likely. Her mother would have her mending basket by her side, telling her husband all about Marion's send off. She imagined her mother rambling on as the fire in the grate hissed and burned.

Fern's
Picks

The train was rather full, but Marion found a seat and settled down to flick through her magazine. Her mind couldn't settle. Through the dusk she watched the alien landscape and houses spool out beside her. Dear God, what was she doing here, so far away from family and home? What was she walking into?

When the conductor walked through the carriage announcing that Windsor would be the next stop, she began to breathe deeply and calmly, as she had been taught to do before her exams. She took from her bag, for the umpteenth time, the letter from her new employers. The instructions were clear: she was to leave the station and look for a uniformed driver with a dark car.

She gazed out of the window as the train began to slow. She took a deep breath, stood up and collected her case and coat. *Come on, Marion. It's only for a few months. You can do this.*

Available now!

Fern's Picks

The No.1 Sunday Times
bestselling author returns

Balmoral, 1932

Marion Crawford, an ordinary but determined young woman,
is given a chance to work at the big house as governess
to two children, Lilibet and Margaret Rose.

Windsor Castle, 1936

As dramatic events sweep through the country and change all their lives
in an extraordinary way, Marion loyally devotes herself to the family.
But when love enters her life, she is faced with an unthinkable choice…

Available now!

Fem's Picks

Our next book club title

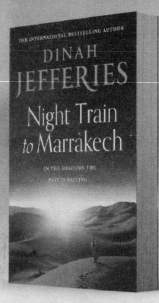

1960s Morocco

Vicky Baudin steps onto the train to Marrakech
looking for the truth about the woman who gave her father
up for adoption decades before. Clemence Petier lives in
a kasbah on the edge of the Atlas Mountains,
her background shrouded in mystery.

But the past holds secrets that threaten them both.

A face from Clemence's childhood threatens to expose
everything she has built a life to hide.

And danger is all around…

When a brutal murder takes place, Clemence
and Vicky are forced to band together. Yet Clemence's own
dark secret must stay hidden at all costs…

HIS DEATH WAS JUST THE BEGINNING...

You know your son better than anyone. Don't you?

When critically ill Jacob Wilson is given a life-saving heart transplant, his parents are relieved that their loving son has been saved.

However, before long, his family are forced to accept that something has changed in Jacob. Their once loving son is slowly being replaced by a violent man whose mood swings leave them terrified – but is it their fault?

Jacob's girlfriend, Rosie, is convinced the man she loves is suffering from stress. But when his moods turn on her, she begins to doubt herself – and she can only hide the bruises for so long.

When a terrible crime is committed, Jacob's family are forced to confront their darkest fears. Has the boy they raised become a monster?

Or is someone else to blame?

AVAILABLE NOW

YOU THINK YOU'RE SAFE, BUT ARE YOU?

Someone is always watching...

Derek Flint is a loner. He lives with his mother and spends his evenings watching his clients on the CCTV cameras he has installed inside their homes. He likes their companionship – even if it's through a screen.

When a series of crimes hits Derek's neighbourhood, DC Beth Mayes begins to suspect he's involved. How does he know so much about the victims' lives? Why won't he let anyone into his office? And what is his mother hiding in that strange, lonely house?

As the crimes become more violent, Beth must race against the clock to find out who is behind the attacks. Will she uncover the truth in time? And is Derek more dangerous than even she has guessed?

AVAILABLE NOW

HE SAYS HE WANTS TO SAVE YOU...

BUT DOES HE?

The
Doctor
LISA STONE

How much do you know about the couple next door?

When Emily and Ben move in next door to Dr Burman and his wife Alisha, they are keen to get to know their new neighbours. Outgoing and sociable, Emily tries to befriend the doctor's wife, but Alisha is strangely subdued, barely leaving the house, and terrified of answering the phone.

When Emily goes missing a few weeks later, Ben is plunged into a panic. His wife has left him a note, but can she really have abandoned him for another man? Or has Emily's curiosity about the couple next door led her straight into danger?

AVAILABLE NOW

One moment she's there

The next she's gone...

Have you seen Leila?

8-year-old Leila Smith has seen and heard
things that no child should ever have to.
On the Hawthorn Estate, where she lives,
she often stays out after dark to avoid going home.

But what Leila doesn't know is that someone
has been watching her in the playground.
One day, she disappears without a trace...

The police start a nationwide search
but it's as if Leila has vanished into thin air.
Who kidnapped her? What do they want?
**Will she return home safely
or is she lost forever?**

AVAILABLE NOW

DO YOU DARE UNLOCK THE DOOR?

Something strange is in the forest...

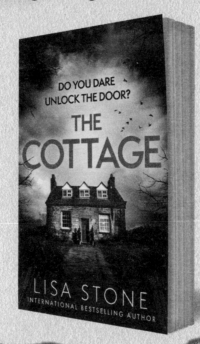

After losing her job and boyfriend, Jan Hamlin is in desperate need of a fresh start. So she jumps at the chance to rent a secluded cottage on the edge of Coleshaw Woods.

Very quickly though, things take a dark turn. At night, Jan hears strange noises, and faint taps at the window. Something, or someone, is out there.

Jan refuses to be scared off. But whoever is outside isn't going away, and it soon becomes clear that the nightmare is only just beginning...